OF THINGS
I DREAMT
LAST NIGHT

OF THINGS
I DREAMT
LAST NIGHT

D. K. Jensen

iUniverse, Inc.
New York Lincoln Shanghai

Of Things I Dreamt Last Night

iUniverse, Inc.

For information address:
iUniverse, Inc.
2021 Pine Lake Road, Suite 100
Lincoln, NE 68512
www.iuniverse.com

ISBN: 0-595-33349-4 (pbk)
ISBN: 0-595-66859-3 (cloth)

Printed in the United States of America

Dedicated to Michael, the brother I never knew

"You must have faith. Only faith will show you the way. If you have faith that it is there, then it will be there for you. Always."

—Giester, from St. Nicholas, Prince of Klause

"It's not the mistakes you make that determine who you are. It's the mistakes you learn from."

—Douglas, from One More Kiss

Contents

▼

THAT DREAM YOU HAD LAST NIGHT (LOVE)

do you remember
the dream you had
late last night
do you recall
the love
the light
do you daydream
of the night scene
dance in your mind
dream one more time

who's face will it be
that makes you think
back to the night
to the dream
that you had
such mystery
such pretty eyes
like stars from skies
stare deep into
the depths of you

do you remember
those pretty eyes
luscious lips
that you kissed
she showed you love

made your heart whirl
when your eyes open
you heart is broken
love can't be found
in a dream

where will you be
when you remember

the dream you had last night

ONE MORE KISS

Ever have that dream where you are falling, and just before you hit the ground, you wake up? Linda doesn't have that dream. She was never afraid of falling; not when she could walk on the clouds at one time. That was a long time ago. Since then, she had fallen about as far as she could in her life. It didn't mean that she was free from nightmares. Hers were just different. Everyone else has nightmare where they barely escape. She was never so lucky.

It was another of these dreams that left Linda sitting on the side of her bed at three o'clock in the morning. Her body was covered in a cold sweat that reflected softly in the blue moonlight shining through her window. She didn't move for several minutes. It wasn't always just a bad dream. It was usually a variation of something from her past.

Slowly she rose to her feet. She reached for her robe at the foot of the bed and slipped it on. Something moved, and she turned her head to see what it was. "Oh, one of those," She whispered to herself while picking up a long white feather from the floor.

She turned to to look at her macaw sleeping peacefully in his cage while whispering, "I guess it's a little big for you." The feather was on the ground near her bed, a good distance from the cage which was sitting on a wrought iron stand next to her dresser. The cage had been there as long as she cared to remember. In fact, she didn't even recall putting it there. The cage was just one of those fixtures in her home that had always been.

She said nothing else, and slowly walked out of her room. The first stop was the kitchen where she made a peanut butter and jelly sandwich, and poured herself a glass of tea. From there, it was a short trip to her couch where she slowly chewed on the sandwich, but took only one sip of her tea. It didn't take long for the food to settle and the night to wear on her before she had drifted back to sleep. She had curled up on the couch, and her eyelids had done the rest; closing out the distractions around her.

It was to be a quick sleep. A sound woke her, though she wasn't sure what the sound was. It wasn't anything loud or abrupt, just a soft sliding sound. She slowly opened her eyes, and immediately felt cold again. As she sat up on her couch, she felt a soft flow of air move past her. That's when she noticed the sliding glass door to her balcony was half way open. The cool night air blew her drapes gently into her apartment.

For some reason, she wasn't as scared as she knew she should have been. She lacked the need to look all around her apartment for any dangers that might lay in wait for her. Something she couldn't explain told her that she was safe. At least, she was safe from physical danger. Mental anguish was another story.

She rose to her feet and walked towards the door. She pulled back her drapes to look out on the balcony of her eighteenth story apartment. Hanging in the doorway, was a thin metal chain. A gold coin was attached to the chain. She ran her fingers down the chain, and held the coin between her index finger and thumb. The coin was simple enough. On one side, there was a cross etched into it. The other side was a bit more intriguing. A single word had been carved into the gold. The shaky nature of the letters suggested that the word had been carved by hand.

"Forgiveness," She whispered to herself while reading the coin. She tugged softly, and pulled the chain from the doorway. She walked onto her balcony and looked out over the city. She rubbed the coin between her fingers as she looked around. A single tear ran across her cheeks as she whispered, "I'm sorry."

She pulled back her arm and threw the coin as far as she could. It fell towards the ground and bounced three times when it hit the sidewalk below. She turned and walked back inside, closing and locking the sliding glass door behind herself.

As the lock clicked, she whispered again, "Why is it easier to forgive others than yourself?" She pondered that question into the night as she slowly drifted back to sleep on the couch.

Her alarm clock was in her bedroom, so it didn't wake her in the morning. However, no one could have slept through the macaw squawking at the alarm clock. It became a typical day with her getting dressed, and heading to her job as a secretary at an advertising firm. Everything was fine until lunch. That's when her fragile world fell completely apart.

She had a quiet lunch at her favorite deli; two turkey sandwiches on a butter croissant with a garden salad, and a piece of cake. All through lunch, she had that feeling of being watched. She kept finding herself glancing over her shoulder to see who was there.

While walking back to work, it all caught up to her in a way that could only be called ironic. She developed that feeling again, and peeked over her shoulder. No one was there. While she was looking over her shoulder, she ran into someone. She was immediately startled, and turned to see a man standing almost seven feet tall in front of her.

"I'm sorry," she said while lowering her eyes. She was about to walk past the man when he spoke.

"Hello Linda," the man said with a deep voice.

Those words physically froze Linda in her tracks. They also caused her brain to freeze for a moment. She managed to slowly stutter the words, "Excuse me?"

"Hello Linda," The man repeated.

She looked up at the man and absorbed the details. He had very dark skin that was only partially exposed under layers of clothing. He wore jeans and boots with a sweater. Over the sweater, he wore an overcoat. His left eye was covered with a patch. Sewn into the patch was the image of a cross.

"Do I know you?" She asked. Her voice cracked on every syllable. She again lowered her eyes to look away. She glanced around quickly, looking for a way out of her situation.

"It's okay Linda," the man said.

She said nothing immediately. He looked familiar, though she couldn't tell why. On a certain level, she felt love. On another level, she could feel a shiver run down her spine. The love told her to run away as fast as she could. The fear froze her in place.

"We want you to come back to work for us," He said softly.

"I already have a job," She replied, unsure of what else to say.

"You belong with us," he replied.

She lowered her head again, and whispered, "I'm sorry, you must have me confused for someone else."

With that, she turned to walk away. He turned his body to let her pass. He said nothing else. He would try again later. He wasn't sure how, but knew he had to get through to her.

The rest of the day dragged on. Her lack of sleep the previous night was catching up with her. Having a good lunch didn't help. The last fifteen minutes of the day were the worse. On one hand she was ready for the day to be over; to go home and get some sleep. On the other hand, She had to admit that she felt a slight bit of apprehension. Would that man be waiting for her? Hopefully, not.

By the time the clock stuck five o'clock, she was already on the elevator. The walk home was uneventful. She passed the usual landmarks; a strip mall, a school, a church, a cemetery, and a park. She paid the usual amount of attention to them, which was almost none. She kept her head down, and her eyes lowered; unwilling to look the world in the face.

Her evening was nothing short of ordinary. She slipped into something more comfortable, her cotton robe. It was two sizes too big, but she liked it that way. It felt lighter on her, and made her feel as if gravity had less of a pull on her.

She sat on the edge of her bed and played with her macaw for an hour. She was trying to get him to talk, but he seemed resistant. That didn't keep her from talking to him. After all, he was her only real friend. It was almost time to cut his wings again, but she resisted. She actually enjoyed watching him fly around her apartment. It made her feel even more free. Besides, it always made a mess when she clipped his wings.

Her lunch was still weighing her down, so she wasn't ready to eat anything until almost eight that night. She was pouring the water from the pasta when she felt a breeze blow through her apartment.

"Not again," She thought to herself as she set the pot on a trivet. She stepped into the living room, and sure enough, the drapes in front of her sliding glass door were blowing into her apartment. The door was open again.

She walked across the living room towards the door. Before closing it, she decided to peek through the drapes, just to see if something was out there. She saw him immediately. He was sitting on the rail with his feet hanging over the edge. He was holding the thin chain with the gold coin in his hand. The chain was wrapped around his fist, and he was rubbing the coin between his thumb and index finger.

"What do you want Douglas?" she asked instinctively. Douglas, his name was Douglas. She wasn't sure how she knew his name. Was it a lost memory, or just an admission that she had never actually forgotten? She did not know.

"I just want to talk," Douglas said.

"I don't feel like talking," She said while lowering her eyes.

"Do you feel like listening?"

"No," She said.

"You don't even know what I have to say," Douglas said softly.

"Maybe I just don't care," Linda replied.

"I don't believe that."

"So you say that I'm lying?" She asked. She paused briefly, then turned back towards the inside of her apartment, "a killer and a lier."

"You are hardly a killer," Douglas said.

"Good-bye Douglas," She said while walking through her drapes.

"I love you," Douglas said in a whisper that only she could have heard.

"I don't believe in love," She replied in an even quieter whisper. He still heard her. A tear fell from his good eye.

She closed her sliding glass door while repeating, "I don't believe in love." Another tear fell from his eye. She heard him leave, and hoped that it would be the last she had seen of him. She would have said a prayer to the effect, if she still believed in such things.

She put it behind her, and went back to making her pasta. An hour later, she was cleaning up behind a meal that had left her stuffed again. The eating filled a void. Somehow, she seemed to be able to eat as much as she wanted without showing any weight gain. It only prompted her to keep eating more.

Before going to bed, she returned to her balcony. It was something she would do from time to time. The night was perfect. There wasn't a cloud to be seen, and the moon glowed brightly as if it might replace the sun. The stars were sporadic, but that was only due to the lights of the city.

She stood by the railing and stared upwards, wondering what else might be out there. Sometimes she thought she had a good idea. Other times, she was scared of what she knew.

She gripped the railing tightly and lifted herself upwards. First she lifted one leg, then the other, over the edge of the railing. She just sat there. It wasn't about jumping. It was about a sense of freedom. The feeling of her legs dangling more than two hundred feet in the air almost took her to another place. Something inside of her said she could float away if she wanted. If she just let go, then every-thing would be fine. Something else always told her to hold on tight.

While holding on to the rail, Linda leaned over to look down between her feet. She could see them down there; scurrying around like ants. She could feel their fears and concerns. She wanted to help them all, but knew she had her own demons to wrestle with. She smiled. It was rare for her, but the freedom she was so close to achieving actually made her lips curl upwards. A loving sparkle floated across her eyes.

The happy moment wasn't to last. She heard a sound. The first noise was that of a door being closed. It clearly came from inside her apartment. She could hear light footsteps being taken through her living room towards the balcony.

"Oh great, now what?" She said with a sigh. She turned her gaze upwards, ready to ignore who ever was bothering her. As she moved her eyes to her left to peek towards the door, she saw her drapes moving. A small hand, only four feet from the ground, pulled back one of the drapes to reveal a girl, maybe ten at most.

The face that only a moment earlier had been smiling, now looked as if it were incapable of producing a look of happiness. She said nothing, and immediately began focusing on a star in the distance. She so wished that she could have been there at that moment.

The girl looked around briefly, as if confused by her surroundings. Slowly, she walked over towards the railing. She put her hands on the railing and lifted herself up on her tiptoes to glance over.

"Cool," the girl said while taking in the view.

"Be careful, you might fall," Linda said while only glancing at the girl.

"What about you?" the girl asked while observing Linda sitting on the rail with her legs hanging over the edge.

"I'll be fine," She insisted.

"Are you sure about that?" the girl asked.

Linda said nothing at first. Somehow, she knew the question had more than one meaning. She glanced at the girl twice before turning back to that star. She just focused on the star, and tried to block everything else out. After several moments of silence, she quietly said, "I'll be fine."

"When?" the girl asked while continuing to look down towards the ground.

Linda slowly turned her head to look at the girl. She was about to ask her a question. She wasn't even sure what question; maybe who the girl was, or what she wanted. Linda never got a chance to speak before the girl did.

"It wasn't your fault," the girl said in a tone so honest that it could have only come from a child.

"What wasn't my fault?" She asked. Half of a memory flashed through her mind. She suddenly felt very scared, and at the same time, embarrassed. She didn't know why.

"Well if you don't even remember, then why are you punishing yourself so much?" the girl asked.

"I remember," Linda said. She did remember, when she chose to. It had just been so long since she had chosen to.

"If you remember, then stop punishing yourself," the girl said. She never looked at Linda while talking. Her eyes seemed to be following something below her when she added, "I really do forgive you. It wasn't your fault."

Linda said nothing. Her brain froze as she tried to recall it all. She swore she could remember, then again, maybe not. Details were of clouds and water. She remembered a decision. She remembered the wrong one. She remembered a kiss.

"Then who's fault was it?" Linda asked. Maybe the girl would say something that would bring back more of the memories.

"It was mine," the girl said. She pulled herself up on the rail a little, as if she were straining to see something. She let a moment hang in the air before saying, "Mom told me not to do it."

"Then why did you do it?" She asked.

"Because I wanted to," the girl said casually.

"You really should be careful there," Linda said while noticing the girl pulling herself over the edge of the railing enough that her toes weren't touching the ground.

The girl let go of the rail and dropped to the balcony. The girl turned to Linda and displayed a serious face while saying, "That's what my mom said."

"You should listen to you mom," Linda said.

"Yeah, I should have," the girl replied, "Like I said, it wasn't your fault."

Linda wanted to say something. She also wanted to not be there at that moment. She wanted to be free, but kept feeling scared. She didn't know what scared her more; feeling trapped, or doing what she had to do to be free. Denial can do that to a person.

She stood up on the railing, and looked out over the city. She felt even more free than ever before. In front of her, there was a two hundred foot drop, and that seemed to free her even more. She turned around again. Suddenly, there was the girl she was trying to remember, or maybe trying to forget. Linda suddenly felt trapped again. She wasn't ready for the freedom she desired. She jumped down from the railing, and landed on her balcony only a few feet from the girl.

"Why don't you go away," Linda said in a dismissive manner.

"Because you went way," the girl said as if that would explain it all. She paused for a moment before adding, "You need to come back."

"From where?" Linda asked.

The girl never answered. Her thoughts were distracted by something on the ground. "Hey cool, can I have this?" She said while picking a feather up from the ground.

"It means nothing to me," Linda said, and almost meant it.

"It should," the girl said while running her fingers along the edges of the feather. She then shifted the conversation in a whole other direction. The young girl dug into her pocket with her left hand while saying, "Oh, here. I have some-thing for you."

"What do you have?" Linda asked, and almost produced a smile in the pro-cess.

"Here," the girl said while pulling a coin out of her pocket. The coin was attached to a long thin chain. It looked like the coin Douglas had offered her ear-lier. When the girl handed it to Linda, it became obvious that it was the same coin.

The girl held it out for Linda to take. Linda never reached for it. She wanted to take it, but knew she wasn't ready for it. "Did Douglas send you?" She asked while turning away.

"No, our father did," The girl said, "he wants you to come back."

"Tell him I don't want it, I'm not ready to come back."

"Very well," The girl said while placing the coin back in her pocket.

"You can leave now," Linda said while refusing to turn around and look at the girl.

Linda watched the stars flicker above her. She wanted to turn around and see if the girl was still there. Again, she was just too afraid. Time passed slowly, and eventually she gave in. She turned her head slowly. Sure enough, the girl was gone.

"Thank you," She said while walking through the drapes.

She poured herself a glass of water and grabbed a bag of chips. She was hungry again. She walked into her bedroom and sat on the edge of her bed. "How are you doing?" She asked while looking at her pet macaw.

The macaw just stared at her. She had never named her pet bird, though she didn't know why. No particular name came to mind.

She reached into the cage and allowed her macaw to step onto her wrist. As soon as she pulled her bird out of the cage, the trouble began. The large colorful bird flapped its wings once and took to flight. She spent almost five minutes chas-ing her bird around her apartment before getting it to come to a rest on her wrist again.

Once she had her bird under control, she gave it a loving stroke down its back while saying, "You're going to hurt yourself if you keep that up."

She gave her bird loving stroke down its back while adding, "I hate to do it, but I'm going to have to trim those wings."

She continued to pet the macaw as she walked towards the kitchen. "Don't worry, it wont hurt," she said while pulling a pair of scissors out of a drawer.

Twenty minutes later, she was standing in a pile of feathers a foot thick on the floor, and admiring the new look of her bird. "There you go," She said with half a smile.

She placed her bird back in his cage, and spent half an hour cleaning up all the feathers. Once she was done with that, she sat down on the couch and allowed herself to relax. She was hungry again, but also tired. She didn't have to go to work the next day, so she allowed herself to fall asleep on the couch.

The sun woke Linda up like a slap in the face. The sun was staring at her, just daring her to keep sleeping. The reason she could see the sun was because her drapes were open. Douglas must have come back to see her again. She hated it when he did that.

Linda tried to climb out of the couch, but her back was killing her. It felt like someone had operated on her spine. She immediately decided that she had to quit sleeping on the couch. Slowly, she sat up, and pondered her day. It was going to be one of those days where anything was possible. The bright sun made her want to be outside. Something else told her to stay inside.

A warm shower woke her up, and made her feel refreshed. She put on a light blouse and a light pair of shorts. She hated the heavier clothes that all the other people wore. She was never able to understand how they could go around feeling so weighed down. She wanted to feel as though she could float away, no matter how afraid she was of the prospect.

When she walked into the living room, the open drapes caught her attention. She walked over towards her balcony to make sure he wasn't there. He wasn't, but something caught her eye. Scattered on the floor of the balcony were a pile of feathers. She instantly panicked, and ran back through her apartment towards her bedroom.

Just as she was afraid, her bird was gone. So was the cage and the stand that the cage sat on. On the wall, behind where the cage had been, there was a floor length mirror. It hadn't been there before. Hanging from the corner of the mirror, was a long chain with a coin attached to it. It was that same damned coin that everyone was trying to give her.

She reached out to touch it, but quickly pulled her hand back. She wanted nothing to do with it. She stared at the mirror, wondering where it had come from. It must have been Douglas, but why? Why had he taken her bird? Most importantly, why did he keep bothering her?

She glanced downward and spotted a feather on the floor. She reached down to pick it up and noticed the blood. The feather wasn't cut or broken at the stem. It looked as though it had been pulled from her bird. She stood up and held the feather in her hand while staring at the mirror. Her eyes kept moving towards the coin hanging from the mirror. She stared at the mirror and the coin for a long time before extending her hand outwards. She reached for the coin. With a slight amount of hesitation, she pulled it from the mirror. She held the coin in her hand and looked at it carefully. She studied the cross.

"It's time to finish this," She whispered to herself.

"What are you going to finish?" A soft voice said from behind her.

Linda turned around, slightly startled, and saw the girl standing only a few feet away.

"Never you mind," Linda said with a rather stern voice.

"OK, but if you don't know, then how are you going to finish it?" the girl asked. Linda said nothing and turned to walk away. As soon as she turned around, the girl added, "You dropped something."

Linda turned around again. She looked downward and noticed another of those feathers on the floor. "I didn't drop that," She said with a hint of confusion in her voice.

She reached down to pick up the feather while explaining, "Douglas wont leave me alone. He left it here."

"Of course he did," the girl said with a wink.

Linda softly stroked the the feather while saying, "I know he did."

"Then who dropped that one?" the girl asked while motioning her head towards the front door to Linda's apartment. There was another feather sitting in front of the door.

Linda turned her head, and became instantly unnerved when she saw the feather sitting by the door. "What did he do to my bird?" Linda asked with a sense of horror in her voice.

"There's a bigger question here Linda," The girl said. She paused until she knew she had Linda's full attention. Only then did the girl ask, "What if you never had a bird?"

Linda turned back to where the bird cage had been. It was still gone, and the mirror was staring back at her. She turned around again, only to find that the girl was gone. "Thank god," she said while walking towards the front door to pick up the feather.

A soft voice that sounded mysteriously like the girl's whispered back to her, "finally."

Linda was rising back to her feet when she heard the voice. She turned around, and saw the girl now standing by the mirror. "I thought you were gone," she said with only a hint of frustration.

"I am gone," the girl said. She walked towards the front door and opened it up. She stepped outside of the door and added, "You should be gone too. You don't belong here."

"And just where do you think I belong?" Linda asked.

"That's a question you have to answer for yourself," The girl said. She turned her head to look down the hallway. Something caught her eye, "Look, another one."

"Another what one?" Linda asked, afraid of what the girl might say.

"You know what," the girl said while stepping to the side, allowing Linda through the door.

Linda peeked outside the door, and sure enough, there it was. Another feather was sitting on the floor at the end of the hall.

"You better go get it," the girl said.

Linda glanced at the girl, then looked down the hall. Slowly, she walked towards the feather which was sitting in front of the elevators. When she got to the end of the hall, she reached down and picked up the feather. She looked back towards her apartment and noticed the girl was gone. As Linda stood up, the doors to the elevator opened. There was another feather on the floor of the elevator.

Linda stepped inside to pick up that feather as well. The elevator door immediately closed behind her. "Now what?" She asked herself as the elevator began descending. There was no one with her to answer the question. Somehow though, she didn't feel as if she were alone.

As soon as the elevator stopped, the doors opened. There was another feather waiting for her. She picked it up and added it to her collection. Something told her that she was being led somewhere. In the very back of her mind, she knew where. She just wasn't quite ready to admit it.

She walked out of the elevator and towards the entrance to her apartment building. Once out on the street, she looked left, then right. There was another feather down the street.

Linda was picking up the feather when she noticed them. There was a couple sitting on the edge of a brick flower bed. They kissed softly. Linda winced as if it were painful to watch. The woman leaned in to kiss the man again. Linda was forced to turn away.

"One kiss is enough," She whispered to herself. She turned her head again, and watched the woman kiss the man softly on his lower lip.

"Don't to it," Linda whispered again.

"It's not that big of a deal," a voice whispered from behind her. Linda immediately recognized the voice as that of the girl.

"You only need one kiss," Linda said without turning to look at the girl.

"And if you kiss someone more than once?" the girl asked.

Linda said nothing at first. She knew the answer. She thought she did. She had to ponder everything to get it straight in her head. Slowly she turned to the girl and said, "More than one kiss makes you selfish."

"No, it just means you are in love," the girl replied as if she could be an expert on such things.

"More than one kiss, and someone gets hurt," Linda whispered softly.

"I already told you," the girl began with a strong tone suggesting she was tired of repeating herself, "it wasn't your fault."

"I was selfish," Linda said as she walked down the street in an almost aimless manner.

"You were in love, nothing more, nothing less," the girl explained.

Linda didn't reply. She could see another feather further down the street. She walked towards it, and pretended the girl wasn't there. It wasn't the first time Linda had ignored the girl. When Linda got to the feather, she picked it up and looked around. She was at an intersection, and couldn't see any other feathers. If someone was leading her somewhere, then the trail was going cold.

"Which way now?" she asked.

"Which way do you think?" the girl replied.

"I don't know," Linda said while looking towards her left.

"Sure you do," The girl replied.

Linda looked around. Her gaze moved back towards her left. Something told her to go in that direction, so she did. She walked a half a block before finding the next feather. She picked it up and looked around for the girl. She couldn't be seen.

Linda pressed on. She walked another block before finding the next feather. That's when she saw the black wrought iron fence. "I can't be here," she whispered.

"Of course you can," the girl said from behind her. "It's my home," the girl added.

Linda froze. Her fingers relaxed and all the feathers she had been collecting fell to the ground.

"Oh don't drop those," the young girl said, "you're going to need them."

"No, I don't need them," Linda insisted. She went on to add, "I can't be here."

The girl reached out and took Linda by the hand, "Of course you can. Don't worry, I'll show you around."

"I can't be here. You shouldn't be here either," Linda said. Her hands began sweating profusely. The girl led Linda along the fence until they came to the gate.

"I'm not going in there," Linda insisted. She pulled her hand away from the girl's.

The girl kept walking through the gate. She looked around at the statues and trees. She then turned to glance at Linda while saying, "See, it's not dangerous."

"I'm not going in there," Linda repeated.

"The rest of your feathers are in here," the girl said.

"I don't want them," Linda said while looking towards the feathers she had dropped on the ground.

"Of course not, that's why you cut them off," the girl said. She turned to walk further past the gate while adding, "You really should stop doing that."

Linda almost wanted to go in. She just wasn't quite ready. She looked around at all the statues. They seemed frozen in time. They were mostly protected under large oak trees. She paused as she walked through the gate. The young girl paused also. She glanced over her shoulder at Linda and cocked her head sideways as if confused.

"Don't worry," the girl said, "It will be ok."

"I can't come in there," Linda insisted for the third or fourth time. She wasn't counting.

The girl looked down the pathway and pointed, "Look, another one."

"Can you bring it to me?" Linda asked.

"No. I can't give you the answers, I can only lead you to them," The girl said while walking towards the feather.

Linda took a few cautious steps forward. She kept looking around as if she were expecting something horrible to happen. She didn't know how bad it could get. She was about to confront her worst fears; facing her past.

She walked up to the feather, and reached down to pick it up. As she was standing up, she saw him. Douglas was sitting on the branch of a large oak tree. Linda turned to look at the young girl. "I don't want to see him," Linda insisted.

"But he has the rest of your feathers," the girl replied.

"I don't want anymore feathers. I want my bird," Linda said.

The girl stared at Linda, and for the second time, asked, "What if there was no bird?"

"I want my bird back," Linda said.

"That's not a bad thing," the girl said. She started walking towards Douglas while adding, "as long as you understand that there might not have been a bird."

Linda extended her hand out towards the girl while saying, "Wait, don't go to him."

"I have to, it's where I sleep," the young girl replied. She walked towards Douglas.

"You sleep here?" Linda asked while looking around.

"Yes, right over there," the girl said while pointing under the tree.

"You don't sleep at home, with your parents?" Linda asked.

"No, I'm not allowed to anymore," the girl said.

"I'm sorry," Linda said while slowly following the girl over towards the tree.

"I already told you, don't be," The girl said.

They walked towards the tree. Douglas only took marginal notice. "You really sleep here?" Linda asked while looking around the tree.

"Yes," came the simple reply.

"But, where?" Linda asked.

"Right there," the young girl said while pointing towards the ground.

"Is that your pillow?" Linda asked while pointing towards a small square rock on the ground.

"No silly, that's my name."

Linda leaned over to look at the stone. There was some writing on it that read, "Miya Hutchison 1994–2003."

"Your name is Miya?" Linda asked.

"Yep," the girl said with a smile.

"What happened in 2003?" Linda asked.

Miya looked up at Linda and said only, "Nothing that was your fault."

"You care to be specific?" Linda asked. She suddenly remembered something about water, but the memory was vague. She thought she could remember some splashing.

"No. You have to remember that on your own," Miya replied.

"I don't want to remember," Linda said. She looked around, then glanced towards Douglas for a moment. She slowly turned her attention back towards Miya while saying, "I just want my bird back."

"What if there was no bird," Douglas asked. It was the third time Linda had been asked that question, and she still didn't have an answer to the question. Her confused look gave her away. Douglas decided to follow it up with, "What if the mirror had been there all along?"

"I don't understand," Linda said.

"You will," Miya said.

Linda turned around to look at Miya, but said nothing. She heard a sound behind her, and turned around again to see Douglas leaping down from the tree. He didn't just fall to his feet like most people do. He appeared to float down slowly, coming to a soft landing on the ground.

Douglas smiled. He knew Linda was close to getting it; close to understanding. Most importantly, she was close to accepting everything. He decided to ask one more question, "What if those were your wings that you had cut?"

"Why would I cut my own wings?" Linda asked, missing the bigger question at first. However, she caught herself, and glanced around confused. She tilted her head sideways and said, "I don't have wings."

"You don't now, but only because you cut them off," Douglas tried to explain.

"Why would I do a thing like that?" She asked.

"This is why," Douglas said softly. He quickly leaned in and gave Linda a soft kiss. His lips barely had a chance to touch hers before she pulled away.

She fell to the ground while screaming, "NO!"

"Don't do it," She said as she fell to her knees. She buried her face in her hands while crying, "Don't do it. We can never kiss again."

"Sure we can," Douglas said.

"No," she said with a voice that cracked through the tears, "Kiss more than once, and bad things happens."

"Like what?" Douglas asked.

Linda looked up at Miya and said only, "Kiss more than once and she has to sleep under a tree."

Miya looked down at Linda while shaking her head, "You still don't get it. It wasn't your fault."

"Then whose fault was it?" Linda asked while crying into the palms of her hands.

"Sometimes, it's nobody's fault. Sometimes bad things happen, and people just go to sleep," Miya said. She kept shaking her head while saying, "I should have listened to my mom is all, so I guess that makes it my fault."

"I just wanted one more kiss," Linda said through the tears.

Miya knelt down to try and look Linda in the face, "And I just wanted to swim in the pool."

"You were too young, you couldn't swim," Linda said.

"See, it wasn't your fault," Miya said while placing her hand on Linda's shoulder.

Linda looked up at Douglas while saying, "I just wanted one more kiss." She turned to look at Miya, "I was going to come save you. I just had to kiss Douglas one more time."

"It was already too late," Miya said, "Sometimes accidents can happen faster than a kiss."

"Just one more kiss," Linda repeated. The tears slowly faded and she almost regained her composure. She tried to repress it all again and looked up at Douglas while saying, "Can I have my bird back."

"There was no bird," Douglas said, "Those are your feathers."

"Don't be ridiculous," Linda insisted.

"Is this ridiculous?" Douglas asked. He pulled his overcoat from his shoulders and showed Linda how serious he was. From under his overcoat, a pair of large white wings unfolded and spread out wide.

She only stared. When his wings fully unfolded, they rose fifteen feet in the air and extended twelve feet out in each direction. That was with them folded in, so she could only imagine how wide he could stretch them out.

He reached out his hand to Linda while saying, "Now come with me. It's time to stop punishing yourself. I forgive you. Miya forgives you. Our father forgives you. You just need to forgive yourself."

"I can't. I made a mistake," She said softly. She didn't immediately take his hand.

Douglas only smiled while explaining, "It's not the mistakes you make that determine who you are. It's the mistakes you learn from."

"It's not your fault," Miya said one last time.

Slowly, Linda reached out her hand. Douglas grabbed a gentle hold with his hand, and slowly pulled Linda to her feet. As she stood up, she noticed several feathers on the ground. She looked around, somewhat confused. Before she could move, Douglas pulled her closer to him. He reached in, and kissed her softly. She didn't resist this time.

As they kissed, one feather after another began falling by Linda's feet. Slowly, two wings began growing from her back. By the time they were through kissing, Linda was wearing a pair of wings as magnificent as Douglas'. She extended them once, and smiled as she did so. She then curled them around her body and stroked them softly with her one free hand. Her other hand kept a tight grip on Douglas' hand. She suddenly felt the freedom she had desired. More importantly, she was ready for that freedom.

She smiled again. That was two smiles in as many minutes. She couldn't remember the last time she had smiled like that. She slowly leaned in, and gave Douglas a soft kiss. She just wanted one more kiss.

ANGEL

In the arms of an angel
I can do no wrong
In the arms of an angel
I can feel so strong

She holds me
Controls me
And keeps me in her heart
She is love
From above
All the way down to my heart

And the robes of an angel
Can dry all the tears
The pure robes of an angel
Can extinguish the fear

There always
Never strays
A guardian to the end

Here for me
Only me
The one I call a friend

When I look at an angel
And I see her smile
I draw such pleasure
I can float for miles

I dream
And she dreams

In that world we can meet

Be silent
So silent

And pay respect to her wondrous feats

The Candle

As the candle burns

And its shadow

Dances on the wall

I dance too

To the beat of the wind

Blowing gently

Through my open window

Making the shadow move

It's the only

Light around me

So my dancing

Has a purpose

To keep it entertained

And prevent it

From ever leaving me

Saint Nicholas, Prince of Klause

Prelude

In 1823, Clement C. Moore wrote a poem called "A Visit From St. Nicholas." Years later, the poem would be known as "The Night Before Christmas." This poem would eventually become one of the major contributors to the commercialization of Christmas. What's not so well known is where Clement C. Moore obtained his inspirations for the poem; until now.

Chapter One—The Lost Explorer

It should have happened a long time ago. Maybe it happened once, and people had simply forgotten. After all, man had conquered most of the other lands. So, why hadn't anyone ever been to the North Pole? It seemed like a simple question for Charles Harris who had set out to be the first person to reach the North Pole. His goal was to get there before the turn of the eighteenth century. That was just the goal.

The reality, at least for Charles, was that he was lost. Not only lost, but alone; long separated from his expedition team for two days now. He was standing on the edge of a low cliff that slanted down into the cold arctic ocean. He reached over his shoulder to pull a diary out of his backpack. With trembling hands, he began to write. He noted his location, and a detailed description of his surroundings. There wasn't much to write about. There was the snow, and there was the ice, and there was the water. That was it. The cliff curved off to the left, though he couldn't tell how far it curved due to the darkness.

For reasons that currently escaped him, Charles had decided to leave at the end of October. The problem of course was that, due to the Earth's tilt, the northern pole was darker in the later part of the year. His line of thinking had been that since it was darker, it would be colder and therefore the snow would be harder, almost like a road. The end result would be an easier crossing. He was wrong, and it looked like he was going to die for the mistake. He made a note of that in his diary as well.

The writing was slow, and he wondered if he'd be able to read his own words later. He also, in a moment of reflection, was curious if someone else would be able to read his dairy later if he were to die. He squinted his eyes as he tried to read what he had written. It was then that he realized the date; December 22, 1798. Christmas was only three days away. As he closed his diary, he began to ponder if he had the gift of being rescued coming his way.

He stepped back from the cliff a little and then began pressing on. He wanted to turn around and walk towards the light, in a southerly direction. Deep down inside, something told him to keeping moving north. The wind speed had started to pick up over the last hour, and now there was even a mild snow fall. He decided the best thing he could do was set up a camp so he could endure what looked like a coming storm. He took a quick survey of his surrounding and noticed a small ridge, barely a hundred yards away. It was only fifteen feet at its highest point, but it would serve as protection against the wind. If he was lucky, he might even be able to build a small fire.

A little more than an hour later, Charles was sitting inside a pitched tent with the ridge behind him and two piles of snow on each side of him. He had dug up the snow piles to make walls that would offer added protection from the harsh weather that he could hear blowing past him with high pitched whistles. He pulled a large piece of jerky from his back pack, and curled up around a very small lantern. The fire was hardly large enough to warm him, but over time the heat built up inside the tent and he could almost say he was comfortable. The small fire also gave him a little light, and he was able to watch the flame flicker from side to side. It provided him with some comfort, and almost acted as a friend.

Charles even caught himself starting to talk to the flickering light, if for no other reason than to hear his own voice. Once he realized what he was doing, he laughed lightly, and went back to nibbling on his jerky. His eyes slowly got heavy. Eventually, the hypnotic dance of the fire, combined with the tranquil hum from the ever strengthening wind, allowed him to relax enough to drift off to sleep.

The sleep wasn't to last. After a little more than an hour of in and out sleep, Charles was awaken by a violent blast of wind. Two large chunks of snow were blown into his tent and sent it rolling, with him inside. The first piece of snow wasn't too large, but it woke him and caused the tent to move. Charles had just enough time to brace himself before another large block of snow hit the side of his tent and caused it to begin to tip over. It only took the wind to blow the tent away from the side of the ridge. Charles did his best to brace himself and let his body roll with the tent, all the while hoping it would stop before going too far.

Charles counted three flips before he realized that counting was the least of his worries. He could feel the wind through the tent, and he knew that his ride was far from over. Flip after flip took its toll on Charles. He could feel one bump as he slammed onto his thigh, then another as he landed on his back. If he had been allowed time to think about it, he would have begun to worry about the cliff that was on the side of the arctic ocean. However, there wasn't time, and Charles never even knew when the tent rolled over the edge of that cliff.

At first, he heard the splash of water. What seemed like an eternity passed before he actually felt the water. His adrenaline kept him from feeling the cold of the water right away. He knew he had to get out of the water in a mater of seconds. It took close to a full minute before he made it to the side of the shore, and almost another minute to find the strength to climb out of the water and onto the narrow edge at the base of the cliffs. It was then that Charles began to know what real cold was all about.

Cold is simply the lack of heat. Even when the average person says their freezing, they still have some heat. There are points though were a person can literally be freezing, and Charles had just crossed that line. The wind was still blowing in a violent manner. There was also a heavy snow storm mixed with falling ice. Charles was soaked, and everything he had with him was now floating in the arctic ocean. He had no change of clothes, no food, and no fire. He didn't even have a dry towel.

His first response was to bring his arms in closer to his body to retain heat. Then, he squatted down and wrapped his arms around his legs. The warmth faded from his body; so too did his strength. In no time at all he was laying on his side, cuddled up into a ball. As he lay there, he focused on keeping his eyes opened. He knew he had to put all his strength into that one task. If they ever closed, even blinked, he risked never opening his eyes again. However, as the seconds, and then the minutes ticked away, he began blinking. Despite all his efforts, his eyes closed. After that day, Charles would spend the rest of his life being thankful that he didn't die then and there. He was about to receive his desired gift, and so much more.

Chapter Two—Shelter

He had no idea how much timed had passed, and never did find out. Eventually, his eyes opened up again. It was a loud popping noise that woke him. His eye lids parted and let a small amount of light rush in. He was greeted by a wall of whiteness. His first thoughts were that he had died, and was in heaven. However, from his left side he could feel some heat. That made him wonder if his post life journey hadn't taken him in a more southerly direction. He pulled his hands away from his chest and could feel he was covered in something. He looked down and saw a large white fur blanket covering his body.

Charles tried to sit up, but still didn't have enough strength to make such a move. He did manage to roll over on his left side and take a look at his surroundings. He appeared to be inside an igloo. It was about fifteen feet across with two cots on the floor, including the one he was on. In the center, there was a small fire with smoke flowing up through a small hole in the center of the roof. On two opposite sides of the hole there were large slabs of what appeared to be meat hanging down. On the other side of the fire, there was a small door with another white fur blanket hanging in front of it. Next to the door there was a large wooden chest. Other than that, the igloo was empty.

Charles first felt comfort, then relief as he suddenly realized he was alive. He laid on his back and allowed himself to relax. As time passed, Charles began to wonder. The igloo obviously belonged to someone, but who? He was alive, and that must have been do to the aid of someone, but who? Just who would have been out in that storm and found Charles in time to keep him alive? He would have to wait to find that answer, but eventually he would find out.

After a long couple of hours, Charles heard a noise. It sounded like a rustling at first, and came from a distance. As the noise got louder, Charles could tell it was something moving through the snow towards the igloo. When the sounds could be heard on the other side of the igloo wall, Charles began to worry. It sounded like a beast of sorts. Charles could hear the heavy foot steps moving around as well as heavy breathing. That is what worried Charles the most, the fact that he could hear the breathing through the wall.

Finally though, his fears were put aside when he heard a voice. He couldn't make out the words, but there was definitely a conversation taking place outside. He just wished he had the strength to rise to his feet and investigate the sounds for himself. He moved his head closer to the wall to try and listen. All he could hear was the breathing and what sounded like chewing. Then, from the other side of the igloo there was another noise. Charles turned his head to see a hand pulling back the fur blanket that draped over the doorway. At last, he was going to meet his savior.

From behind the fur, there appeared a man. He was short in height, standing just barely five feet tall. He was also slender and had a long, thin jaw. His eyes were set back behind a narrow, but well defined nose. His hair was dark, neat, and went beneath his shoulders. The man's skin looked to be lightly tanned, though not dark like an Eskimo or any other native. However, as he looked at the man, Charles suddenly realized that he could, in fact, see the man's skin. He was wearing only tanned leather pants, moccasin boots, and a leather top that looked like a vest with sleeves. There was a stripe of white fur down the sides of his legs, apparently sown onto the pants. He also had two small stripes of fur that came down over his shoulders and across his chest. Down his right arm, he had a long tattoo of a cross with a star in the top left corner of the cross. On his left forearm he had a bracelet that looked like a cross with the shorter bars wrapping around his arm. Around his neck there was a necklace with a small cross pendant.

He looked like no man Charles had ever seen before. The man brought with him a presence of both fear and comfort. Charles only stared. After completely entering the igloo, the man looked at Charles. At first he shook his head. He walked over to Charles who only stared up at the man, not knowing what to say.

The man studied Charles from his head to his toes. Then, he looked deep into Charles's eyes and said only, "You need sleep. Tomorrow I will take you to the prince. But sleep now." His words were barely understandable to Charles. They carried a European accent, almost Prussian. However, Charles never had a chance to respond. As soon as the man spoke, he extended his right hand, and waved his fingers. Charles swore he saw stars fly from the tips of the man's fingers, but that was the last thing he remembered. His eyes closed again and he drifted off to a deep, yet comforting, sleep.

It felt like he had been sleeping for days, or maybe even weeks, when Charles once again awoke. In fact, it had only been a few hours, and he was awoken by the soft nudge of his strange savior.

"Here, eat this," the man said with a forceful accent as he handed Charles a makeshift wooden bowl filled with berries on one side, and a piece of meat on the other.

"Thank you," Charles moaned as he accepted the bowl. The man didn't reply. He simply turned around and walked over to his cot. He had his own bowl of berries and meat which he set on his cot. He then walked over to the wooden chest which now had a large leather satchel on top of it. The man reached into the bag and pulled out a book that measured close to six inches in thickness. It looked old and ragged, though it had an antique quality to it.

The man sat down and opened the book towards the back. He slowly began reading, only occasionally reaching for a single berry. Once in a while he would stop and take a large bite from the piece of meat. Charles watched while eating from his own bowl. Finally, the silence began to get to him and he asked, "So what's your name?"

The man never looked up. He reached for a single berry as he said, "Mien namen ist Geister."

"I see," Charles said, not knowing what else to say.

There was a long period of silence as Charles ate slowly. He continued to glance around the igloo. His eyes kept coming back to Geister. There really wasn't much else to look at in the small round room. He still couldn't fathom how the strange man was able to live in such a harsh environment without any protection. After another long period of silence, Charles spoke up, "So where are we?"

Again, Geister never looked up as he replied, "We are not too far away."

"Away from what?" Charles asked, very curiously.

Geister glanced at Charles, and with a smile, answered only, "The Prince."

"The prince of what?"

Geister looked back at his book as he replied, "You ask too many questions. You should rest." He again waved his hand, and Charles again saw a series of stars fly at him.

Immediately, Charles was out. As he slept, he dreamed, but only about being lost in the snow. He saw himself searching for something, but never knew exactly what. Eventually the dream ended. His eyes opened at the sound of a thunderous boom. In his dream it was a bolt of thunder, but in reality it was Geister opening his wooden chest. He had his leather satchel strung over his shoulder, and appeared to be looking for something.

Charles sat right up as his dream quickly merged with his reality. He glanced over at Geister who looked back and almost appeared to smile as he said, "Sorry."

"It's okay," Charles replied as he wiped a small amount of sweat from his brow. He was surprised at how much heat the igloo held from the small fire. Combined with the fur blanket, he was almost uncomfortably warm. He still remembered falling in the water and being cold, so he wasn't about to complain.

Slowly, he pulled the fur blanket away from himself as he watched Geister dig through his chest.

After a few minutes of searching, Geister closed the chest, then walked over to Charles. "You feel better? Warmer? Stronger?"

"Yes," Charles replied as he completely sat up in his cot. It wasn't until then that he noticed he was wearing only his long underwear. "My cloths, where are my cloths?" He asked as he pulled the fur blanket over himself in an effort to keep covered.

"They were wet, so I burned them."

"Oh, I see," Charles replied with a little confusion. He wasn't upset by any means. After all, Geister had saved his life and taken him in.

He just sat there on the cot with the fur blanket wrapped around himself and rested his head in his hand. He was pondering his situation while also keeping a loose eye on Geister who made his way casually out of the igloo with his leather satchel. Charles moved his head a little to try and see where Geister was going, but to no avail. The hanging fur blocked any view of the outside, and Charles just didn't yet have the strength to be too curious.

A few moments later, Geister reentered the igloo with a different satchel. He walked over, and handed it to Charles while saying, "Here, you can wear this?"

"I can?" Charles replied as he took the satchel and looked at it, wondering exactly what he was supposed to wear.

Geister didn't answer, rather he turned and again exited from the igloo. Charles laid the satchel down on the cot next to himself and opened it. First, he pulled out a pair of fur pants. They were black, unlike the blanket he had wrapped around himself. Charles wondered where Geister would have gotten the black fur from this far north. Just about every animal in the arctic was white. Before pulling anything else out, he went ahead and slid into his new pants. To his surprise, they fit perfectly, almost as though they had been made for him. Again, he reached into the satchel and this time pulled out a moccasin vest and a long sleeve moccasin shirt. At first he questioned them, but decided to go ahead and put them on. There were already enough things for him to be confused about, and he didn't want to add to the list by worrying about his attire.

The last thing in the bag was a pair of moccasin boots. As he was sliding the second boot on, and marveling at the perfect fit, Geister again entered the igloo. This time, he was carrying a pail of water which he slowly poured over the fire. After setting the pale down, he looked at Charles and asked, "Are you ready?"

"For what?"

"I am going to see the prince. You will come with me."

"Very well," Charles said in an agreeable manner.

Geister didn't say anything else. He turned around and proceeded out of the igloo. Slowly, Charles rose to his feet. He still felt tired, but was able to get up and move around some. He made his way past the smoldering ashes that had been the fire, then pulled open the hanging fur that served as a door. He was greeted by a short tunnel, then a few steps which he climbed before finally being out in the open arctic air. It was different this time. The snow seemed to have a purity to it, and the wind was moving at a slow, friendly speed. Also, the sky was lit up by a glow of colors that Charles had heard tales of in the past. They were the Northern Lights; also know as the Aura Borealis. Few men had ever seen them, though many had speculated about their nature. Charles joined those men as he awed at its presence. It looked magical and had a quality unlike anything he had ever seen.

Off to his left, there was another light. When he turned, Charles saw it was a large pole with a torch on top. Next to it was a trough with water in it, and a small fire beneath the trough to keep the water melted. Beside the trough, there was a large pile of hay. Charles nodded his head as he realized the noise he had heard when he awoke the first time must have been a horse. He looked back to his right, then again to his left as he tried to find Geister. After deciding to circle the igloo, he heard someone call from behind, "Charles, come now. We go."

"Oh, huh?" Charles mumbled, confused about the source of the words. When he turned around, his eyes saw the horse that he had heard and seen traces of. However, it wasn't like any horse he had ever seen. In fact, it wasn't much of a horse at all. It stood close to eight feet at the shoulders. This might have made it just a big horse, except it had large branching antlers. Geister was already on the back, and there were two packs on each side of the animal. Charles was immediately struck by the fact that Geister was wearing the same cloths, and not bundled up at all.

"What kind of a horse is that?" Charles asked with great curiosity.

"Not a horse, a reindeer."

"I see, well he's big," Charles said, trying to find a way to comment on the situation.

Geister only patted the large reindeer on the back and added, "Yes, but very gentle." He then snapped the reins, and the large reindeer leaned down; allowing Charles to climb on behind Geister. Once on top, the reindeer stood up straight. Geister turned and smiled at Charles while asking, "Ready?"

"I guess."

"Very well then. Hold on."

Geister snapped the reins while saying, "Geht Donnert!"

Then, with great speed and power, the reindeer named Donnert began running away from the igloo. Within the first few steps, Charles swore he heard a giant clap of thunder. They moved swiftly across the snow, and despite the speed, it was a very smooth ride. Charles wanted to ask where they were going, but two previous attempts to find out resulted in only a vague mention of a prince. He simply decided relax and enjoy the ride.

Chapter Three—The North Pole

They rode for close to three hours. It was quiet, except for the occasional burst of thunder. Charles said little, and Geister said less. Charles watched the sheets of snow and ice go by, and marveled at the dancing lights in the sky. A little off to the left, there was a large plateau, and he noticed Geister was slowly steering Donnert towards the raised surface. After another half hour, Charles could see them approaching closer and closer to the plateau. Within a short time, Donnert was slowing down at the beckoning of Geister. Finally, the large reindeer had slowed to a trot as they stood not far from the plateau which measured a quarter of a mile across.

"Do you like?" Geister asked as he glanced over his shoulder at Charles.

"Like? Like what?" Came the slightly confused response.

"The castle," Geister said rather bluntly. His voice sounded almost as though he was frustrated over having to clarify something so obvious.

Charles saw no castle, and responded likewise, "What castle? What are you talking about?"

Geister looked at Charles, then up at the top of the plateau, then back at Charles again. "You really don't see it?" he asked sincerely.

"All I see is snow. What should I see?"

"What do you want to see?"

"Huh?" Charles asked, obviously confused. If there was anything he wanted to see at that moment it was a big steak next to a soft warm bed. He didn't see anything.

Geister turned and looked directly at Charles before stating, "You have to concentrate. You have to want to see it."

"Concentrate on what? See what?"

"The castle, the prince's castle."

Charles, now frustrated, only shook his head. He looked up at the plateau, and again only saw the snow, ice, and the Northern Lights. He then looked back at Geister and stated simply, "I'm sorry, but I don't believe I see anything."

"That is your problem, you don't believe. You must have faith. Only faith will show you the way. If you have faith that it is there, then it will be there for you. Always."

"Faith?"

"It's the only way."

"Very well, I will try."

"Don't try. Succeed. It's the only way," Geister said in a convincing manner.

Charles shrugged his shoulders, then looked towards the top of the plateau. He watched the Northern Lights dancing high above, and tried to figure out what exactly he was supposed to see. He looked across the plateau from the left to the right, then back again, but didn't see anything. He began to get discouraged, and slowly closed his eyes. He relaxed his shoulders and took a deep breath. He looked up, and opened his eyes. Still, he saw nothing; at least not at first. However, as he moved his eyes across the top of the plateau, he began to see several flickers. He thought it was just the Northern Lights, but quickly realized they were being reflected off of something.

Charles blinked and did a quick double take. He closed his eyes, and tried to relax even more. He took another deep breath and then opened his eyes again. This time, he saw something. The whole plateau lit up, and brightly reflected the Northern Lights. The light was being reflected off a structure that was unlike anything Charles had ever seen before.

Geister had said there was a castle, and sure enough, Charles was looking at one. It wasn't a castle of stone though, rather one of ice. In fact, It almost looked like a diamond structure because of the way the light reflected off the crystal clear ice. Charles could only marvel at the beauty. Slowly, Charles moved his stare across the structure. The entire plateau was a high wall with a tall tower approximately every hundred feet. On one end, there were several structures, and the other end, there was one large building. The exact details of the castle weren't immediately visible because of the darkness and the flickering Northern Lights. Even without the details, Charles could tell it was a thing of pure beauty.

"I see it," Charles exclaimed. He was still in shock that what had appeared as simply a snow covered flat rock, now appeared as a large magnificent castle. Charles turned to Geister while saying, "There really is a castle." His voice carried the tone of surprise, but also of relief that it was there.

Geister smiled while stating, "Yes, it is. Now, you see what faith gets you?"

"I guess," Charles replied, still in disbelief. He couldn't help but wonder if he wasn't just seeing things as a result of his recent misfortunes. He had to admit that since his fall into the water, everything he had seen had been something out of the ordinary. A bump on the head would have explained a lot. He went so far as to wonder if perhaps he hadn't died.

Charles didn't have long to question things. His mindset was disrupted by a clash of thunder. Immediately, Donnert began running straight towards the plateau. Charles watched intensely as the the large reindeer showed no sign of slowing down, despite the approaching structure. As they were about to make contact with the frozen rocky base of the plateau, Charles felt himself suddenly being thrown back when the reindeer lifted up. Charles fought off the urge to let out a scream as he was now in a more horizontal position, and riding straight up the side of the plateau. Then, as quickly as he had been thrown back, he was again sitting in a vertical position as the horse slowed at the top of the plateau.

Charles was amazed. The view that he had of the arctic world just kept getting better and better. Donnert turned around in a slow circle, and Charles was able to look down from the plateau and see the long trail of footprints that Donnert had left behind. The scene was both beautiful and tranquil as the Northern Lights danced across the snow. Donnert kept spinning around, and Charles' eyes were moved to the walls of the castle. The walls were carved from clear blocks of ice with each block being about ten feet long, and five feet tall. It was unclear how thick they were.

Charles' eyes moved along the wall until he saw a gate. The gate was also made of ice, though it was lined with silver and adorned with a gold cross. In the upper left corner of the cross, there was a silver emblem of a star. It was similar to the tattoo on Geister's arm. Donnert stood in front of the gate and moved a little from side to side as Geister reached down by his side, and pulled up a small curled horn. He then looked up at the gate and blew the horn softly. The sound that flew out was not the normal loud and obnoxious sound that comes from a horn, rather it was somewhat tranquil, soft even.

It only took a few moments after the horn sounded before the large gate began to open. The golden cross that was embroidered across the gate split in half as the two sides of the gate swung inward. Once the gate was completely open, the large beast known as Donnert began moving again. Slowly they rode into the fantastic castle.

As they entered, Charles could see a near mirror image of Donnert. On the new beast's back was a man, similar in build to Geister, though with fiery red hair. His attire was slightly different to Geister's with the fur down his pants and over the top of the vest being darker. Geister maneuvered Donnert closer to the reindeer as both men reached out and shook hands.

The two men exchanged words in a language that Charles didn't understand. It sounded European, but he couldn't place it specifically. As the men spoke, the two reindeer seemed to also be communicating. Their faces moved close together and they rubbed each other's cheeks. It was a rather affectionate sight, Charles noted. The moment was a brief one and the two men concluded their discussion rather quickly.

"Is everything all right?" Charles asked while continuing to stare at the man with the fiery red hair.

"Yes. All is well," Geister said.

"Who was that?" Charles then asked. It was only one of a thousand questions he could have asked at that moment.

"His name is Baldrich. He is the keeper of Blitzen and the first priest of the palace," Geister explained.

"Blitzen?" Charles asked.

"Yes, Blitzen," Geister said. He patted Donnert on back and added, "This is Donnert. Baldrich rides Blitzen."

"I see," Charles said as if he were really starting to understand. As they rode further into the castle, Charles continued to look around in awe. The gates opened up into a large circular courtyard. On the left of the courtyard there were four small buildings, each measuring about fifty feet across.

What stood out most to Charles was that even the inside of the castle was made of ice. There were traces of gold and silver in various places, but that was just for adornment. The most notable, and most consistent adornments were the crosses and stars. On every door, Charles could see the symbol of the golden cross with the silver star in the upper left corner.

To Charles's right, there was a small fenced in area filled with small statues. Next to that was another single building that looked remarkably like a church. It was made of masonry of some kind. Charles couldn't fathom where anyone could have quarried so much stone this far north. Even at its thinnest points, the depth of the ice was measured in yards, not inches.

Charles could not see what was along the back wall of the castle because his field of view was obstructed by a tree. Not just any tree, but an evergreen. Here he was in the middle of the northern arctic, and Charles stood face to face with the largest evergreen tree he had ever seen. It rose more than a hundred feet in the air. The trunk was ten feet across, and rose fifteen feet before the first branches sprout out twenty feet in every direction.

"What kind of tree is that?" Charles asked.

"Tis Ygdrassil, the tree of life," Geister replied dismissively.

"But how did it get here?" Charles inquired.

"The prince planted it when he first came here. Since then, it has just grown."

"How long does it take to grow a tree that big?" Charles asked to himself.

Wrapped around the tree was a short wooden post fence. Within the fence, there were six more reindeer eating from a large pile of hay.

"How many reindeer are there?" Charles asked as they rode up to the large pile of hay.

"Only eight," Geister said.

"What are the names of the other six?"

"There is Dasher, Dancer, Prancer, Vixen, Comet, Cupid," Geister pointed as he named them off. He paused and added, "Of course we cannot forget Donnert and Blitzen."

Charles cocked his head to the side as he listened to Geister. "What kind of names are those?" He asked.

"Names the prince likes."

"Do I get to meet this prince?" Charles asked again.

"Yes, but not now," Geister said as he climbed off Donnert. Before Charles could say anything else, Geister waved his hand in front of the eager explorer and said, "Right now, you need more rest." And with that, Charles was out like a light.

Chapter Four—Man, Myth, or Legend

Charles didn't know what time it was when he woke up. The darkness was constant, so it always felt like eight o'clock at night. It was most likely the silence that opened his eyes. Even for a place that sat in the middle of nowhere and surrounded by nothing but snow, it was still too quiet. He sat up in his bed and looked around. The window was covered and the door was closed, so all he could see was darkness. He managed to feel his way to the window where he pulled the drapes to the side. The Northern Lights filled his view. They glimmered across the horizon; dancing like ferries performing a Shakespearean play.

The light let him find his way around the room, and eventually his clothes and boots. Once dressed, he slowly opened the door and peeked outside. No one could be seen, so he proceeded down the hallway. He came to a circular intersection and turned left, confidant he knew where he was going. Fifty feet down that hall, he came to a pair of double doors. The blast of cold could be felt as soon as the doorknob was turned.

Once outside, he immediately closed the door behind himself. He was standing at the main entrance to the castle. This left him staring at the large tree which was in the center of the courtyard. The smaller houses were off to his right and the church was to his left. He looked up and could see what appeared to be a bright light at the top of the tree. It was pure white, and left a halo glowing around the upper most part of the tree. It was a minor contrast to the flicker of color that could be seen on the horizon.

There was another building that looked very much like a church to Charles' right. Between him and that building, there was a collection of statues. He had noticed the statues when he first entered the castle and was drawn towards them. He approached slowly, and never stopped looking over his shoulder. He knew he had been invited to this place, but still felt like an intruder.

Charles stood in front of the snow covered statues and stared. The ever shifting Northern Lights caste an eerie illumination over the collection of stone statues. Charles counted twenty-eight different statues, all lined up seven across and four rows deep. Each statues was different, though they all had a few things in common. All of the statues were of children, and they were all depicted on their knees with their hands clasped in front of their chests. However, each statue was different in features, as if they were each representing a different child. They were close to being evenly split between boys and girls, though a variety of ages were represented.

It presented a very tranquil visualization for Charles. He couldn't help but notice how close to a cemetery it appeared, though he suspected there was more to the statues than that. He slowly turned around and his attention was again drawn to the large tree in the center of the courtyard.

Beneath the tree, Charles could see the eight large beast that Geister referred to as reindeer. They were powerful to say the least, but they carried a peaceful presence that night. Seven of them were sitting under the tree, sleeping the night away. An eighth one was pacing slowly back and forth in front of the tree. She was larger than the others which seemed to contradict most species where the males are always larger. After a few moments of studying her, Charles remembered her as being the reindeer that Balderich has been riding. Her name was Blitzen.

Charles took slow steps as he walked towards the Blitzen. He held his left hand out and maintained eye contact with the reindeer who kept pacing back and forth, almost in a nervous manner. "You doing all right there?" Charles asked as he reached over the fence to gently pet the large animal.

"She's expecting," A raspy voice said from behind Charles.

Charles' heart stopped beating from the shock of hearing another voice. He turned around slowly to see Balderich standing ten feet behind him. "Good lord, you scared me," Charles said while placing his hand on his chest to make sure his heart was still beating.

"I'm sorry," Balderich said. He never moved and stared at Charles with a harsh glare. "Is everything fine out here?"

"Yeah, it's fine," Charles replied with a stutter.

"If you need anything, just ask," Balderich said without breaking the stare.

"Sure will," Charles said.

Balderich didn't reply. He turned around and walked away. Charles went back to admiring Blitzen who continued her nervous pacing. The fact that she was expecting explained both her large size and her nervousness. Charles reached across the fence to try and touch her again, but just as his hand made contact with her chin, she turned to walk back in the other direction. Charles moved slowly around the fence while watching Blitzen. As she turned around to walk back the other way, Charles saw something else move in the distance.

He tilted his head to the side and squinted his eyes to try and make it out, but all he could see was a flicker of red near the church. He saw a brief wave of light that seemed to come from the inside as the door to the church was opened quickly then closed. Naturally curious, Charles made his way towards the entrance to the church.

At the front of the church was a pair of large wooden doors. Stretched across both doors was the now familiar emblem consisting of a large cross with a star in the upper left corner. The cross was steel in both color and texture. When Charles touched the cross with his hand, he could feel the cold of the arctic north absorbed in the hard metal. Slowly, Charles turned the handle that opened the door. The heavy door made a loud creaking sound, the kind that penetrates the quiet night like a scream. He only opened it up enough to slide in before slowly pulling the door shut again.

Charles stood in a round vestibule that was lit up by candles. There was a small door to the left and a larger doorway directly ahead of him that led into the main body of the church. There was a shimmer of light coming from the other side of the doorway, though not enough to illuminate everything. As soon as Charles passed through the doorway, he froze in his tracks. In the center isle between the rows of pews, there was a man. He was no more than ten feet away from the alter, between the first row of pews.

He was kneeling down on one knee with his head lowered in prayer. Though he was kneeling, Charles estimated the man's height at well over six foot tall. He was wearing a large red robe with a silver trim to it. The robe had a hood on the back to cover the head.

There were a small row of candles lined up around the alter, illuminating the front part of the cathedral. Behind the alter, there was another large cross. Like the rest of them, it had the emblem of a star in the upper left corner. The only difference from the other crosses is that this one was gold with a silver lining. The symbol was also on the front of the alter. Along both walls, there were a series of sconces. The sconces were wrought iron, and in the shape of a cross. Every other sconce had a candle burning in it. This partial illumination gave the church a warm, yet mysterious feel to it.

From what little Charles could see, the cathedral had a very elegant appearance which kept consistent with everything else he had seen in the castle. The sides of the pews were all lined in gold and silver. At the end of each of them was the all too familiar symbol of the cross and the star.

Charles remained completely motionless as he watched the man do nothing. He would occasionally glance upwards at the cross before him, but promptly lowered his head again each time. He wanted to approach the man, but he also wanted to quietly slip away; more out of respect than fear. Surely a man kneeling in front of an alter wouldn't harm him. However, the decision to leave or stay was not going to be left to Charles. Through the silence of the night, the man spoke.

"Can I help you?" The man asked with a graveled voice that carried a heavy accent with it.

At first, Charles was stunned. Maybe he was talking to someone else. There was no one else. He was talking to Charles, but that didn't prevent the frightened explorer from asking, "me?"

"Yes. Is there something I can do for you Charles?"

"How do you know my name?" Charles asked as he took a careful step towards the man.

"Because, you are a guest at my home," Came the reply from the man as he slowly rose to his feet. Once standing, Charles could tell that the man stood close to seven feet tall. He towered over the 5'6" would-be adventurer.

"So this is your place? All of it?" Charles asked respectfully.

"Yes."

"And you are the prince?"

The man turned around to look at Charles. As he turned, he pulled the hood back from his robe. His face was covered in a white beard that was sprinkled with hints of silver. His eyes carried a glow to them, but also sagged a bit, as if worn from a long life. Across his forehead, Charles could see a long scar.

"Yes. I'm Nicholas, Prince of Klause," the man said.

"This is Klause?" Charles asked.

"No, I'm afraid not," the man said.

"So you are a prince somewhere else?" Charles pondered out loud.

"Another place, another time," Nicholas said with a long face.

"I see," Charles said, and was immediately lost for any other words.

"This is just a place where I live," Nicholas said, "a place where I hide."

"Hide? Who do you hide from?"

Nicholas walked slowly past Charles while casting a hard stare, "A lot of people."

"I didn't mean to pry," Charles said softly.

"You're not prying. I have no secrets to hide, just a past that will always haunt me." The words Nicholas spoke came out slow, almost as if it hurt to even talk about his past.

"Is someone after you?" Charles asked, now wondering if he was as safe as he thought he was.

"I doubt it. Not anymore. They are long since gone," Nicholas said, though his face didn't show the signs of relief that would comfort Charles. He only momentarily glanced at Charles while continuing to walk towards the vestibule.

"Then why are you hiding?" Charles asked, more out of concern for his safety than anything.

Nicholas froze in his tracks. He turned around and looked downward at Charles. His eyes stared into the very soul of the explorer, "Don't be fooled. Evil is everywhere."

"That sounds a little paranoid," Charles suggested, though he was careful to speak with respect.

Nicholas said nothing at first. He pulled down the collar of his robe to reveal a scar that ran the full length of his neck. "Does this look like just a little paranoia?"

"What in the hell?" Charles whispered in amazement. The scar was two inches thick and wrapped around Nicholas' entire neck.

"Hell indeed," Nicholas said as he again turned to walk into the vestibule of the cathedral. "You die once Charles, then we can talk equally of paranoia." Nicholas spoke slowly, almost begging Charles to understand. He never once came across as arrogant, or as if he felt above Charles. He had a perspective that he knew few people could and would understand.

"What happened?" Charles asked, then quickly added, "If you don't mind me asking."

Nicholas paused mid-step. They were standing next to the last row of pews in the body of the church. He turned again to Charles and said, "I don't mind you asking. And, I don't mind telling you. But do you mind listening?"

"Not at all."

Both men took seats on the last row of pews. Charles sat on the left side of the aisle, and Nicholas sat on the right side. Nicholas took several deep breaths before finally saying, "I am a Christian, you understand that?"

"Yes, of course," Charles said.

"Well, I wasn't always such," Nicholas said with a bit of confession in his voice.

"No one is perfect," Charles said in an attempt to be understanding.

"I killed a man. I killed more than one in fact," Nicholas explained, "It's nothing that I am at all proud of, but something I tell everyone. I have made peace with this fact a long, long, time ago."

Charles listened to the narrative that Nicholas presented. "I was a man still in my teens, but ready to take on the whole world. That whole world included the Romans."

"Romans?" Charles asked with clear confusion.

"Yes. They had made their way to the southern most parts of what is now called Denmark."

"When was this?" Charles interrupted.

"I forget. The early part of the first millennium of our Lord."

The idea that Nicholas was so old hit Charles like a slap in the face. Surely something was amiss, but Charles said nothing. He decided to let Nicholas relay the whole story before jumping to conclusions.

"They had set up a small camp near our village and we decided to send an early message that they weren't welcome. In the dark of night, we struck."

Nicholas paused to reflect on his words before going on, "I killed three men before being captured myself. In the end, I think it was only my youth which saved me. A priest took pity on me, and decided my soul was worth saving. I spent the next seven years learning languages, arts, and science. I also learned the bible and the word of our Lord."

Nicholas paused. He looked up at the large cross hanging behind the alter before turning back to Charles, "I learned what morals were, and was taught the difference between love and hatred." He squinted his eyes while adding, "On a very fundamental level."

He then relaxed a little before going on, "Ten years later I returned to what was left of my village and set up a monastery of my own. The Romans had never been able to conquer my people. On one level, it made me proud. On another, I felt sadness."

"Why sadness," Charles interrupted.

"I despised much of the Romans and who they were. But still, if not for them, I would have never found my way to God. I took it as a personal challenge to spread the word to my people. If I could have saved just one soul, I would have been happy."

"How did you do?" Charles asked.

"Within two years, I had a school of children. I taught them, I worked with them, and I prayed with them."

Nicholas' eyes lowered a little as he mentioned praying with the children. He looked up at Charles and began to speak before getting interrupted. Balderich came running into the church while shouting, "Come quick. Blitzen is about to give birth."

Chapter Five—The Birth of Fire

Nicholas followed Balderich out of the church. Charles walked behind them, but at a much slower pace. He didn't feel directly connected to anything going on in or around the castle. At best, he was an outside observer to a world he was still trying to understand.

Once he passed through the doors of the church, the harsh cold fell upon Charles immediately. Nicholas and Balderich were standing near the large tree. Blitzen could be seen laying on her side next to them. Geister and a few others were running outside from the main entrance to the castle. Charles remained standing by the church. His curious instincts were to be as close to the action as possible, but something else told him to keep a respectful distance.

He watched for close to five minutes as everyone gathered around the mother to be. Finally, he saw Nicholas walk over to Blitzen and kneel down. He rose back to his feet and lifted a young reindeer off the cold snow. Charles was hypnotized by the sight. From the sky, the scene was illuminated by the dancing flicker of colors, like a rainbow twisted into a knot. This light shined down on the large tree that served as the back drop for it all. Encircling the tree was the small group of large reindeer, all waiting anxiously to see the newest member of their herd.

In the center of it all, was a man of almost mythic proportions. Charles walked slowly towards the scene, now allowing his curiosity to take over again. Charles approached Nicholas who was carrying the newborn reindeer away. As Nicholas passed, Charles leaned in to get a good look. The newborn calf opened his eyes and looked back at Charles. It was an eerie stare, and Charles swore he could see a series of bright fiery sparks fly from the eyes of the young reindeer. Charles followed Nicholas and Balderich as they walked away from the scene.

"Where are you taking him?" Charles asked.

"Somewhere warm. He'll never survive the night in this cold," Nicholas replied as he walked in the direction of the church.

"With the storm approaching, I'm not sure how the the others are going to make it," Balderich added.

"How bad is the storm?" Charles asked.

"Bad," Balderich said with a harsh tone showing his frustration with the uncontrollable weather conditions.

"Is he going to be okay?" Charles inquired while running ahead of Nicholas to open the door to the church.

"If he makes it through the night, he'll be fine."

"What are the odds of that?" Charles asked while holding the door open for Nicholas and Balderich.

Nicholas walked through the door, and Balderich followed. "It's out of our hands now," Nicholas said. He walked all the way to the front of the church and knelt down before the alter, carefully setting the newborn calf on the ground. Balderich never left Nicholas' side. Charles kept a fair amount of distance from the two. He had gotten caught up in the rush of the moment, but was once again feeling like a third wheel; the lonely observer that he was.

What he witnessed next put everything he was experiencing, and everything he was in the middle of, into a perspective. Simultaneously, Nicholas and Balderich knelt down next to the young calf and lowered their heads in prayer. Charles had never been an active church patron. He would usually show up for either a Christmas or Easter mass, nothing more. Now though, he was not just witnessing, but experiencing something else; something different.

He could hear them each speaking, apparently saying their own prayers. The specific words eluded Charles, but he could tell they each said a prayer of thanks for the calf and a separate prayer for the health and well being of this newest resident. Maybe it was guilt, or maybe it was a new awakening, but Charles found himself slowly kneeling down to say a prayer of his own. His was different. He said a prayer more of thanks. He was alive, and he was seeing something magical, something that would change his life forever. He was truly grateful.

Several long moments passed. Charles watched as Nicholas and Balderich both rose to their feet. Ever the follower, Charles also rose, but kept a fair distance. "Seeing as how Blitzen is yours, I see it only proper that you be given the right to place a name on this newborn," Nicholas said to Balderich as he stepped off to the side.

"My grandfather made me the man I am today," Balderich began as he watched Nicholas reach for a small decanter of water.

Nicholas held the decanter with his left hand and poured a small amount of water into his right hand as he asked, "What was your grandfather's name?"

"Rudolph," Balderich said softly.

"So be it," Nicholas said as he sprinkled some of the water over the head of the calf, "I Christen thee, Rudolph."

Almost on cue, the young calf raised its eyes and looked directly at Charles. Again, the calf's eyes flickered with fire. "What's wrong with his eyes?" Charles asked.

Nicholas knelt down next to young Rudolph and Balderich leaned in over Nicholas' shoulder. Nicholas grabbed a firm hold of Rudolph by the back of his head, trying to get a close look at Rudolph's face, "Let's see what we have here."

Naturally, the calf was still trying to find control of his senses and his motor skills. Slowly, and with great care, Nicholas pulled back Rudolph's eye lids to open his eyes. A flash of fire flew from his eyes that was so bright, both Nicholas and Balderich were thrown back to the ground.

"Dear lord," Nicholas exclaimed.

"Where did that come from?" Balderich asked as he rose to his feet.

Nicholas also rose to his feet and looked down at Rudolph. He tugged on his beard in a thoughtful manner before suggesting, "I believe, from his very soul."

"Tis evil," Balderich said with great caution.

"Nay, tis righteous; the touch of God," Nicholas commented. His eyes wandered up towards the large cross that hung behind the alter. He turned to Balderich and politely asked, "Can you please bring Blitzen in here. I'm sure young Rudolph is hungry."

Balderich said nothing. He turned to walk away. He exited the church and left Charles and Nicholas with Rudolph who was struggling to stand for the first time. "Are you sure that he should be in here?" Charles asked.

"He'll never make it out there. Not in this cold," Nicholas said while looking at Rudolph with sympathy.

"But, in a church?" Charles asked.

Nicholas turned his head to Charles and said only, "What is a church if not a place of refuge?"

He let a quiet moment hang in the air before saying, "Jesus was born in a manger. I doubt seriously that he would question a calf being born in a church."

Nicholas turned to look at Rudolph before adding, "Especially one as special as this."

There was a quiet moment that was only interrupted by the door to the church being opened. Balderich led Blitzen into the church, tugging gently at the harness around the new mother's neck.

"Come now girl," Balderich said as he walked, "Just taking you to your boy."

Half way down the aisle, Balderich let go of the harness and allowed Blitzen to walk the rest of the way down the aisle alone. Nicholas and Charles both stepped aside to give the mother some room with her child. Charles swore he could see a smile on her face, proud of her young calf who would one day grow up to be the dominate buck in the herd.

Rudolph was standing, but too afraid to try and move. Three previous attempts at walking had failed, so he was content where he was. Blitzen lowered her head and gave a loving lick across Rudolph's face. He turned to his mother and looked up at her. When he opened his eyes to see her, another flash of light flared outwards. Again, out of instinct, Rudolph closed his eyes. At first Blitzen turned her head. It was a natural reaction to such a bright, almost blinding, light. Once the light had faded, Blitzen again looked at her son. She stared for a moment. She turned her head, followed by her body, and began to walk away.

"She's abandoning him, isn't she?" Charles asked with a whisper.

Nicholas nodded his head slowly, "Yes, it appears as though she is."

"What will happened to him?"

"Nothing," Nicholas said bluntly, "We'll raise him. He'll be fine."

"What about his eyes?"

"He'll be fine," Nicholas repeated as he turned to look at Balderich who was opening the door to let Blitzen out of the church. She actually paused at the door, and looked over her shoulder at Rudolph. She stared for a second, then lowered her head, and walked out of the church.

Chapter Six—Rebirth

Balderich held the door open for Geister and another man who Charles had only seen once when they first arrived. They all walked down the main aisle of the church. Balderich led, followed by Geister, and the other man. Charles could see something in the third man's hand. It was a long tube, or maybe a scroll.

The third man didn't look like Geister or Balderich. He resembled Nicholas, only thinner. Below his left eye, a long scare ran down his cheek. His hair hung long down his back and over his shoulders, though it was neatly groomed above his face. He wore far more clothes than any of the others, suggesting that he was not as accustom to the cold as anyone else. He had high boots on with several straps holding them tightly fit. Tucked into a few of the straps were what looked to be mid sized daggers. Besides the long scroll, he also had a brown leather back-pack strung over his shoulder.

"How is he?" The third man asked as he looked down at Rudolph who was still trying to master the fine art of standing.

"He'll be fine Vincent," Nicholas said for the third time, showing a kind of optimism that even Charles could almost find comfort in.

"Glad to hear," Vincent replied. He spun the long scroll in his hand as if it were a baton before asking, "Are you ready to go over the list?"

"Is that it?" Nicholas asked.

"Yes. It's the master list put together by myself and the others."

"Are your notes in here Geister?" Nicholas asked as he extended his hand and took the scroll from Vincent.

"Of course," Geister said.

Nicholas began unrolling the scroll and took a bare moment to peek at its contents. "Long list," He said begrudgingly.

"It's a bigger world. More people means more bad people," Vincent replied.

"Do we have enough books?" Nicholas asked while looking at Geister and Balderich.

"We believe so," Balderich said.

"Very well. Load them. We'll depart in a few hours," Nicholas said. He rolled the scroll and set it on the front row of pews. He glanced down at Rudolph who was making a valid attempt at walking.

"Are you sure you wouldn't rather wait?" Geister asked.

"Why? Tis Christmas Eve," Nicholas said, turning his attention to Geister.

"Yes, and it's tradition, but the storm will be out in full force in just a matter of hours. I doubt it will be clear enough."

Nicholas again tugged on his beard as he looked down at young Rudolph, "I think we'll be fine." He smiled when he said that, and for a second, Charles thought he could see a sparkle in Nicholas' eye.

"We'll prepare everything," Geister said before turning to walk away. Balderich followed Geister, though Vincent remained behind.

He said nothing, but kept a careful eye on Balderich and Geister as they walked out of the church. Only after they had left did he speak, "I'm sorry, but this is the last time I will be able to help." Vincent had a very apologetic look on his face, as if he were deeply embarrassed.

"Can I ask why?" Nicholas pressed.

"I only have so much time, and other obligations keep me busy. I'm sorry. I want to help, but I just can't balance it with my other duties."

"I understand, I really do," Nicholas insisted. No other words were spoken. None were needed. Vincent lowered his head in a polite bow, then turned to walk away.

Once he had left the church, Charles asked, "What does he do for you?"

Nicholas paused and tugged on his beard as he thought for a moment. He wasn't exactly sure how to answer the question. After a long moment's pause, he said only, "Vincent is a note taker of sorts."

"Note taker?"

"Yes. All he does, all he's ever done, is travel the world and record his experiences."

"So he's like a historian?" Charles rationalized.

"You could say that," Nicholas began, "Except he has a gift. Vincent can see things that others miss."

"What sort of things?"

"Future things," Nicholas said. He knelt down next to Rudolph and began petting him under the chin.

"He's psychic?" Charles asked.

"No, just very intuitive. He can look at people or places, and see what the near future holds for them."

"So it's not something like magic?" Charles tried to understand.

"No, far from it. It's more like wisdom, built in an age of a thousand years and counting."

"A thousand years? You've got to be kidding?"

Nicholas kept petting Rudolph, trying to offer some affection to the calf. He paused for only a moment to glance up at Charles. The look on Nicholas' face said everything, "I couldn't be more serious."

"No one lives that long? I mean it just isn't possible," Charles insisted.

Nicholas nodded his head towards the large cross hanging behind the alter, "My dear Charles, with faith, all things are possible."

He turned back to look at Charles, and with a twinkle of light in his eyes, asked, "How old do you think I am."

"I don't have a clue," Charles confessed. He went on to add, "You look to be in your fifties, but from what you have told me so far, I could only guess."

"Go on, take a good guess," Nicholas challenged with a smile.

"Well, you already told me about living with the Romans, so I would assume something in the order of fifteen hundred years old."

Nicholas kept on smiling, but said nothing.

"Am I right? Close?" Charles asked.

"I don't know," Nicholas said with a shrug of his shoulders, suggesting that it didn't even matter to him.

"You don't know?" Charles asked. His curiosity was more than peaked. How could someone not know how old they were?

Nicholas went back to petting Rudolph as he explained, "I know how old I was when I died."

"Died?"

"Yes," Nicholas said before pausing, "I mean, my heart can't honestly tell any man that it stopped beating. But, I touched death."

"What happened?"

"I was fifty six, and had been running a monastery for more than half of my life. My main focus had been trying to show my people the way to Christ. I had had some successes, and some failures."

Nicholas kept petting Rudolph. Charles took a seat on the pew next to Nicholas. Cautiously, he reached out his hand and also began to gently pet the young calf. Nicholas seemed to get lost in thought. After a few quiet moments, he continued, "Not everyone in the community appreciated my attempts to change them. There was always ridicule, but that slowly turned to something a bit darker. For reasons that I still don't understand, word spread through my homeland that I was a spy for the Romans. These rumors eventually widened to include the children that I taught."

"Everyone thought you were teaching a spy school?" Charles asked for clarity.

"In essence, yes," Nicholas said bluntly.

"What did they do?"

"One night, in the dead of winter, they came. There must have been fifty of them. They burned down my monastery." Nicholas then paused in a moment of reflection. He looked up at the cross hanging behind the alter, searching for support. The quiet moment froze in time.

"So they torched everything, and you were burned in the fire?" Charles speculated.

"No," Nicholas said. Again there was a pause.

Charles looked at Nicholas and beckoned him to go on.

"They burned everything down and made me watch as they did it. They killed everyone in the monastery, and made me watch as they did that. Then, then killed me."

"How?" Charles asked. As outlandish as the story was, Nicholas spoke with such sincerity and such pain, that there had to be at least some truth to it.

Nicholas again pulled down his collar to reveal his neck. The scar spoke for itself. "They hung you?" Charles asked.

Nicholas only nodded with his eyes. "For a week I hung from a tree. If I didn't actually die, then I came as close as any man ever has."

Nicholas shook his head with disgust, "I was blinded by my own blood. For that week, as I was bound to the tree, the only thing I could see was the memories."

"What memories?" Charles asked.

"Memories. Images. The sights and sounds of horror. I had watched as twenty-eight children had been brutally murdered."

Charles flashed back to the statues he had seen only a couple of hours earlier. He had counted twenty-eight of them, and now they had been put in their proper perspective. He didn't say anything though. He could see how it was all coming together.

Nicholas caste a hard stare at Charles, "It's not something you ever forget. Even the smallest details of such an atrocity won't fade."

"How did you survive?"

"Vincent and Geister," Nicholas said with a nod of his head. "Geister passed by and found me. He cut me down and took me back to his home. Apparently, Vincent told him where I was."

"Did you know Vincent before this?"

"Yes. I did."

"How?"

"He was the priest who originally took pity on me. He led me to Christ."

"And he just knew you could be found hanging from this tree?" Charles asked with some degree of skepticism.

"Yes."

"How did he know you were there?"

Nicholas turned to Charles, and with a twinkle in his eye said only, "Probably the same way he knew Geister would find you in that frozen water."

Charles' brain froze, not from the cold, but from how it all fit.

Chapter Seven—The List

There was another moment of silence. Nicholas was focused on Rudolph. Charles was pondering his surroundings, and absorbing everything. It seemed so real, but defied so much. There were no more questions to ask. So far, each question had only been met by answers that were open to criticism to say the least. Nicholas stood up from petting Rudolph and broke the long silence, "I'm going to get him some food."

"You want me to come along?" Charles inquired.

"No, please stay here with him," Nicholas said.

Charles continued petting Rudolph as Nicholas walked out of the church. The young explorer kept roaming around the church with his eyes. It only took a minute before Charles was staring at the scroll sitting on the pew just a few feet from him. Everything told him to leave it alone, that it was none of his business. However, he was an explorer; a man driven by curiosity about the world around him. That meant that it only took another half a minute for Charles to pick up the scroll and examine the contents.

The paper was very rigid and rolled around a gold wand. At the top of the paper, there was the now familiar symbol of the cross with the star in the left corner. Below the cross were three columns. The tops of the columns had three headings; name, offense, and age. Listed below the name column were naturally the names of people. Below the heading of offense were a few simple words detailing some offensive act such as stealing, or hitting, or lying. Under the heading of age were numbers.

"They're all children," Charles observed out loud after noting that not a single person listed was over the age of twelve.

"Indeed they are," A loud and scratchy voice echoed from the back. Charles knew that voice all too well. He was less than surprised when he turned around and saw Nicholas walking down the aisle of the church. He had a small bail of hay in one hand, and a large bottle of milk under his arm.

"I'm sorry," Charles said as he rolled the scroll up.

"Don't be. You are a naturally curious person," Nicholas said as he dropped the bail of hay in front of Rudolph.

"Thanks," Charles said softly. He set the scroll back on the pew where he had found it.

"Of course Adam was also curious," Nicholas added as he watched Rudolph begin chewing on the hay. He turned his eyes to Charles and added, "Curiosity is just another word for temptation."

"I guess you're right," Charles admitted in a moment of self reflection.

"Never guess, always know," Nicholas said softly. He lowered the bottle in front of Rudolph and waited for the young calf to begin to nuzzle the milk.

"Can I ask you something?" Charles asked.

"You can ask anything," Nicholas replied.

"Who are those people in that list?"

"Kids, children. Potential saints, and potential devils," Nicholas replied.

"What do you mean?" Charles asked.

"I mean every child is nothing more than clay, waiting to be molded into the person they will become. If you want a child to be righteous, you mold them in that manner. Otherwise, you do nothing and let them become whatever fate has laid out for them."

"If you wait until they're an adult, then it's like molding a finished pot?" Charles asked, suggesting he was understanding the point Nicholas was making.

"Exactly. You have to break the pot, just as you would have to break the man. It's much easier to do something while their will is still soft as the clay of their skin," Nicholas said, completing the analogy.

"And what do you do?" Charles asked, trying to get at what seemed to be the heart of everything.

Nicholas smiled, and with a twinkle in his eye said, "I make sure they get the message."

"What message?" Charles inquired.

"The word. The word of God."

Charles flashed back to earlier when Nicholas was talking to Vincent. He had asked if the books were ready. That prompted Charles' next question, "You give them bibles?"

"Yes." The smile on Nicholas' face was one of pride.

"So you find bad kids and give them bibles?" Charles asked rhetorically before asking a real question of interest, "What about good kids? Why not give them something?"

"Living well is their gift. Besides, if I have to reward you to be good, then how honest are your actions?" Nicholas pressed with a wink.

Charles nodded as he too seemed to find a smile in everything. Though unbelievable to no end, everything began to make sense to him. He had always heard stories of a saint who traveled around on Christmas Eve and brought gifts to everyone. Yet, here he was, standing in front of a real saint; a man of myth who had a real presence in the world.

Charles looked again at the scroll and was left with but one last question, "How do you know who's done what?"

"Geister, Balderich, and several others. Vincent takes their notes and compiles a master list," Nicholas shrugged as if it were no big deal.

"So if they didn't see it?"

"Then I don't know about it," Nicholas interjected. He went on to add, "It's a big world Charles. I can't, and I wont even try, to change it all. No man should take on that task. But still, I can play a roll, and that's something all men should at least attempt."

On those words, everything fell silent. An aurora of reflection fell across the room. Nicholas was focused on Rudolph. The young calf was going after the hay with all the hunger of a full grown buck. This brought another smile to Nicholas' face.

For his part, Charles found himself again looking around the church and taking it all in. He longed to know more about this magical place he had found himself in. He also longed for home. He had no wife or kids, but had brothers and sisters and friends. He suddenly missed all of these people, and couldn't wait to recount his story to them. Nicholas could see it in his eyes.

"Homesick?" The wise old man asked.

"Yes," Charles replied through a pair of red eyes that wore the signs exhaustion.

"I can take you home," Nicholas said, though he quickly added, "But you are more than welcome to stay here as long as you like."

"Thanks, but I have friends and family I want to be with."

Nicholas smiled upon hearing this. He could tell that Charles was someone who would carry a message of faith to his family and his friends. He believed that Charles would also go the extra step to carry the word to others that Charles didn't know.

"Well rest Charles. You'll soon be with your loved ones," Nicholas said with a smile and a now familiar twinkle in his eye. That was the last thing Charles remembered of the magical place he had found only by accident.

Chapter Eight—Home

The next time Charles awoke, he found himself in his own bed. His head was groggy, but he wasn't sure if it was from the exhaustion, or from too much sleep. He kept running his hands across his face as he sat up in bed. It wasn't until he went to climb out of bed that he noticed the package sitting at the foot of his bed.

The package was a small rectangular object wrapped in golden paper with a bow around it. A sheet of paper was folded in half and tucked under the bow. As soon as he picked up the package, Charles knew what it was. He pulled out the card and read the short note written inside.

"Maybe you were right. Sometimes the good kids should get presents too. Sincerely, Saint Nicholas, Prince of Klause."

Charles would read that bible more than once in the course of his life, and always remember what faith really meant.

DINE'
(THE PEOPLE)

though they may be

so far gone

not been seen

in so long

their spirits

do live on

hear their whispers

in the wind

their history

is spoken

their spirits

never broken

they move into

the future

their history

the teacher

like a reflection

from a mirror

DESERT STAR

on a lonely desert dirt road
he's wandering again

looking for another place
that he has never been

and he looks upon a desert star
looking for the light

to take him to a place
where he can spend another night

the wind it blows so softly
tells him where to go

and where he'll be tomorrow
he doesn't really know

because he's chasing that desert star
lighting up the night

he doesn't have a reason
just knows that it feels right

and the star it calls down to him
follow me tonight

It'll show him exactly how
to make his life feel right

he knows he'll never be alone
last thing on his mind

with his eyes upon the star
he'll chase it for all of time

THE CANYON

It was August, 1872. Summer was at its hottest point, and thick lines of sweat ran down the sides of his face. He couldn't tell how much of the sweat was due to the heat, and how much was due to his being nervous. Sadness and fear could also have been at play.

Robert watched from a distance. A crowd had gathered on top of the hill. They all wore their best clothes, though black was the predominant color. A single wagon drawn by two horses approached the crowd of people. When the wagon stopped, six men approached the back. Slowly, in an almost ritualistic manner, they pulled a long wooden box from the back of the wagon.

Robert pulled lightly on the reins to his horse, indicating it was time to move on. As the box was carried through the crowd, Robert rode through the streets of the empty town. When the box was placed into the ground, Robert would be almost a mile away.

The town was completely empty. Everyone was on top of the hill. It had been a tragic event, one that had shook the entire town. It had also shook Robert's entire world. As he rode away, he wondered if anyone would miss him, or if they would even care that he was gone. It was an accident he kept telling everyone. He was just trying to protect her. It really was the other man's fault; the man who was trying to have his way with Robert's wife. Robert just wasn't as good of a shot as people in the so called wild west have been made out to be. The fact was, as many people were killed by a poorly aimed shot as were killed by the so called, "steady hand". This was no exception.

Robert headed west. He didn't know why, and wasn't sure exactly where he was heading. He just knew he couldn't look anyone in the face ever again. Two months later, he was in northern Arizona. He had just left a small town called Chinle where he bought a few supplies with the last of his money. He had decided to turn north from there, maybe head to Denver.

Clip-Clop, clip-clop, clip-clop. The hooves of the large horse made a rhythmic sound as it moved along the hard red rock. There weren't many other sounds. The wind blew ever so gently that afternoon. In the distance, a large bird made its presence known with an occasional squawk. Mostly, there was just the sound of the horse's feet on the hard red rocks.

The sun was beginning to set in the distance, and the night was already beginning to cool down. It was late October, and the sun was loosing its influence over this high desert. As it lowered in the distance, the rays cast longer shadows. The sky turned brighter colors, and set the tone for the impending end of warm days. The first snow was only a few weeks away.

He was looking off to his left and observing the bird as it passed in front of the sun. The entire sky was turning bright orange as the sun became lower on the horizon. Even the clouds shifted from white to orange and red. It looked both ominous, and peaceful at the same time. He was trying to reconcile this contrast when his horse came to an abrupt stop. He turned his head to look forward. That's when he saw it.

His horse was standing on the edge of a cliff. The drop was near vertical, and he estimated it to be about a thousand feet. It was a canyon, roughly a half mile across. At the bottom of the canyon, he could see flat plains of green grass. There was a small creek that wound its way through the canyon. Juniper trees gathered along the edge of the water, but mostly the bottom was flat and grassy.

It seemed appropriate. It was time for him to start thinking about a place to sleep for the night. What better place to set up camp than near water. The tricky part would be in getting down the canyon. He steered his mustang to the left, guiding it along the cliff in search of a way down into the canyon.

After thirty minutes, he stopped his horse. Something in the distance caught his eye. He pulled on the horn of the saddle to look up over the horse. The shadows caste by the sun slightly obscured everything, but he swore he could see a structure. He leaped off of his horse and walked closer to the edge of the cliff. He covered his eyes with his hand as he stared across the canyon. Sure enough, there was a building. It looked to be made of brick. The odd part was the building was half way up the cliff on the other side of the canyon.

Part of him wondered how, and another part wondered why, someone would build a house half way up the side of a cliff. As curious as he was about it, he knew that he needed to find a way down into the canyon before it got too dark. There was water down there, and his canteen was down the the last few drops. Just when he was ready to give up, he noticed a large boulder near the cliff. Etched into the boulder were a pair of zig-zag lines that someone had obviously carved onto the side of the boulder. It had to be there for a reason.

He carefully walked towards the edge of the cliff. A few feet from the boulder, he could see a trail leading downwards. He couldn't tell if it went all the way to the bottom or not, but figured it was worth taking a chance. He walked back to his horse, and took hold of the reins. The trail was narrow, only three or four feet at its widest point. He decided to lead his horse down the trail instead of riding.

For close to fifteen minutes, the trail switched back and forth, from one direction, to the other, as it wound down the side of the cliff. That's when he came to the tunnel. It was only twenty feet long, but low. The man, standing well over six foot tall, had to duck slightly to make it through the tunnel. He kept a careful eye on his horse who also had to lower his head while passing through the tunnel.

Once he was out of the tunnel, he could tell he was close to the bottom. There were a few tricky sections of the trail where it narrowed to barely two feet across. He was able to make it fine, but it took some convincing, and even some tugging, to get his horse to navigate those parts.

The bottom gave him an entirely new perspective of the canyon. He couldn't help but feel consumed by it all. In the center of the canyon, there was the water he was so desperate for. He approached the slow moving stream, and dipped his canteen into the water as his horse drank directly from the stream. With his thirst quenched, and his canteen full, he set his sights on finding a good place to sleep.

He climbed onto his horse, and headed to the left, in an easterly direction. For another twenty minutes, he meandered through the canyon until he came on something that stopped him dead in his tracks. In the center of the canyon, there was a towering rock. It was made of the same red rock that the cliffs were made off, and rose as high as the cliffs; almost a thousand feet by his reckoning. He rode his horse in a full circle around the rock, and finally decided it was as good of a place as any for him to set up camp.

Within a few minutes, he had a small fire going with a tin pan of beans sitting on it. His horse was tied to a juniper tree near the creek, and Robert was sitting on a log on the ground. The fire made little pops and crackles that echoed through the quiet canyon. Red sparks would fly into the air and fall slowly to the ground, dancing in the light breeze like fairies before fading to a small piece of charred wood.

He scrapped the last spoon full of beans from his tin pan, and stared across the fire at his horse. That's when he heard a snapping noise. It sounded like just another noise the fire would make, except that it came from behind him.

He stopped chewing, and moved only his eyes; first left, then right. He saw nothing, and heard nothing. He was ready to believe that it was nothing until he heard another sound from behind him; this time more of a crack. Slowly, he turned to look over his shoulder while reaching for his gun that was tucked safely away in a holster on his hip. He stared through the darkness as he chewed. There had to be something out there. He was almost ready to convince himself that it was nothing more than some small rodent when he heard a voice.

"Hello Robert," a female voice said through the distance.

Robert said nothing. He stared through the darkness, searching for movement. There had to someone there, they had spoken. By the sound of the voice, it had to be a beautiful someone. Suddenly, he saw something.

At first, a leg revealed itself as the woman stepped out of the shadows of a juniper tree. It was a slender leg, tone and smooth. He could see her leg all the way up to her mid thigh. Smooth became sensual. An arm, a body, and eventually a face slid out of the shadows. Her face was slightly round, and as beautiful as her voice suggested she would be.

She had a dark tone to her skin with long straight black hair. Over her body was a simple clothe dress that extended down to her mid thighs. Robert only stared. She stopped moving as soon as she knew he could see her.

He lowered his gun, and placed it in his holster. It wasn't as if the gun were loaded anyway. He hadn't placed a bullet in his gun since the accident. He definitely didn't want to pull the gun on another woman.

"My apologies ma'am," Robert said.

"None needed," the woman said.

Robert still couldn't get over how beautiful she was. He also couldn't understand why she was out in the middle of nowhere with him. She stood still, and only stared at Robert. It looked as though she were observing him, possibly equally confused about his presence in the canyon.

"What brings you here?" She asked.

He thought about it for a second. He really didn't have an answer to that question. Instead of thinking about it, or making up a lie, he instead asked, "Do you object to my being here?"

"No," the woman said with her usual soft voice. She took a single step forward and added, "But she might."

"Who might?" Robert asked.

The woman looked over her shoulder in the direction of the large towering rock and said, "The Spider Woman."

"Spider what?" Robert asked, obviously confused.

The woman turned to look at Robert as she said, "Spider Woman. She protects Dine' from monsters and outsiders."

"Who is Dine'?"

"I am, all of us that live here are," the woman said with a smile, "You would call us Navajo, or any of a hundred names. We are simply Dine'; the people."

The woman smiled again, and took another step closer to the man while saying, "You are an outsider, so you could be considered a threat. Besides, you are also armed."

"It's not loaded anyway," Robert said with half a smile, almost embarrassed over having to admit such a thing.

"Why isn't it loaded?" the woman felt compelled to ask.

Robert didn't answer immediately. He pondered the question. "So I don't hurt anyone," Robert finally said, though he hesitated on every word.

"Then why carry a gun in the first place?" the woman was quick to ask.

"So people leave me alone."

The woman smiled a bright smile as she said, "You just defined irony."

"What do you mean?" Robert asked.

The woman took another step closer to Robert and explained, "You carry a gun so people will leave you alone. Because you carry a gun, people will perceive you as a threat." The woman paused her thoughts.

The pause gave Robert just enough time to ask, "Yes, and?" He made no attempt to hide the irritation in his voice.

"And, the gun is unloaded so you can't protect yourself if attacked," the woman concluded. She shrugged her shoulders and said only, "Sounds like a man who is looking to bring hardships on himself."

"What do you know about hardships," Robert asked.

The woman stood almost motionless as she said, "Close your eyes, and I'll show you."

"I'm not closing my eyes. There's no telling what you might do," Robert said.

"Do I scare you?" the woman asked.

"No," Robert said simply. What he didn't say was that he felt at least a little uncomfortable talking to her. She had come out of nowhere in place where no one else should have been. She also knew his name, a fact that didn't stop bothering him. Robert went on to add, "I'd just rather be alone if you don't mind."

"I don't mind if you don't mind," the woman said. She turned around, and stepped back into the shadows. Like that, she was gone.

Robert found it incredibly easy to dismiss the encounter. Maybe it was his desire to be alone that made it easy. Then again, maybe it was just a fear of being near another woman. He didn't want to hurt anyone else. He just wanted to be alone.

He turned back to the fire and watched the flames dance around. As he did so, he reached towards his neck. He had a necklace around his neck. Attached to the necklace was a shell casing from a bullet. He reached for the casing and rubbed it between his fingers. He watched the flames of the fire, and was taken back to two months ago.

They were memories he tried to forget, but couldn't. They were memories of a hot August day in northwest Texas. He could remember how the heat was visible as it rose from the fields in waves that obstructed his view, and kept him from seeing things as they really were. He remembered coming in from the fields after a long day.

He closed his eyes from the pain. That's when he remembered seeing his wife. He also remembered the strange man. He could still hear her screams for help. His thoughts froze as he watched sparks fly from the fire. It was like watching the fury in his wife's eyes as she struggled to get away from the man.

Robert didn't want to remember anything else. He had come to the desert to forget it all, to hide from it. He was again faced with irony as he realized his attempts to hide from his past had brought him to that canyon. It was in the canyon that he had found the mysterious woman. She reminded him of his horrible past.

It all ran full circle. The fire let loose with a loud pop, and that brought back memories of the gunshot. His wife was screaming for help. She didn't want to be with the other man. Robert wanted to hurt the other man.

His shot missed. The man got away. His wife was not so lucky. A loud squawk from a hawk in the distance reminded Robert of his wife's scream. Robert never did find the man. He didn't even look for the man that had forced himself on his wife. She died in Robert's arms.

Robert had chosen to run away that day, abandoning his farm, and his life he had lived. Robert fell over to his side and curled up in a ball. He began crying. There was no shame. He was alone there in the canyon. He cried for almost an hour, and would have cried himself to sleep if he hadn't been disturbed.

"It seems as though you aren't much of a threat after all," the female voice said.

Robert looked up, and saw no one at first. He glanced behind himself, and still saw no one. He then slowly turned his head towards the fire. On the other side of the flames, he could see the woman again.

"I thought you were gone," Robert said as he fought to regain his composure. He ran his hands across his face to wipe away the tears.

"Your crying woke me," the woman said simply.

"You sleep around here?" Robert asked.

"Yes, I do," came the soft reply from the woman.

Robert reached for his canteen. He took a sip of water, and splashed a small amount on his face. As he closed the canteen, he asked, "I thought you were going to leave me alone."

"I was, and I did. As I said, your crying woke me. So now the question is; who is disturbing who?" The woman asked. She stood almost perfectly motionless as she spoke. Her tone never changed, it was always soft and smooth, just like her skin.

Before Robert could say anything, the woman began explaining, "You might end up bothering her."

"Bothering who?" Robert asked.

"The Spider Woman," the woman said. Her voice had a slight inflection as if she were pointing out the extremely obvious.

"Whatever," Robert said.

"Show respect Robert. You are a stranger in the land of the Dine'. You are armed, and that could make you appear as a threat. You are also making loud noises in the middle of the night. That could confuse you for a monster."

The woman leaned in a little, and stared at Robert through the fire. "She will protect Dine' from monsters and threats."

"I'm no monster," Robert said with a very dismissive tone.

"Oh really now," the woman said. She displayed a smile that was just a little too wide for Robert's comfort.

"You can leave me be now," Robert said with a hint of force to his voice.

"My dear Robert. You are in my land. If you are unhappy here, then you can leave," the woman said. She paused and looked upwards for a moment before glancing back at Robert, "I'd suggest you leave before she comes for you."

"Whatever," Robert said for the second time. He was growing more and more weary of her idle threats that some strange woman was going to hurt him.

"Very well then. I will leave the monster to be," the woman said.

"I already told you, I'm no monster," Robert said while looking towards the woman. She was already gone. He looked all around, but saw no one.

Then, from nowhere, he heard the voice. "Of course you are no monster. Only a normal man would kill his wife in cold blood," the female voice said from behind Robert. The voice seemed to ride a soft wind that blew through the canyon.

Robert turned to look over his shoulder, but saw no one. As he turned, he saw the light fade. He turned around again, and saw the fire fading to nothing more than a pile of wood that glowed red.

Robert scooted closer to the fire, wondering what could have caused the flames to suddenly be extinguished. He reached out, and held his hand over the smoldering wood. As soon as his hand was over the wood, the fire erupted again. Robert instantly pulled his hand back, and rolled away from the fire while screaming in pain.

Robert jumped over the small log he had been sitting on as the fire grew even higher into the air than it had been earlier.

"I think she wants you to leave," a female voice said from behind Robert.

Robert jumped to his feet as he looked around for the woman. He turned towards the fire that rose almost eight feet high. He could see her through the flames as she stood on the other side of the fire.

"I'll leave in the morning," Robert said.

"No, you should leave now."

"I need to sleep," Robert begged.

"She can arrange that. She can arrange that you sleep forever," the woman said. She stepped closer to the fire and added, "You can arrange it also."

"What do you mean?" Robert asked.

"Your gun. It has one bullet left in it," the woman said.

"It's not loaded," Robert said while glancing down towards his gun.

"You kept one bullet," the woman insisted.

"I haven't loaded it since the accident," Robert said.

"What accident?" the woman asked. She walked closer to the fire. She was now close enough that she should have been singed by the heat. She didn't even appear to feel the heat. "I don't want to talk about it," Robert said as he backed further away from the fire.

"Because it was no accident Robert," the woman said.

"What are you talking about?" Robert asked.

The woman stepped into the flames. She spun a slow circle, almost enjoying the heat of the fire. When she turned to face Robert, she said, "There was no accident. There was no strange man."

"There was a strange man," Robert said.

"No. You knew him. You shared his blood even," the woman said. She took another step and exited the fire.

"You don't know. You weren't there," Robert said while continuing to back up.

"I can look into your eyes and see what happened Robert," the woman said. She stepped completely out of the flames. As her body cleared the flames, the fire died again, and was reduced to smoldering logs that glowed red.

Robert kept backing up. His emotions were shifting from confusion to fear. Surely he couldn't be seeing what he thought he was. There was no way that the woman could have walked through the fire. More than that, he couldn't believe that she knew what really happened.

"He was your brother, wasn't he?" the woman asked.

Robert said nothing. He tried to block it all out, pretending she wasn't there. He moved towards his left, trying to circle around the woman and make it to his horse. The woman kept walking towards him.

"He wasn't forcing himself on her either, was he?" the woman asked.

"Stop it," Robert shouted. He pulled his gun from his holster and pointed it at the woman. She stopped walking towards him.

"You weren't there. You don't know what happened," Robert yelled while waving his gun around.

"No Robert. You were there. And yet, you don't know what happened. You've been blinded by vengeance," the woman said calmly. Her voice and her actions were a direct contrast to Robert who was shouting and moving around radically.

Robert kept walking towards his horse. He moved sideways, occasionally glancing towards his horse. Mostly he kept his eyes on the woman while waving his gun at her.

"You were angry, weren't you?" the woman asked.

"Shut Up!" Robert shouted.

The woman moved closer towards Robert who was now only a few feet from his horse.

"While they were at the height of passion and happiness, you shot them," the woman said.

"You shot your brother, and you shot his wife," the woman said simply just as Robert was grabbing a hold of the reins of his horse.

Robert suddenly let go of his horse. He turned to the woman and cast a hard stare at her. "She was my wife," Robert shouted with special emphasis on "my."

"No Robert, she wasn't," the woman said.

"She would have been if my brother hadn't stolen her."

"She went where her heart took her," the woman explained, "And you replied by taking her heart's blood."

The woman paused for a moment, took a single step closer to Robert, and said, "They were happy, and you took it from them for your own bitter form of happiness."

Robert raised his gun at the woman as he said, "I should shut you up right now."

"You have one bullet don't you?" the woman asked.

"Yes," Robert said coldly.

"Then use it Robert," the woman said. She smiled again, and turned to walk away. As she walked away, a single tear ran down Robert's cheek. The woman walked back towards the smoldering wood that had been the camp fire. She walked across the wood, and as she did, the fire roared back to life.

As soon as she cleared the fire, a single shot rang out through the canyon. It echoed on the walls of the red rocks. The horse screamed out into the night, and reared up on its hind legs. The horse then took off to running down the creek, away from the small camp.

It didn't matter how far the horse ran. The horse's rider lay dead next to the cold water of the creek. The woman smiled when she heard the shot fired. She knew her people were safe from the monster. She returned to her home atop the towering spider rock, deep in the heart of the canyon where she could watch over and protect Dine'.

MOTHER

she watches
she laughs
she cries
he dances
he plays
and he cries

what's he doing
where did he go now
just ask his mother
she knows somehow

she holds
she hugs
she cries
he smiles
he grows
and he cries

what's he doing
where did he go now
just ask his mother
she knows somehow

So New

so new to me
and new to he
a world out there
but does he care
so small to me
so big to he
there is no fear
cause we're both here
he cries to me
I sing to he
I try to soothe
I sing so smooth
does he know me
like I know he
I hope he does
at least feel my love

BECAUSE

As If more needed to be said

"Mom," he moaned while struggling to climb to his feet and rubbing his tired eyes.

"What honey?" mom instinctively said. She was sitting on the couch and watching a movie, but turned to look down at her three year old son.

"I wanna watch another movie," the son said with a touch of pleading in his voice.

"Just finish this one son, okay?" Mom said with a sympathetic voice.

"Okay, but I wanna watch this many," the son replied while holding up all ten fingers.

"We'll see," mom said with a smile. She then turned to look at dad who was sitting in the recliner. "Oh dear. Tonight's going to be another fight night trying to get him to go to bed," she whispered.

"It'll be okay," the dad said with a confidant smile, "It won't be that hard."

"Oh really now?" Mom asked with wide eyes.

"Yes really. He just needs to learn that when it's bed time, then it's bed time. Period, end of story."

"So it's that easy?" Mom asked with a clear tone of skepticism.

"Yeah," dad said with a shrug of his shoulders, suggesting that it couldn't possibly be so difficult.

"I suppose you can teach him this?"

"Sure," dad said, "It's not that hard."

Mom said nothing. She let her silence speak for her as she looked at dad with a pair of eyes that said, "We'll just see about that."

The movie wound down over the next ten minutes, and finally gave way to the scrolling credits. By the time the second set of names appeared on the television, the son was up on his feet.

"I wanna watch another movie," the son said to no one in particular.

"Come here son," the dad said while sitting up in his recliner and folding the foot rest below the chair.

"I wanna watch another movie," the son said again as he walked towards his father.

"I don't know," the father said slowly.

"Please," the son said with a hint of begging in his voice.

"It's getting awfully late," the father said.

"No it isn't," the son said, clearly oblivious to time.

"It's after ten," the father tried to explain.

"No it isn't," the son said again.

"You know what that means?" the father suggested more than asked.

"But I wanna watch another movie," the son said in an attempt to get away from talking about time; clearly a subject he knew little about.

The father held his ground and said only, "No, it's nite-nite time."

"Nooooo," the son whined, "No it isn't nite-nite time."

"Yes it is."

"No it isn't," the son insisted.

"Yeah," the father said with a smile.

"No it isn't!" The son screamed as if an argument could be settled by volume.

"Do we have an attitude?" father asked before glancing at mom.

Mother said nothing. The smile that she made no attempt to hide said enough.

"No," the son replied.

Father moved his gaze back towards his son who was standing in front of dad with his head hanging down.

"Then what's wrong? Why do you have an attitude?" dad asked while trying to make eye contact with his son.

"I don't have an attitude!" the son snapped back while waving his index finger at his dad.

"Looks like you have an attitude to me," dad said softly.

"No I don't," the son said as he lowered his head again, "I'm just grumpy,"

"Why are you grumpy?" father asked while glancing at mom. She was still smiling.

The son never looked up as he said only, "Because."

"Because what?"

"That's why," the son replied while fidgeting slightly.

"Why are you grumpy?" the father asked again.

"Because I am," the son tried to explain, "because I just am."

"Are you grumpy because you're sleepy?"

"No."

"Then why?"

The son said nothing at first. He looked up at his father, then looked back down again before asking, "dad?"

"Yes son?"

"Can I watch another movie?"

"Not tonight son, It's time for nite-nite."

"No, I don't wanna go nite-nite!" The son exclaimed while falling down on his rear.

"I know, but you need to get some sleep," the dad said in a gentle voice.

He glanced at mom who never stopped smiling. She whispered, "he's still not in bed."

"We'll just see about that," he whispered back.

"Oh we will, huh?" Mom replied a bit above a whisper.

"Mom?" The son asked after hearing her voice.

"Yes son," Mom said softly.

The son scooted around so that he was now facing his mom, "Can I watch another movie?"

"Did dad tell you that you could watch another movie?" Mom asked with a careful tone suggesting that she already knew the answer.

"Yes," came the quiet reply.

"Did he?" mom asked again.

"But mom, I just wanna watch another movie. I just wanna watch one more," the son pleaded.

"You can watch another movie tomorrow," the father cut in.

"But I just wanna watch one more," the son replied without turning to look at dad.

"Nope. It's time to go to bed," the father insisted.

"No, I don't wanna sleep in my bed," the son snapped, conceding one fight, but ready to start another.

Deciding to play along with his son, the father asked, "Why not?"

"Because," the son said as he raised his head just a little.

"Because of what?"

"Because my bed scares me," the son said as he lowered his head again.

"And why does your bed scare you?" the father asked.

"Because it does, because it just does," the son said as he raised his head again.

"Well where do you wanna sleep?" the father asked.

"I wanna sleep on the couch," the son said as he climbed up on the couch.

The father glanced at mom with a confused look. She still said nothing, and once again had to hide a smile of amusement. Her face told the story of a woman who had been here many times in the past.

"Why do you wanna sleep on the couch?" the father asked. He quickly followed it up with, "why does your bed scare you?"

"Because," the son said simply.

"Because what?"

"Because it has a monster," the boy explained.

"What?!" the father asked before adding, "It does not."

"Does too," the son replied in a manner that just dared his father to prove him wrong.

"There's no such thing as monsters," the father replied.

"There are too," the son said. His words sort of dragged on as if he were offering a warning about the monsters.

"Oh come on. You're too old to believe in monsters," the father said before glancing at the mother with concern. Mother's face changed expressions as she gave the father a look that said, "actually, he's the perfect age to believe in monsters."

"Now son, there are no monsters in your room," the father insisted, almost showing his frustration over such a notion.

"Yes there are," the son said as he sat up on the couch.

"We'll why don't you just show me then," the father said in an effort to cut through everything.

"No," came the quick reply.

"Why not?"

"I don't want to."

"Why don't you want to?"

"Because I don't, I just don't," the son said.

"Maybe I don't believe you. I bet there are no monsters in your room," the father said in a very doubting manner.

"I'm telling you they're in there," the son insisted.

"Then you need to show me," the father pressed on.

"No, I don't want to," the son snapped before turning around on the couch to face away from his father.

The father put his hand on his son's shoulder and pulled slightly while saying, "Come on, just show me where they are."

"Leave me alone," the son said as he scooted away from his father, and towards the corner of the couch.

"Boy, you do have an attitude," the father said.

The son didn't say anything, but simply let out a "Mmmrrpphh," sort of squeak in defiance of his father.

"I'm going to count to three, then I'm just going to carry you in there," the father said while looking down at his son.

"No!" the son snapped.

"One."

"Go away!"

"Two."

"Stop that!"

"Two!"

The father paused before using an elevated voice to repeat, "TWO!"

"Leave me alone!" The defiant son shouted.

"Three," the father said out of frustration before reaching down and grabbing his son under the arms.

"Stop it! Leave me alone!" the son shouted as his father picked him up. Both parents began to wonder if their child would make as much noise if he had been attacked by a real monster.

"I gave you a chance," the father said as he began walking towards the hallway.

"No! I don't wanna sleep in my room," the son screamed as he was being carried down the hall. "I want my mom," he then added as he saw his mom disappear when his father rounded the corner to his room.

"Don't do it!" he shouted again as his father flipped on the light switch.

The father sat his son down on the ground just inside the boy's room that was covered in toys and stuffed animals. "Now show me where the monsters are," the dad said softly while trying to make eye contact with his son.

"NO!" The son snapped as he fell to the ground and sat on his rear.

"Why not?"

"Because."

"Because of what?"

"I don't want to."

"You don't want to? Or, because the monsters aren't real," the father suggested.

"Yes they are too real," the son said while nodding his head.

"Well, where are they?" the father asked while looking his son square in the eyes.

The son looked around the room some before pointing in a seemingly random manner and saying, "There, and there, and there."

The father had to glance away to keep from laughing. He looked up and around at where his son had pointed, both to stall for time, and to play along with his son. Once he had his composure together, he looked back at his son and said, "I don't see any monsters."

"They're there."

"Naaaaa," the father said in an almost playful manner.

"Yeaaah," the son said back in a slightly more serious tone.

"Are you sure?" the father asked.

The son only nodded his head in the affirmative while staring back at his father. It was then that the son noticed his mother standing a few feet outside his room.

"Mom," the son said as he looked up at her.

"Yes son," the mother said.

"I wanna watch a movie."

"No son, it's time for nite-nite," the mother said as she looked down at her son with sympathy.

"But I just wanna watch a movie. I just want to," the son pleaded.

"Nope. Sorry," mom said with a nod of her head.

Dad went ahead and cut in, "Stop playing around, let's climb up in bed and go nite-nite."

"NO! I don't wanna sleep in my bed," the son protested while turning his back to his father.

"Come on. There are no monsters. Now let's go," the father said again while patting his son on the rear, somewhat pushing the young boy towards the bed.

"There are too monsters," the son said. He was clearly frustrated, and showing the signs of a child about to burst out in tears.

"Show me," the father said.

"Right there," the son said while pointing in the direction of his bed.

"Right where?" the father asked.

"Right there!" the son shouted while still pointing towards his bed.

"Come on, let's go look," the father said while picking his son up and carrying him over to the bed.

"Noooo!!" the son screamed through tears, "I don't wanna go in my bed," he continued while being carried across his room.

"Stop it," the father said before setting him down on the bed.

"I don't wanna sleep in my bed," the son said as he stood up on his bed and waved his index finger at his dad.

"Yeah, well that's just too bad. Now lay down and go nite-nite."

"No, you can't make me," the son said while continuing to wave his index finger at his dad.

"That's enough. Your acting like a baby now," the father said as he began to be less amused by his son's antics.

"It's time to go nite-nite, so lay down and go to sleep."

"But I don't wanna sleep in my bed," the son said for what seemed like the millionth time that night.

"Well you're going to, so lay down and go to sleep," the father insisted.

The son dropped down to sit on his rear as his arms fell to his side. He began crying loudly and slowly raised one hand and stuck four fingers in his mouth, "I don't wanna sleep in my bed," he whimpered through the tears.

"Why not?" the father asked, hoping to get a different answer.

"The monster's gonna get me," the son said while continuing to cry.

"Where is the monster?" the father asked.

The son stood up on his bed and and tried to control his crying as he said, "right there."

"Right where?"

"Right there," he said again while pointing directly at the wall. His fingers were only an inch from the wall next to his bed.

"What color is the monster?" the father asked as he looked at the solid white wall.

"Purple," the son replied. His crying slowly faded as he came under the impression that his dad was ready to believe him.

The father looked around the room and noticed that there wasn't a purple piece of anything to be seen. "Where do you see purple?" the father asked.

"Right there," the son said again while pointing at the same spot on the wall.

"All I see is a white wall," the father tried to explain.

"It's right there. It's going to come out and get me," the son tried to explain.

"How do you know?"

"Because."

"Because what?"

"That's why."

"What's why?"

"I told you, that's why," the son said as if it were all he needed to say to prove his point.

"Because why?" the father asked, hoping that would get him somewhere. It wouldn't, he had met his logical match in his son.

"Because I do, that's why," the son said.

"How do you argue with that?" the father mumbled as he looked over his shoulder at the mother who was leaning against the door frame. She only shrugged her shoulders.

"Okay son," the father began, ready to put an end to all the nonsense, "There are no monsters..."

"Yes there are," the son interrupted.

"No there aren't," the father replied sternly.

Again, the son only dropped down and began crying. The father took a slight advantage of this and used his hands to gently lay his son down on the bed, "Let's go nite-nite. You need to get some sleep," he explained.

"I don't wanna go to bed. I wanna watch a movie," the son cried out into the night as his father tucked him in bed.

"You can watch a movie tomorrow," the father said as he took several quick steps towards the wall and flicked off the light switch.

"No dad, don't do it," the son cried after the lights were turned out.

"Don't do what?" The father asked as he walked back over towards his son who was laying in bed and crying.

"I don't wanna sleep in my bed," the son said again.

"It will be okay," the father explained. He gave his son a quick kiss on the forehead before saying, "Love you."

The son just rolled over on his side and kept crying with a squeaking and whimpering sound.

"Nite-nite," the father said as he walked across the room towards the door. He and the mother took a few steps away from the room as the father pulled the door shut, though he stopped just short of closing it all the way.

"Now was that so hard?" the father asked.

"Looked like it to me," the mother said as they took a few more steps down the hall.

"I got him to go to bed."

"Oh you did?" the mother asked, obviously confused.

The father only pointed over his shoulder towards their son's room as he said, "he's in there isn't he?"

"Yeah, but you didn't get him to do anything," the mother said with a light chuckle.

"What do you mean?"

"I mean, I watched as you picked him up and carried him to his room. I also watched as you had to physically place him in bed and tuck him in."

"Yeah, and?"

"And you didn't get him to do anything."

"It's a beginning. He'll learn. Besides, I'm sure he's just about cried himself to sleep by now," the father said with confidence.

"Probably," the mother agreed.

There was only a moment of silence before a light whisper came from behind them, "I wanna watch another movie."

POSSUM

"Look at that," Gina said while pointing upwards.

"Yeah, it's just a big bird," Jeff said as he reached down and picked up a rock from the gravel road. He looked off to his left at a field of cows. He eyed the one closest to him, a bull who was sitting peacefully and grazing on some high grass. Looking the bull square in the eyes, Jeff threw the rock towards, though not directly at, the animal.

"He's just looking for some food," Jeff then added in an almost dismissive manner, referring to the bird.

"Maybe he wants some cereal," Gina said as she looked up at the bird while scratching her head.

"Naa, birds don't eat cereal, only five year olds do," Jeff replied as he picked up another rock.

"Oh. Well what do they eat then?" Gina asked.

"I dunno," came the admission from Jeff as he pulled back to throw the rock. He paused to look up at the bird before speculating, "Maybe they eat other birds. I know they eat bird seed, but I dunno where they get it."

He then looked back at the cow and did the best job that he could in measuring the distance between himself and the bull. This time he aimed directly for the bull as he threw the rock, though he missed by more than a few feet. The bull barely noticed, and continued grazing on the grass in front of him. Jeff picked up another rock while glancing at Gina. She was focused on the bird circling overhead.

"I hope he doesn't want to eat us," Gina said as she looked straight up. She had her small hands held over her eyes to block the sun.

Once again, Jeff pulled back his arm, and proceeded to throw the rock with all his might. Though he missed again, he did at least come close enough to get the cow's attention. The bull raised his head and looked around while chewing. Jeff was now more determined than ever to hit the cow with a rock. He really wasn't trying to be mean, it was just a goal for him. As with most eight year olds, once he sets a goal for himself, he will stay occupied until he accomplishes it.

He was reaching down for another rock when something caught his eye. "Hey what's that," He asked out loud as he stood up and began walking towards a large piece of gray fur in the road.

"What is it?" Gina asked as her attention also shifted from the bird to whatever her older brother was looking at.

"I dunno. Maybe it's a dog," Jeff speculated.

"It sure is an ugly dog," Gina said as she walked next to her brother.

"Look at its tail," She then added as she pointing to the long, thin, hairless tail.

"Maybe it's dead," Jeff speculated as he picked up a small pebble. He gently tossed the pebble at the animal in an effort to get some kind of reaction. No reaction was to be found. Jeff, now more curious than ever, took one more small step towards the animal before beginning to lean over and poke the animal with his finger.

Gina, ever the scared five year old, reached up and grabbed Jeff by the tail of his shirt to hold him back. "Don't," she said with genuine concern for her brother.

"I just want to see," Jeff said in a dismissive manner.

"No, don't," Gina insisted before adding, "I'll tell mom."

"Don't be so stupid, mom's dead," Jeff said as he poked the animal in the belly. There was still no response from the animal. However, he did get one from his little sister who backed up a few steps and displayed a very serious look on her face.

"What do you mean?" She asked with eyes that just stared at Jeff.

"Huh?" Jeff asked as he turned around to glance at Gina. She was looking at him while scraping the gravel around with one foot. She was obviously confused and waiting for her big brother to explain it to her.

"What do you mean about mom?" Gina asked.

"She's dead, don't you remember?"

"No."

"You're so stupid," Jeff began, mostly out of instinct, "We just went to her funeral a while ago."

"Oh," Gina said as she stared at the animal.

"What does it mean?" She asked while looking down at the ground.

"Just that she went away."

"Where?"

"I dunno," Jeff admitted with a shrug.

"Is he dead?" Gina asked while pointing at the animal.

"I think so," Jeff said as he glanced behind himself at the animal still laying there.

"Is he going to go away also?"

"Probably."

"With mom?"

"I guess so."

"Then I'll wait here so I can see her."

"What are you talking about?" Jeff asked while looking at his sister; trying to make sense of the conversation.

"I'm going to wait here for mom to come and get him."

"I don't think it works like that," Jeff tried to explain, though he was at a loss for what else to say.

"Why not?" Gina asked.

"It just doesn't."

"But why not?" This was one of those times where she just wasn't going to settle for a simple answer.

"Cause he's just an animal."

"And?"

"Mom is mom. She's special."

"Yeah, she is," Gina said with a sigh.

There was a moment where the conversation started to fade. Gina tilted her head to the side and stared at the animal.

"What now?" Jeff asked. He could see the look in Gina's eyes that told of an impending question.

"What if it's a mommy?" Gina asked, somewhat reluctantly.

"Huh?" Is about all that Jeff could reply as he glanced over his shoulder at the animal behind him.

"If it was a mom, wouldn't that make it special?" Gina asked.

"Oh geezzzz," Jeff said as he shook his head. He reached down to pick up another rock from the ground.

"What?"

"You're so stupid?"

"So I'm not special then?" Gina asked.

"No, you're a stupid sister."

"That's not nice. I'm going to tell mom."

"I already told you, she's dead," Jeff insisted as he glanced at Gina while holding his arm back, preparing to throw the rock. He then looked towards the cow which was still sitting peacefully in the field and chewing the grass in front of it.

"I'll just wait for her, and tell her then," Gina said while folding her arms across her chest.

"That's stupid," Jeff said as he threw the rock. This time he had the distance, but his aim was off. The rock went wide, missing the bull by a good ten feet to the left.

"Mom is in the ground. We buried her at the funeral. Don't you remember anything?"

"I don't know," Gina said as she thought hard with a blank stare.

"You remember the big field, with all the square rocks?" Jeff asked, trying to jog her memory.

"OK, I remember," Gina said as she turned again to look at the animal.

"Lookie," Gina said as she pointed at the ground.

"Hey, where'd it go?" Jeff asked. He turned around and noticed that the animal was no longer laying where it had been.

"It died. It went away just like you said it would," Gina tried to explain while still pointing at where the animal had been.

"But where did it go?" Jeff asked with a confused tone.

"I dunno," Gina said. She looked towards the sky, then paused a moment. She squinted her eyes as she held her hands over her forehead and looked around. After seeing nothing, she turned to Jeff and noted, "The bird is gone also."

Jeff looked up and said nothing. Instead, he only shrugged his shoulders before reaching down and picking up a rock. He eyed the bull, and once again he pulled back to throw the rock. Just as with before, it fell a bit short and missed the bull.

"Oh well. No big deal," Jeff said as he turned to continue down the road. Gina followed behind her brother while looking over her shoulder at where the animal had been.

"I miss mom," She whispered as she turned around one last time to follow her brother.

SNOW

snow falls in June
sun fades away

darkness takes over
a soul slips away

it was too early
it was too soon

no one expected
the snowfall in June

she was too precious
always so bright

snow fell in June
and closed out her light

so very young
so full of hope

so little future
no one could know

she will be missed
cause she left so soon

she slipped away
when snow fell in June

TICKLE ME SINGLE

"I guess I just wasn't ticklish enough," She said with one of her wide smiles that she was so well known for.

"That's one way of looking at it," her long time friend replied.

"There's actually some truth to that," She then said while adjusting herself in the recliner.

"What do you mean?" her friend asked while also moving her body some on the couch. Apparently, age had only been so accommodating for these two life long friends. Neither one of them looked to be in their upper fifties, though they both felt it.

Sue's back preferred the slow motion of the rocker recliner that allowed her to rock back and forth. She would only occasionally have to shift her body in order to avoid constant pressure to the same point. Her friend, Laura, had spent most of her life working in the garden, and her knees were paying the price for that constant crouching, squatting, and crawling. When visiting Sue's house, Laura usually sat on the couch so she could stretch her legs out across the three person sofa. They always had a pitcher of sun brewed tea, and they always kept their glasses full.

Sue took a sip from her glass of tea and smiled as she said, "Someone told me that once."

"You're kidding," Laura replied.

"Nope," Sue insisted, "I mean, I wish I was."

"Who? When?" Laura asked, somewhat surprised that there was something about her friend she didn't know. It was only a little ironic.

Sue thought for a second as she tried to recall the details of an event long gone by.

"Brad Carlson," She finally said.

"Did I know him?" Laura asked as the name failed to register with anything from her memory.

"No, I don't think so," Sue said before correcting herself, "Wait, we all went to the beach together once." There was another pause as Sue reached for a glass of tea.

"Remember? He was the one who got the speeding ticket on the way back, and tried to get us to flash the cop so he could get out of it."

Laura reached down for her own glass of tea as it slowly started coming back to her, "Okay, that's right. He had blond hair right? Kinda short?"

"That's him," Laura admitted.

"So he said you weren't ticklish enough?" Laura asked again.

"Yep, said it was too hard to get me to laugh. It really bothered him," Sue paused to take another sip of her tea, "I can't even get you to laugh when I tickle you," She said in a mocking voice as she quoted him verbatim. She even went so far as to hold her left hand up to make quote marks in the air.

"It takes all types," Laura suggested as she pondered the long line of men she had run through. A reflective moment passed before she asked, "but still, there had to have been someone."

Sue shrugged her shoulders with a smile as if to say, "sorry," before verbally offering, "Nothing dramatic. Nothing that said this is it, this is the one guy that I want to spend the rest of my life with."

"What about that Daniel guy?" Laura then asked abruptly. She glanced away casually as she mentioned his name, almost as if embarrassed to bring it up.

"Daniel," Sue said with another smile, "Five years of joy, two months of misery."

"Oh it wasn't that bad," Laura said as if she were an authority on the subject.

"No it wasn't," Sue agreed, "But it obviously wasn't good enough to spell forever."

"Not ticklish again?"

"Not enough I guess," Sue said with a sigh as she reached for her half empty glass of tea. She took a long sip before setting the glass down, "I never did find out what his problem was."

She went ahead and poured more tea into her glass while making brief eye contact with Laura, hoping she would change the subject. Laura's eyes said, "go on."

"Those last two months were the worst. At first I was so afraid of loosing him. When he finally ended it, I only felt relief. Nothing else," Sue explained. The smile was still on her face, but it was showing some signs of pain.

"I remember you were kind of out of it for a while after that," Laura said respectfully.

"Yes, it took some time to get over," Sue admitted.

"I still can't believe what he did to you," Laura commented in passing while reaching for her own glass of tea.

"He got cold feet," Sue suggested while shrugging her shoulders, "it happens when a relationship drags on for too long without going anywhere."

"So that's all that happened?" Laura asked.

"Yep."

"Really, that's it?"

"Yeah, why?" Sue asked of Laura who seemed to be fishing for further details that weren't there.

"You really don't know, do you?" Laura asked sincerely, "I mean, he never told you?"

"Don't know what?" Sues asked as she adjusted herself on the recliner to sit up.

"Sue, I don't know how to tell you this," Laura said slowly.

"Tell me what?" Sue asked, not ready to take the news that Laura was about to give her seriously.

"Daniel," Laura began before pausing to catch her breath, "He, ummm, he made a mistake." Her words seemed to stumble together.

"I guess you could say that," Sue commented.

"No Sue, this was really serious. I can't believe he never told you," Laura began explaining. Sue sat and listened patiently, all the while wondering what had Laura so shook up.

"He had an affair," Laura finally came out and said bluntly.

"What do you mean?" Sue asked. Her tone carried a genuine disbelief. Certainly Laura had to be joking.

"I mean he had an affair. He became intimate with another woman," Laura said with a stutter.

"No," Sue said as if discounting it would simply make it not so.

Laura's face said everything. The brows above both eyes lifted ever so lightly and her lips produced a nearly perfect horizontal line that showed no emotion. She said nothing, and yet spoke volumes at the same time.

"No," Sue said again, almost smiling as if it were all a joke.

"I'm afraid yes," Laura finally confirmed.

"He cheated on me?" Sue asked.

"Yes."

"But why?" Why didn't he ever tell me?" Sue wondered out loud.

"He didn't want to hurt you," Laura said.

"He what?"

"He was too afraid of hurting you to tell you."

"But he didn't worry about hurting me by cheating on me. He also didn't worry about hurting me by lying about it." There was a pause as Sue stared at Laura. She never stopped smiling.

"What's the smile for?" Laura asked.

"It's just all so amusing," Sue said with the wave of a hand.

"So you don't care then?" Laura asked with a bit of relief in her voice.

"Oh I care, just not enough to get all bent out of shape about it. I mean I'm a little upset that you knew and never told me. But, I understand."

"I've always worried about that," Laura said as she felt even more relief about unloading this burden from her shoulders. "I wanted to tell you this for some-time now."

"But you didn't want to hurt me. I understand," Sue interrupted.

Laura smiled a content smile while reaching for her glass of tea. Sue also reached for her own glass, allowing a moment of silence to pass. It was while she was setting her glass down that Sue asked, "So how is it you know all this?"

Laura held a firm grip on her glass as she looked away from her friend. She used a soft and calm voice to say only, "I'm sorry."

500 HOLES

500 holes deep in the ground

filled with dirt and wood

clay returns to where it was found

500 souls rest under these trees

they entered by parade

and left unseen

500 stones mark where they lay

spirits long gone

but here their bones still remain

500 times they entered this place

carried in by parade

and left without a trace

just 500 holes

where they went

no one knows

REQUIEM

Son I have now grown old
My final day is here
But I do have one last wish
Please take me to a place
Where I may rest in peace
Help me on this trip
With your still youthful strength
I will show you the way

To a place you must see
As the tradition goes
My father before me
Once led me to this site
And as he passed he spoke
Of the secret he had learned
A secret passed to him
That I now pass to you

[Father and son
then walked down
a trail known only
to the one of age
and wisdom]

Now look to the distance
Look through the breaking woods.

[and before his
unbelieving eyes
was a site of pure

inspiration
the trees opened
into a field
and upon this field
there sat a cemetery that had an element
of purity
tranquility
and everlasting peace]

Make no noise for they rest
Save those given a task

Forgotten
Is this place
By all but one above
Here to rest
Here to sleep
Without a beat
In their hearts
They await
For the day
When the one returns
To take them home

[From around
the corner of
the far end there
approached a man
riding upon a
horse as white
as a pearl
he rode proudly
and the young one
stood in awe]

Watch as he approaches
Riding upon his steed
His life has passed him by
But he's forbade to rest
Instead he's forced to ride
Around the outer grounds
To keep the evil out
And keep the sleeping in
The task is without end
A burden he must face

[The father then
paused as the
rider passed
in front
of the two
he wore no
emotion just a
stare so blank
yet the one
of youth could
feel the pride
possessed by the
rider eternal]

He does it with pride
Keeping his head raised high
For it's the only way
To justify his life
And the mistakes he made

[The rider then
disappeared around

the corner at
the other end]

Forgotten
Is this place
Save those sleeping within
They rest alone
With pride inside
And comfort as they dream

[The two continued in
closer to the gate
the soft sound
of music could
be heard
to the
amazement of
the one without
age, the music was
that of a woman singing]

She sings a requiem
To keep them all asleep
And to prevent their souls
From ever wandering off
This task was handed down
A sacred family heir
desire fills her heart
And comes out through her voice
Each passing day and night
Those within can hear her song
It's sung without an end
Its only goal—subdue

Now hush my son you'll hear
This tranquil song she sings

[Then both fell
silent so that
they could hear
the joy within
her song]

Forgotten
Is this place
But done so for a cause
To keep it safe
For those who rest
And away form those who pry

[The father then
raised his hand
to point to a tree
and below the tree
there sat a man
weeping like no
man ever had before]

A tear strolls down his face
One followed by the next
Each one represents
A deceased laid to rest
This task he cannot help
He's merely overcome
With regret for all mankind
Who will one day lay down
That final time to rest
So he weeps forever
And for humanity

This man will never rest
Some might call it a curse
But he calls it his pride

[The son then felt
the desire to weep too]

Forgotten
Is this place
And all those
Laid to rest
But they know
Where they are
And where they were before

[the father then
turned to his son
and began to speak
in a more firm, but
still gentle voice]

Son you can go no more
From here I go alone
But you must not forget
This place you have now seen
Keep it safe in your heart
But never tell a soul
Until your final day
This you must show your son
And lead him here alone
And pass it on to him
It's a tradition passed down
from father then to son

a cycle like life

[Only then did the
son realize the
severity of the
current events
for it was something
he had always feared
yet now it was less
of a burden and in
fact relieved him
of the pressure of
facing his own time
this would allow him
to live a more fulfilling
life than he could ever
imagine]

Forgotten
Is this place
By all but one above
Here to rest
Here to sleep
Without a beat
In their hearts
They await
For the day
When the one returns
To take them home

THE GATHERING STORM

It was getting late, and she was ready for bed. She made sure all the lights were out downstairs before making the trip up to her second floor bedroom. She spent her normal hour reading a book before she went to sleep. As she read, she could hear the wind slowly picking up outside.

The wind was always different for her. Her house was in the middle of a mostly open plain, surrounded by only four trees. This gave little break or resistance to the wind, allowing it to blow directly against her hundred year old home. It usually just gave the house a slight shake, sent a howling sound through the air. This wind was different. It was bringing something bad. She just didn't know it yet.

The first sign of trouble came from the branches of a tree brushing against the window of her second story bedroom. It was a large oak tree, one of four. They had been growing long before the house was built. The smallest of the trees was just over three feet thick while the largest was close to five. There was no real pattern to their arrangement. Ironically, the smaller tree was the one with the most past. It was also the tree closest to the house, and whose branches were rattling against the window.

The trees continued to grow more and more restless as the wind gathered the brewing storm. This was hardly the first, and certainly not the worst storm that any of the trees had ever seen. She had also seen her fair share of storms, though this was shaping up to be stronger than most. It was just the beginning.

It was obvious that the sounds she heard was only caused by the branches blowing in the wind. She really didn't need the flash of lightening to display the silhouettes of the branches against the drapes that covered the window. More than that, she didn't need to hear the crackle of thunder that came moments after the lightening.

For twenty minutes, it was the same thing over and over. The tree branches would slam against the window. The sound was occasionally interrupted by the loud clash and crackle of thunder. Only occasionally did the thunder come out of nowhere. Usually, it was announced by a flash of lightening. Instead of helping by serving as a warning, it would only end up making matters worse. There was actually a tranquil kind of contrast to it all. One second it would be pitch dark, the next bright as day. One second it would be quite as night can be, the next the sky would literally scream at her.

She tried to dismiss it and allow the storm to sway her to sleep as storms were prone to do. This was no ordinary storm. Twice she felt her eyes begin to close and carry her to dreamland. Each time, a terrible thunder would bellow through the sky, shaking the windows in a manner that suggested they might break. She quickly decided to give up sleeping until the storm could calm. Unfortunately, there was to be no calming of this storm.

She laid in her bed, and watched the lightening. Seconds would pass slowly as the tension built up in her shoulders. Her eyes would squint in preparation. When the thunder would finally rumble through the air, every part of the two story house would shake. Most times, she would even shudder with the house.

When the rain started, it came in sheets of water falling against the roof and side of the house. The wind seemed to blow it in every direction. This was the point when most storms would settle into a routine of wind, water, thunder, and lightening that would slowly fade away. However, this was to be the exception to most storms. The rain only brought more thunder which only got louder. The thunder only brought more lightening which only got brighter.

That's when the scream came. It flared up and came out of a burst of thunder. At first, it even sounded like part of the thunder. The third time, it was clearly something else. The thunder faded from the loud crackling sound like that of a sheet ripping, to the distinct sound of someone screaming out of tremendous pain and suffering. Slowly, the sound faded to that of just the wind and the rain.

She sat up in her bed and looked around her room. Her eyes moved towards the window where all she saw was darkness. Then the lightening came, and she saw the silhouettes of the branches banging against her window. This time, the lightening hung around an extra second to reveal the image of something moving quickly past her window. It was small, and moved fast.

When the lightening was gone, she sat frozen in the center of her bed with her eyes wide open. She glared at the window through the darkness. She was waiting for the thunder, but only heard the rustling of the branches and the loud splatter of the rain. Seconds passed slowly, and she swore that it was way past time for the thunder. The only thing worse than a lot of noise, is the total lack of any sound. Just as she was about to relax and let her tense shoulders sag a bit, the silence was destroyed. There was no thunder at all this time, just the sound of pain.

The scream moved slowly from a deep growling roar that echoed through the night to a high pitched, ear piercing, screech. When the scream peaked, her windows began to rattle. Sitting on her bed, she pressed her hands over her ears and closed her eyes from fear.

Again, the terrific scream faded through the night, and an eerie silence fell into place. The rain was still pounding the house and the wind continued to bang the branches of the tree against her window. Compared to the horrific scream, this sound was nothing more than a comforting white noise in the background.

Her hands fell away from the side of her head, and slowly she allowed her eyes to open. With a hypnotic stare, she gazed at the window, and waited for the next flash of lightening. She didn't have to wait long. When the lightening came, it wasn't simply a bright flash that faded away. Instead, it was a series of lightening streaks that illuminated the sky like a strobe light.

Amidst the flashes of lightening, she could see something out there. She couldn't tell what it was, but with each flash of lightening it got bigger as if it were moving towards, not past, her window. The lighting came to an abrupt end, and she braced herself for what she hoped would be thunder. Her hopes would be let down.

Another bright, lingering, streak of lightening flashed through the sky. She could now tell that that the object outside her window was a bird of some kind. The lightening displayed the silhouetted image of the bird opening its wings wide as it moved towards the window. The lightening faded to darkness, and the night was ripped apart by another loud scream as the bird came crashing through her window. Pieces of glass flew in all directions, and the wind blew the drapes into the room behind the bird.

The darkness was once again removed as another bolt of lightening displayed the bird; a solid white owl, perched at the foot of her bed. Though the light faded, she could still see the outline of the bird sitting there, staring directly at her. Another flash of lightening raced across the sky, and the owl spread its wings wide as if to say, "hi."

She tilted her head to the side, and looked at the owl in amazement. She inched her way across her bed to get closer to the owl. Slowly, she extended her left arm in the direction of the bird. Just as the tips of her fingers were a bare inch away from the owl, another flash of lightening flew across the sky. The roar of thunder echoed through the air like a warning. Instinctively, she pulled back her hand.

The night once again fell silent, but her eyes never left the owl. She inched even closer, and again she reached out her hand in an attempt to touch the owl. This time her fingers came within a hair of the owl when the lightening again flashed and the thunder again crackled. With a single flap of its wings, the owl glided from the foot of the bed to the window ledge where it perched peacefully between the two drapes blowing into the room.

The bird continued to stare at her, and she never stopped staring back. She slid her body to the edge of the bed where she paused and allowed her legs to dangle over the side. She looked down at all of the glass on the floor. Almost on queue, the lightening again lit up the night in a series of flashing strobes. She watched in amazement as the glass shards began sliding across the floor so as to make a pathway from where she was on the bed to the window where the owl was. The lightening stopped. The thunder roared, and once again the owl spread its wings wide as if to say, "Come on."

Her first steps were taken with caution. She still had a youthful curiosity in her, but she was old enough to know when to go slow. As she moved her leg forward, she held onto the bed with her hand, just in case. By the time she took her fourth step, she realized that she was half way between her bed and the owl who was still perched on the window ledge. She also noticed that she hadn't seen any lightening, or heard a hint of thunder since stepping off the bed.

She eased through the next two steps, bringing herself even closer to the owl. She was almost within reach, but not quite. One more step took her close enough to actually touch the bird, though she was afraid to make any sudden movements towards the owl. It hardly mattered at all. As soon as she stopped moving forward, the owl moved from the center of the window to the far left side.

The rain was still falling and the wind was still sending the tree branches on a collision course with the side of house. She was now close enough to feel the rain as it blew in through the shattered window and splattered against her face. All the while, the owl continued to stare at her with those cold dark eyes.

She took the last step that would move her to the edge of the window. When she paused again, the owl finally broke its stare. The bird turned its body a little and its head even more to look out through the window. She followed the gaze of the owl, curious as to what had caught its attention.

By now, she was more than just a little damp from the continuous splatter of water blowing in through the window. She was drenched, and her face was covered with sting spots from where the heavy rain drops had collided with her skin like little bullets from the sky. As she gazed out through the window, she saw only darkness and the silhouettes of the trees in front of her. That's when the night once again erupted with the crackle of thunder and a simultaneous flash of lightening. With the light in the sky, she saw something.

There was movement, though she only saw it out of the corner of her eye. By the time she moved her head, the light had faded, and no movement could be seen. The sky fell silent just long enough for her already peaked curiosity to be raised even further.

She turned to look at the owl, hoping it could offer some sort of explanation. She was met with only a blank stare. Suddenly, the owl spread its wings wide, like a conductor raising his wand. Out of nowhere, the sky erupted into a thunderous chorus of song. The lightening shot through the air so as to illuminate the show below.

The first bolt of lightening lit the sky as bright as day. Again, she saw movement. The light hung in the air just long enough for her to get a good look at what appeared to be something swinging from the main branch of the tree next to the house. It looked like a rope, or maybe a chain. She couldn't tell exactly. The lightening bolt faded into darkness. Her eyes maintained their constant stare at the branch while she waited for the next flash of lightening.

Her fears were slowly giving way to curiosity, and she found herself looking forward to what ever this storm might bring. Another flash of lightening shot across the sky and she could tell that it was, in fact, a rope swinging from the branch.

The light faded for a second, then reappeared in another series of strobing flashes. When the first flash came, the rope was suddenly gone. She found herself asking if it had really been there in the first place. The second flash disputed this as the rope became visible once again. With each alternating flash of light, the rope would appear and then vanish.

Just as fast as it had come, the light disappeared into darkness and the thunder faded away. The only thing that could be heard was the sound of the rain, though it seemed to be slowing down. She stared at the tree branch, waiting for the sky to light up again. A long minute went by, then another, and nothing happened. She turned to look at the owl who was still perched on the window ledge. Its eyes were closed, as if it were sleeping.

She tilted her head sideways, somewhat confused. Again, she decided to try and touch the owl, just to see if it was really there. She extended her hand towards the owl which she had yet to be able to touch. This was to be another attempt that failed at the last moment.

Her hand froze when she noticed movement in the owl's closed eyes. They slowly opened, revealing the dark black eyes that stared at her intensely. The eyes became wider. The rain began to fall harder as if the storm was reawakening with this mysterious bird.

She pulled back her arm as the owl continued to stare at her with those cold eyes. By now, the rain was back to its peak intensity. She turned her head to look out through the window, and when she saw nothing, she looked back at the owl. The bird seemed almost frozen in place until it once again spread its wings wide.

With this, the night erupted. The thunder came first, though it faded quickly into another sound. It was like the screaming she had heard earlier, though it seemed closer than before. The scream reached its highest pitch, and the sky once again lit up with a brief flicker of lightening. She looked out her window again and saw more movement; this time beneath the tree. A thunder-like noise could be heard coming from the ground.

When she stared though the rain, she could see several horses approaching the base of the tree. She could hear their heavy breathing and even see the steam of their breath through the cold rain. The silhouetted images of men could be seen on the backs of the horses. She moved her gaze across the scene and counted eight horses.

A streak of lightening flashed across the sky to reveal the details of the men. Their skin was fair. Their hair was trimmed, and while some had black hair, most wore the red and yellow colors of the sun. Their clothes were all blue and gray; covering their entire body with the exception of the random rips and tears. Something told her to run and hide. Certainly these men had no right to be on her property. Something else told her to keep a careful eye on what was happening; that maybe she was about to learn something.

A deep thunder bellowed through the sky and a single bolt of lightening flew low across the horizon. The lightening bolt back lit the arrival of a ninth horse. Behind this horse, there was another man. This man was obviously different than the others. Even through the rain, she could tell that his skin was darker. She could also see more of his skin because he was only wearing what appeared to be moccasin pants. His hands were tied by a rope that led to the back of the horse.

The man riding that horse dismounted from his horse, and jumped to the ground. When his boots hit the mud, the sky went dark. The lightening stopped and the thunder slowed to a soft rumble that faded into the sound of just the pouring rain. She leaned through her window to get a better look at the ground, but saw nothing. It was as if the men and horses had disappeared into thin air.

Confused, she turned to the owl. The mysterious bird was perched on the window ledge and staring up at her. Despite the fierce rain and wind, not a single feather moved on the owl. This lack of motion, combined with the cold stare, gave the owl an aurora that sent a shiver down her spine. The bird appeared to have a presence that was outside of the storm.

A sudden streak of lightening caught her eye, and again she looked below her window, but saw nothing. A second bolt lit up the scene and this time she could see movement. The white men were no longer mounted on their horses. Instead, they were all circled around the horse with the darker man tied to the back. They pointed at him, and waved their arms at him.

Through it all, the lone man stood strong. One of the white men walked up to him and kicked the man in the gut. The man collapsed to his knees and looked upwards before standing again. The defiance that he presented was awe inspiring. Then, everything fell black. She turned to the owl again, begging to know what happened next.

The thunder was to answer that question. As with earlier, the thunder started as a deep roar and peaked as a high pitch scream. She looked down and saw nothing. She turned to the bird and saw only the cold blank stare. That's when the bird blinked. When the owl opened its eyes again, all hell broke loose.

The thunder shot across the sky in a rolling manner that didn't want to stop. The lightening flickered like a child playing with a light switch. With each flash of light the men below her would appear and disappear. Through a strobing light show she watched as the white men took turns hitting and kicking the lone man who had been tied to the horse. She watched as the man dropped to his knees, and two of the other men began dragging him towards the tree.

Suddenly, everything went dark again. She had to lean over the window ledge to look down, curious as to what was really out there. As fast as the storm had died, it suddenly started with a thousand flashes of lightening flying from everywhere. It was like a swarm of fire flies that called to her; just daring her to venture into the heart of the storm. With most things that night, the images were short lived and left her mind plagued with thoughts. Fear told her to stay where she was. Something else, something she couldn't explain, told her to move forward.

The window was a standard four foot by four foot frame, so she had to squat some as she stood on the ledge. She actually felt rather comfortable perched next to the owl. She held on to each side of the frame with her hands. That's when her left leg actually brushed against the owl. She felt its soft feathers.

She quickly glanced down to see if the owl reacted in any way. It hadn't, and was still there. She had tried to touch the owl on three separate occasions, and had failed each time. It didn't seem like that big of a deal. She had touched and held birds before, but not like this one. This bird was different. It was trying to show her something.

It had been her hopes all along that she'd touch the owl, and it would disappear. She'd wake up, and be in her bed. Her window wouldn't be shattered, and there would be no loud screaming sounds. It was too surreal to be just a dream. She had felt the bird. It was real. This was real.

It was then that she suddenly felt a return of the fear. She was also curious, and for some reason, the curiosity outweighed the fear. Why else was she be perched on the ledge of a shattered window during the middle of a serious thunder storm?

She had to know what was out there. The storm sure wasn't telling her anything, and neither was the owl. She turned to look down at the owl, wondering why the storm was slowing down. Again, the owl seemed to be falling asleep. As the owl slept, so too did the storm that was winding down to a slow drizzle. That didn't change the fact that something was out there, something strange, and something she wanted to see.

She carefully stood up on the window ledge as she reached for one of two branches. She had made this escape plenty of times before, so it was almost routine for her. First she would grab the the higher branch with her hands, then she would use that to keep her balance as she did a careful hop from the window ledge to the tree limb. When she landed on the limb, the branches shook, and this apparently reawakened the owl.

Those eyes slowly came open. That's when she felt the wind start to pick up again. She could also feel the little drops of water bombarding her like pellets falling from the sky. The night even let loose with a slow bellow of thunder, possibly just to let her know that it wasn't over.

For a second, she pondered jumping back though the window where she could be safe from the elements. That second passed quickly, and she turned her attention back to the tree she was standing on. The branch that she had seen the rope hanging from was on the same tree, but on the other side of the trunk. It would take some careful maneuvering, but she knew she could make it from the branch she was on to the one she wanted to be on.

She was holding onto the trunk and twisting her body around the tree when a crackle of thunder screamed out from the sky. It had been the first such sound that she had heard in almost five minutes. Her guard was down, and her grip on the tree was almost lost as her entire body shook from the startling sound. Somehow, she managed to hold on, and even got her body moved from one branch to the other.

Now, she had to wait. It's never easy waiting, no mater what the reason, but waiting through nervousness is even harder. Waiting through fear can take the mind to previously unknown places. Throw something more than just idle curiosity into the mix, and the mind is apt to take the imagination anywhere and everywhere. Her mind was racing somewhere in between.

The sky once again erupted into a show of light and sound. Streaks of lightening chased each other across the sky. The thunder roared louder and louder. At first she looked up, but a sudden movement below caught her attention. When she looked downward, she saw what she had been so afraid of seeing before.

Sure enough, there was a rope wrapped around the branch of the tree. The rope hadn't been there five seconds ago. Even more disturbing, at the other end of the rope, there was a man. It was the same man that had stood so defiantly. The defiance had faded, and now he was fighting for his life.

The lightening faded and so too did the man. It was only for a brief second, just long enough for a single heart beat. Three streaks of lightening flew across the sky, one after the other. This fire show brought light to the darkness and she was able to see the details of the man. Below his left eye was a marking similar to that of the wing of a bird. It was a single vertical line that gave way to three separate lines that arched downwards and came to a point. A single tear ran down from that eye, though it was quickly lost in the drops of water raining onto his face.

She glanced downward and saw the men below her. They could be seen pointing up at the man hanging from the tree. They appeared to be shouting. The odd part was that she couldn't hear what they were saying. Even through the storm, she should have been able to hear them shouting. There was only the thunder and the rain. She watched closely and noticed something that was truly terrifying. Every time one of the men would appear to shout, the thunder would roar louder, as if they were shouting the thunder.

She turned her attention again to the man hanging from the rope. His hands were desperately grasping at the rope around his neck as his body swayed in the gusts of wind. Down each arm was another black mark similar to the one below his eye, only it was longer with less of a curve. She so wanted to help him, but was overcome with a single thought. Was he even real?

She turned to the owl for answers and noticed a deep stare in the bird who was sill perched on the branch of the tree. The owl swelled its body, becoming almost half as big again. He then spread his wings wide and leaned forward as if to fall from the branch. The bird glided along the wind in a direction that seemed to put it on a collision course with the girl. At the last moment, the owl arched upwards. Fear overcame her. In an effort to move out of the bird's path, she lost her footing and was faced with the option of either falling from the branch of the tree, or jumping with at least a small amount of control. She landed, and rolled through the grass.

She regained her footing and was able to stand again. She looked up and saw only the shadows dancing in the darkness. There was the frantic movement of raindrops falling at a slight angle. Nothing else moved. She ran both hands across her face, creating a moment of dryness that was quickly washed away by the onslaught of the rain.

A slow step was taken to move her closer to the tree. Her eyes never left the branch that she could see only in shadow. Clearly there was no one hanging from it. In a pattern already repeated countless times that night, the darkness gave way to lightening that streaked from one side of the sky to the other.

That light illuminated everything in a whole new way. Again, she could see the man struggling to free himself from the rope that was slowly draining away his life. The owl could also be seen again, this time perched only inches away from the rope that was tied to the branch. The owl now seemed less interested in her. The bird stared over its short beak to observe the man.

The last thing she saw was the lightening fading from the sky. That allowed the darkness to remove any clarity from what she was seeing before her. She thought she could see the silhouetted image of the bird still perched on the branch high in the air. Everything else disappeared. The man swinging from the tree was gone. Even the men that she knew were surrounding her seemed to have vanished. Confused, she tilted her head to try and gain a better perspective. She slowly looked all around herself, but saw nothing. It was then that she noticed the owl once again outstretch its wings as wide as it could.

Just as the owl brought its wings back into its body, the night erupted with all kinds of violence. A wave of sheet lightening turned the night into day. There were no streaks, simply a panoramic view of whiteness surrounding everything. This was followed quickly by a sharp break in the silence that rumbled through the air. She could feel her skin shake from the vibrations caused by the thunder. The first outburst had only partially faded when it was followed by three more. No sooner had the thunder began to roll away softly than the night again lit up. Three bright streaks of white lightening flew from the clouds above to the ground below. They struck barely twenty feet from where the girl was standing.

A cloud of dust flew through the air, and the force of the blast knocked her to the ground. By the time she knew what had happened, she was trying to again climb to her feet in complete darkness. She looked up at the man and swore she could see a flash of light flicker in his eyes as he fought to free himself from the rope. Suddenly, this light faded from his eyes, and the entire sky turned pitch black. Thunder rumbled softly across the sky, but faded without event. A second wave of thunder passed with a mere flicker of lightening that flew through the clouds.

An eerie silence again fell over everything. She knew that the white men were surrounding her, but couldn't see them. That was the worst part. It wasn't just the silence, but the lack of any feeling what so ever. Even the rain had stopped. She was almost ready to believe that it was all over when a flash of light flew through the clouds. A second later, a single bolt of lightening flew towards the ground. There was no thunder, just the sudden flash of light that hit the ground and caused a cloud of dust to rise into the air.

Slowly, the rain started again. A series of thunder bolts rolled across the sky from different directions. Subtle flashes of lightening flickered through the clouds and caste a small amount of light on the subject. That's when she saw them.

Three men, all on horseback, rode out of the falling dust. They looked rather similar to the man who was hanging from the tree. The dark skin, the long flowing black hair, even the markings below the eyes were all the same. They were also bare from the waist up, and only marginally covered below the waist. All the horses were mustangs with eyes as wild as the storm. Their eyes even glowed a soft blue color. The horses also carried markings similar to the men that road them.

This left her in the precarious position of being between the three men on horses and the nine men beneath the tree. She was facing the nine white men, but kept peeking over her shoulder at the three men on horseback. For several long moments, time hung in the air, like a raindrop not sure where to land.

She watched as the white men each turned their heads and took notice of the arrival of the three new men. The white men immediately returned their gaze to the man in the tree. It was only then that she began to wonder why the man was being hung. It was nothing more than a fleeting thought. There was something missing from the reality of everything, and that removed any empathy she might have had for the man. The only thing she felt was curiosity. The numerous whys, and hows flew through her head. She had no answers, only questions, and there appeared to be as many of those as there were rain drops that night.

Everything froze in the darkness. Even sound was absent from the rain that seemed to be absorbed by the ground as it hit. The man in the middle held out his arm, and she could feel the air move above her as the owl flew from its perch on the tree to land gently on the man's outstretched arm. As soon as the bird landed, it cast another of its deep stares at the girl. She had learned that this was always the sign of something to come.

She kept her eyes on the nine men while slowly backing in the direction of the men on the horses. Even then, she moved a bit to the side so she could put distance between herself and everyone. Something told her that this was no place to be. When she looked at the owl and saw the stare, she only had that point reinforced.

Again, the bird stretched out its wings in a moment of silence. The owl held its wings outwards longer than usual. She only assumed that whatever was about to happen, was going to be big. She sped up her retreat, moving further away from everyone, the trees, and even her house.

The first clap of thunder knocked her to the ground. Hey eyes never left the owl, and to her total surprise, the bird still held its wings stretched outwards. The second clap of thunder was less of a surprise, but the ground shook fiercely. She didn't even try to stand up, and instead used her feet to push herself further back away from everything.

The third clap of thunder was the worst. As the sound first cracked the silence, the owl lowered its wings. The show was on. The clouds above could be seen swirling into action, almost as if their very movement was producing the ear shattering noises. Like sparks from a machine, giant streaks of lightening came winding down towards the ground. Unlike most lightening, there was nothing random about where they hit.

The bolts of lightening could be seen curving under the tree to hit men who felt protected by the large round branches. One by one, the men standing under the tree were evaporated into dust as hot flashes of energy crashed down on them from the sky. The first four happened so fast that they never knew what hit them. The men had started to scramble away from the tree. The next two men vaporized into clouds of steam as they were hit by the lightening and the rain.

She watched as two of the men took off running. One of the men dove to the ground twice, actually dodging a lightening bolt each time. He stood up and began to run off through the field when two separate bolts of lightening hit him. They smashed into him from opposite directions and reduced him to ash. It was like a soft sandstone being squashed between two baseball bats. Small pieces of the man flew off in different directions, glowing incandescent as they fell to the ground.

The second man only made it a few feet before the first bolt of lightening stuck the ground behind him. This bounced him into the air where a second bolt of lightening flew through him. He was instantly scattered like dust to the wind.

Through it all, her eyes never blinked. The sight was both frightening and amazing at the same time. It was so real that she could feel the tremors running through the earth each time a bolt of lightening exploded to the ground. The colors and sound were so vivid, that it seemed like a dream. Surreal was the closest word that fit her experience at that moment.

It only took seconds for the sky to find and remove the last of the nine men. There was literally nothing left of them when it was over. Like the battle of a time gone by, she watched as hardy men were reduced to the earth that had given birth to them.

Her gaze moved again to the man still hanging from the tree. That he was alive was amazing. That he still had enough energy to be able to pull at the rope around his neck was beyond comprehension. She was so focused on the man that everything else was missed on her. She didn't notice as two of the men on horseback began slowly backing their horses up. The owl, still perched on the arm of the man in the center, was also out of her view. She didn't notice as the man threw up his arm, tossing the bird high into the air.

When she finally did turn to look at the three men, she saw the owl circling high above the man in the middle who was now the only one close to the tree. The sudden silence was lost on her as even the rain fall went unnoticed. There was so much to take in, and she was trying to absorb it all at once. Details were lost. She became focused on the owl who had taken to flight. The look on her face showed her confusion as she was left wondering, "Was it leaving, or was there something still left to come?"

The sky would answer her with one last outburst of anger. From all four directions, a slow rolling thunder descended upon everyone. Sporadic waves of light flickered across the sky. It wasn't lightening, and wasn't like anything she had ever seen. The bird circled, and gained more speed until it finally broke the circle.

The owl began flying in a straight line towards the man who was still trying to free himself from the death grip that the rope had on him.

The middle man on horseback also began moving. He pulled the reigns of his horse, and the giant beast reared up to stand like a man on two legs. As his front legs crashed back down on the ground, a giant crackle of thunder erupted from the sky and the man began charging towards the tree.

For a second, the sky glowed incandescent. This allowed her to see both the man on his horse, and the owl, charge towards the man hanging from the tree. Suddenly, the night was overtaken by a darkness like she had never before seen. Not even shadows were visible.

A final outburst of thunder cracked the sky and gave way to a streak of fire from above. The bolt of lightening struck the tree at its very base. The light caste on the night allowed her to watch in amazement as the owl flew directly into the chest of the man. From there, the owl vanished. In the snap of a finger, it was gone. The force of the impact from the owl actually ripped the man away from the tree, snapping not his neck, but the rope that held him.

The man never landed on the ground. His companion on horseback caught him in mid-air and whisked him away from under the tree that was being split down the middle by the bolt of lightening. Half of the tree fell in the direction of the girl who found herself running even further from her house to escape being hit by the falling branches.

She dove to make a final attempt at escape, landing only a few feet from the closest branch. The other half of the tree began falling in the opposite direction; towards her house. A strong gust of wind blew from across her house and held the tree in the air for a moment. A second gust of air blew against the tree, sending it falling away from the house. The tree fell to the ground with an eerie creaking sound of the wood cracking and twisting. It landed with a thud, and sent a large cloud of dust into the air.

And like that, it was over. A final gust of wind blew away the clouds, giving way to the light of a full moon and the stars. She rose to her feet and tried to find the men on their horses. They too were gone. The next morning, she would awaken and ask herself if they had ever even been there. She had a feeling that only the large oak tree laying on the ground would ever know for sure.

She would never look at another storm the same. She'd also never sleep through another storm. She always wondered what stories the wind and rain were trying to reveal. Even if there wasn't an owl present to show her the details, she would look hard for what wasn't there. Sometimes she'd see something. Other times, she would only be left wondering what else was out there. At the end of the night, only that gathering storm really knew.

-fin

THE BOOK

Prequel to "Power And Responsibility"

The anger in her voice was clear and pointed, "You have two carts of books to put up and only thirty minutes to do it."

"Don't worry, it'll only take ten," he had offered in an almost dismissive manner.

"Then do it," came the stern order from Mrs. Clairborne, the assistant head librarian. "I have to close everything down in the back, then we need to get out of here," she added in a terse voice as she turned to walk away.

She wasn't always so rude. In fact, she was usually a fairly pleasant person. He had seen her greet one visitor after another to the library with a smile and a friendly voice. When it came to Chandler though, something changed. She always managed to reach down and find a harsh reception for the sixteen year old boy.

He had been working at the library during the summer to earn extra credit for school. The deal was that he'd spend four hours a day helping to keep the library clean. He'd also read one book a week. When it was all over, he'd write a short paper detailing his experiences at the library. In return for this, he'd pick up the extra credits that would help him graduate a year early. It had all been worked out by Mrs. Boyles, the head librarian of the newly built library.

Mrs. Boyles had taken an immediate liking to young Chandler. He was athletic enough to be on whatever sports team he wanted, but he had taken a far more academic approach to school. So far, he had received only one 'B', but he swore it was a fix by his freshman history teacher who Chandler had kept correcting throughout the class. He had shrugged it off a long time ago. Who could really worry about a single 'B' when they had a GPA of 3.95.

At 16, he was all set to leave high school a full year earlier than the rest of his class. The best part was that he would still be at the head of the class he graduated with. All he needed, was to remain strong through his last year, and survive one more month with Mrs. Clairborne.

"What a pod," He said to himself as he eyed the two carts of books. It would take him 5 minutes, if that. In barely seven weeks, he had memorized the location of every book in the building. He had always had a good memory. Sometimes he considered his ability at near perfect recall to be a gift. Other times, he considered it a curse when all the facts in his head became cluttered, and one of his thunderous headaches would take over.

By the time he finished the first cart, Chandler could feel one of those headaches approaching. As he put up the last book from the second cart, Chandler had to steady himself against one of the large bookcases. The headache was at its peak, and had brought a fair dizzy spell along with it. This was nothing new, and didn't concern him in the least. Chandler had learned to live with the headaches and the dizzy spells for a long time now.

Once he had steadied himself, Chandler slowly made his way to the water fountain where he took several long sips of cool water. He then slipped into the restroom so he could splash some water on his face. As soon as the restroom door closed behind him, Mrs. Clairborne appeared from the back; purse in hand, ready to go.

"Chandler?" she called, but got no reply. She saw the two empty carts and rolled her eyes, wondering where Chandler had thrown the books. She stepped closer to the rows of bookcases and called his name again.

Her low opinion of him dropped even further when she got no reply. She muttered a few choice words about the reliability of teenagers before calling his name one last time. With no reply, she assumed he had left already.

"Oh Chandler? I'm leaving," she called out in a half informative and half threatening voice. Again, she got no reply.

She walked towards the front door. One by one, she turned off each of the eight light switches. The library got darker with every flick of a switch. With a pitch dark building, and still no sign of young Chandler, Mrs. Claiborne walked out through the front doors. There was a loud, echoing "boom," as she closed the solid oak doors. Another loud sound, this one more of a "clang", announced the doors had been locked.

Chandler never heard the calls. He was tucked away in the restroom with the water running. The lights to the restroom were controlled by a switch on the wall just a few feet away, so he never noticed when Mrs. Clairborne turned off the lights in the library. He went right on splashing water on his face as the headache slowly subsided and the dizzy spell faded. He wiped away the water with a facial towel and threw it in the trash.

When he opened the door, Chandler was met with near total darkness. Instinctively, he ran towards the front doors, though it only took one tug for him to realize that they had been locked. He wasn't worried, but more annoyed by the situation. Mrs. Boyles had entrusted him with a key when he started, just in case of an emergency.

With his backpack strung over his shoulder, and his skateboard by his side, Chandler made his way towards the door. Just for fun, he glided across the floor of the library on his skateboard. There was just enough light shining through the round skylight in the roof to allow him to see the outlines of any obstacles. He stopped five feet shy of the door before using one foot to pop the skateboard up in the air, catching it with his left hand.

Chandler was reaching in his pocket for the key when he heard a noise at the front door. It was a rattling sound, like someone messing with the front latch. A couple of seconds later, there was the loud sound of the main lock being turned.

"Cool," Chandler thought to himself, believing that Mrs. Clairborne must have realized she had forgotten about him, and was now coming to let him out. It was actually for the best that someone was there when he left. This way, no one could accuse him of any wrong doing on the way out.

Simultaneously, both doors slowly swung open. Chandler waited to see the face of Mrs. Clairborne, who he knew would be unhappy about having to come back for him. As the doors opened wider, Chandler was met with a face, but it wasn't Mrs. Clairborne's. The face was older like hers, but wasn't even that of a woman's.

Standing ten feet away from the door, and fifteen feet away from Chandler, was a man. His face was worn. It looked to belong to a man in his upper forties. His hair was dark brown with a few streaks of solid gray. Though long, he wore his hair neat, pulled back in a ponytail with just a few strands hanging over his face.

He wore black pants that were loose. A pair of straps ran down, and wrapped around, each leg. All the way down each of his legs, various objects either hung from, or were tucked into, these straps. There were three daggers, several leather pouches and satchels. On his left leg, there was a three inch wide silver cross tucked into the strap. On his right leg, there were a pair of five inch long bones hanging from the strap just above his calf. The bones looked like teeth, though they were a bit large for that.

He wore a solid gray wool turtle neck shirt. Hanging from around his neck was a sterling silver chain with a long but thin silver cross. Strung over his left shoulder, was a back pack. His forearms were each wrapped in leather straps and he wore rings on three of his fingers.

The man held up his left hand as if he had just pushed the doors open. He hadn't. He was standing too far away to even touch them, and yet they were slowly opening.

When the doors were completely open, the man lowered his hand and took one deliberate step after another towards the doors. As he moved forward, Chandler backed up, though at a slower pace. By the time the man was inside the library, he was less than eight feet away from Chandler.

"Can I help you?" Chandler asked with a trace of fear in his voice.

The man didn't reply verbally. Instead, he slowly raised both arms up by his side. As his arms moved up, the doors also moved, and slowly closed again. When both doors were firmly closed, the man dropped his arms by his side. A loud "clang" could be heard as the doors locked.

Believing that the man may not have heard him the first time, Chandler again asked, "Is there something I can help you with?"

The man never looked at Chandler as he said simply, "No," in a deep voice that carried a distinct European accent to it. He moved forward towards Chandler, though he turned his body just enough to avoid running into the boy. Chandler stood frozen as the man walked past him. He found himself slowly turning around to look at the man who walked further into the library.

"I'm afraid that I'm going to have to ask you to leave," Chandler said with enough conviction to suggest that he really meant it. The man paused for only a moment, just long enough to look over his shoulder at Chandler and cast a stare that was half curious and half dangerous. He immediately dismissed Chandler and went back to walking into the heart of the library.

Chandler followed behind at a cautious distance and again said, "You're going to have to leave." This time he went on to add, "We're closed for the night."

The man didn't even look back at Chandler. He continued walking; past the help desk, past the rarely used card catalog, and past the four rows of computers that everyone now used in place of the card catalog. Apparently, the man didn't need a catalog. He knew exactly where he was going. Chandler followed, though he stayed mindful about keeping a safe distance. Something told him to leave then and call the cops. Something else told him to hang around and watch the man. If the man was going to do something, then at least Chandler would be a witness.

The man walked towards the rows of book cases, then paused as if he had forgotten what he was looking for. He glanced up and around. His gaze moved in Chandler's direction, though they never made eye contact. The man's stare then moved up towards the ceiling where there was only a small amount of light shining through a round glass window in the ceiling. He held both hands up in front of himself and snapped his fingers. Nothing happened, and he tilted his head to the side as if confused.

He turned his body to the side and looked over his shoulder towards the door. He extended his left hand towards the light switches by the door. He closed his eyes and appeared to concentrate for a second. Simultaneously, all the switches popped up and the darkness in the building faded to light.

"Wow," Chandler said in a soft whisper.

The man went back to looking around the library, obviously searching for something specific. He came to the first row of books, and paused for a moment. His eyes scanned across all the shelves. Apparently, he didn't find what he was looking for, and moved on to the next row of books.

The man was walking along one end of the rows of books. Chandler stayed at the other end of the rows, but followed along to keep an eye on the man. When the man got to the fifth row, he apparently found something. He turned to walk through the rows of books, moving slowly and deliberately as if each step had been planed well in advance.

Chandler was at the other end of the row. He had to decide if he was going to stand his ground, or back up as the man came walking down the row towards him. The man walked about two-thirds of the way down the row before pausing. He turned to his left and looked up and down at all the books. He stared at the books for almost a full minute before turning around and looking at the books behind him. He studied those books for only a second before extending his left hand outward.

On the top shelf there was a large book laying on its side. As the man extended his hand outwards, the book began to shake. At first it just vibrated slightly, but as the man stretched out his arm more, the vibrating book began to shake intensely. The shaking book moved slowly forward and seemed to almost float towards the edge of the shelf. When more than half of the book had crossed the edge of the shelf, the book dropped and the man reached out with both hands to catch it.

Chandler noticed that the book was at least six inches thick with a profile of fourteen inches long by ten inches wide. Two other things stood out to Chandler. First, it was odd that the man could make the book float through the air, but had to use both hands to catch and carry it. What was he thinking, it was just odd that the man could make the book float through the air in the first place. However, the combination, or contradiction of factors did leap out at him.

The second oddity was that the man found the book in the first place. He went right to it. Sure he looked in the wrong place at first, but that was just a simple mistake. He still knew the book was there. That was more than Chandler could say. Chandler knew where every book in the building was. Certainly he would have noticed a book of that size. The design was also different. The pages had gilded golden edges and the cover of the book was trimmed in silver. There was no way that Chandler wouldn't have ever noticed that book.

The man carried the book with both hands as he walked down the isle towards Chandler who instinctively backed away from the man. The young teen gained some relief from noticing that the man seemed far more interested in the book than him. The fact was, he had only once even acknowledged the teens existence. Chandler watched as the man carried the book over to the tables and chairs. He dropped the book on one of the tables with a loud "Thud." A large cloud of dust flew up into the air from the book. The man pulled out a chair as he dropped his backpack on the floor, obviously settling in for a long visit to the library. He paused for a moment and rubbed his temples while looking around at his immediate area. He reached into his backpack, and pulled out a thin leather pad.

Chandler took a few steps closer to the man who first opened the thin pad, then carefully opened the large book and began flipping through the pages. As Chandler took another curious step forward, the man stopped flipping through the book. Apparently, he found the page he was looking for. He reached down to his left leg and pulled a pen out of one of the leather straps.

The young teen had slowly made his way to within ten feet of the table where the man was. He could hear the soft sounds of pages being turned and even of the man's cloths moving as he reached down for the pen. The sounds were normal in a place such as a library where people were expected to remain silent. The sound that Chandler wasn't expecting to hear was of the man saying something. But, that's exactly what he did. His words were brief, quiet, and even somewhat muffled, so Chandler heard only his voice, not what was said.

Chandler didn't say anything immediately. He didn't offer any kind of response either, since he wasn't sure if the man was talking to him or just thinking out loud. A long collection of moments passed before the man turned his head slowly to look in Chandler's direction.

Once he had made eye contact with the young teen, the man asked, "Can you get me a glass of water, please?"

The question was simple enough, but still it perplexed Chandler. Why did this man think Chandler would be willing to offer any sort of help? How long was this man going to be there that he needed something to drink? What was next, a sandwich? Most perplexing of all was the fact that he had asked so nicely. He was much larger than Chandler, and armed as well. Why not just bark out an order with an "or else" attached at the end? It was this point that actually prompted Chandler to go and get the man a glass of water. If the man was going to be nice, then there was certainly no need to agitate him.

Chandler walked to the small break room by the offices and filled a styrofoam cup with water. He carried it back to the table where the man was still sitting. The man was running his fingers down the leather notepad as he wrote in the larger book. It seemed odd. Most people, actually everyone, brings a note pad to the library and copies information from a book to their pad. The man was doing just the opposite.

"Here you go," Chandler said softly as he set the cup of water down on the table next to the man's book.

"Thank you," the man said without even looking up at Chandler.

"You know, we're closed," Chandler both asked and suggested.

"Yes," the man replied softly. His eyes never looked up, but instead continued to glance back and forth from the leather bound pad to the large book he was writing in.

Chandler pulled out a chair and sat across from the man. He moved slowly, ready to bolt if the man gave the slightest hint that he objected to Chandler's presence. He didn't even seem to notice, let alone care. Chandler could feel himself becoming rather at ease with the man.

After turning to a fresh page in the large book, the man paused. He reached over and picked up the cup of water, barely glancing at Chandler while taking a sip. As he sat the cup down, the man made momentary eye contact with the young teen, but he went immediately back to reading from the leather note pad and writing in the large book. Having made eye contact, Chandler felt even more comfortable with the man. He watched the man for a few more minutes, staying quiet and moving little.

Chandler strained his neck a lot and his eyes even more in an attempt to read what the man was writing. It was obviously not English, though Chandler couldn't figure out what language it was. The writing had a lot of curves and swirls to it. There were occasional dots, though they appeared in what looked like a random manner. The oddest part was that the man was writing backwards; from right to left. It looked familiar, but Chandler just couldn't make it out.

The man was apparently not copying everything from the smaller book to the lager one. His hand would slide down the pages in the leather note pad. Sometimes he would pause and begin writing in the larger book. Other times, he would skip over paragraphs, occasionally even whole pages.

Finally, the curiosity got the better of him and Chandler asked, "What language is that?" There was a slight crack of hesitation in his voice.

"Greek," the man said without slowing down.

"Of course," Chandler whispered to himself. He recognized it then. Of course it was Greek.

He watched for another minute as the man copied an entire page from the leather bound pad. The man turned the page and copied another paragraph or two. He then read from the note pad without writing anything for a while. After finishing the page, he paused to take another drink of water.

Again, he glanced at Chandler, but only made brief eye contact. He turned his attention back to the smaller book and began reading from the right side of the page. He just read, but didn't copy anything. This prompted another question.

"Why aren't you copying everything?" Chandler asked with a bit more confidence than he had put into his last question.

"Because it's not all relevant," the man replied without looking up.

"Relevant to what?" Chandler asked, cutting to the heart of the reply. Sure he could have just asked, "why not," or some other mundane follow up. Chandler wasn't mundane. The man wasn't ordinary, and Chandler knew this was no ordinary encounter. Ordinary questions would get him no where.

The man finished reading the page he was on before turning the page. It was only then that he took the time to look up at Chandler and say, "Relevant to those who might read it later."

"Who's going to read it later?" Chandler asked.

"I don't know," the man began to explain, "but I do know that they won't want to wade through a large amount of useless information."

"What kind of information is it?" Chandler asked.

The man displayed a slight hint of a smile as he said only, "All kinds."

The answer was vague and Chandler took that as a hint that the man didn't want to share too much. He wasn't rude, in fact rather polite. He was just private.

Chandler said nothing for close to five minutes as he watched the man continue to copy information from one book to the other. Chandler studied the man, making mental notes about every detail. There were so many questions that could be asked, he just didn't know which ones he'd get an answer to.

Eventually, Chandler couldn't take it anymore. He took advantage of a time when the man paused to turn a page in the larger book, then took a sip of water. When the man made eye contact with the young teen, Chandler asked, "How did you know the book was there?"

"My brother left it there for me," came the soft reply.

"Why did he leave it there?"

"So I would find it."

Chandler was stumped as to how he could continue the conversation further. However, he caught himself just before the man could go back to writing.

"Who is your brother?" Chandler asked.

"His name is Justyn."

"Does he come here often?"

"I don't know," the man began as he looked up to think. "I suppose he tends to spend most of his time in this part of the world."

"This part of the world? You mean Houston?" Chandler asked for clarification.

The man smiled politely, "The world between the oceans, the Americas. He often speaks fondly of the southern parts."

"South America?"

"Yes."

Chandler paused as he took it in. The man had a brother named Justyn, and he lived somewhere in South America. It wasn't much, but it was more than he knew about the man in front of him.

"So what's your name?" Chandler asked.

"Vincent."

"Hi, hey Vincent. I'm Chandler."

Again the man just smiled. It was a polite smile, an honest smile even.

"What part of the world do you live in?" Chandler followed up.

"All parts."

"That's pretty vague," Chandler said. He was now much more comfortable talking to the man.

"I don't have a favorite part, but I spend most of my time around Europe."

"Why there?"

Another smile, "More to write about," and with that, the man looked downward and went back to copying from one book to the other.

Chandler let the silence hang for a moment before taking a hold of the man's cup, "I'll get you some more water."

"Thank you," the man said softly without looking up. Chandler turned to walk away, but froze in his steps when the man added, "And don't worry. He won't hurt you."

"He?" Chandler asked.

"You'll see," the man said with a smile as he continued writing.

"Okay," Chandler said slowly. The apprehension in his voice was as much from irritation as concern.

Chandler made his way across the main lobby and towards the water fountains next to the restrooms. He first got a drink for himself and then filled the cup with water. He listened to the sound of the water running into the cup and when it was full, he stopped. That's when he heard something else. It was the sound of water running, but it was coming from the men's restroom.

The sounds lasted several seconds before Chandler could hear the water being turned off. The brief silence was interrupted by the sound of two footsteps followed by the sound of the hot air drier. As soon as that sound faded away, Chandler heard more footsteps.

Each step sounded louder and louder as whoever was in the restroom moved closer to the door. Chandler, only a few feet away from the door, began to worry about who was in the restroom. Something said freeze, and something else said run. Those two signals crossed each other and Chandler only took a few steps back. "Don't worry, he won't hurt you," Chandler whispered to himself.

The door to the men's room swung open and Chandler saw another, even stranger, man. He was well over six foot tall, though thinner than Vincent. He was wearing black boots that each had what looked like metal bars running up the front. The legs of his denim pants were tucked into the boots, though they were ripped and torn. The shirt was black, and just as torn and tattered as his pants. The left sleeve was completely ripped to shreds. The left part of the collar was also torn off. The man had more than one fresh scar. His hair was wet, and the visible parts of his body showed the signs of having just been washed.

Chandler's eyes froze as he stared at the man who was obviously not expecting to see the young teen standing there. The disappointment was written all over the man's face. Chandler took a single step backwards. The man took four quick steps towards him, and in doing so displayed a severe limp in his left leg.

As he closed in, the man reached out and grabbed Chandler by the collar of his t-shirt. He pulled the young teen closer, causing Chandler to drop the cup of water.

"Who are you?" The man asked. His voice showed signs of genuine confusion.

"My name is Chandler," the teen said with a hint of a stutter.

"Are you with the them?" The man asked.

"Them?"

"The others," the man clarified with a kind of vagueness that Chandler was almost used to.

"What others?" Chandler asked with a pleading tone.

The man rolled his fist over, tightening his grip on Chandler's shirt collar. That also tightened the collar around Chandler's neck. The man leaned in a bit more so that Chandler got a good look at the fresh scars on the man's face. They seemed more liked welts, or even burn marks, than cuts.

"The other children. Are you with them?" the man asked in a slow and clear manner.

"No, I'm all alone," Chandler replied in a voice that the man had to believe was honest.

"You're not alone," the man said while letting go of Chandler's shirt and pushing the teen away. "You're with him," he then added.

"You mean Vincent? Yes, he's here."

"Where else would he be," the man commented while walking past Chandler.

Chandler didn't offer any reply. He let the man walk past before picking up the cup and refilling it at the water fountain.

He quickly turned to walk back towards the heart of the library where Vincent was. "He won't hurt you," Chandler kept thinking as he remembered what Vincent had told him. Chandler followed the man at a distance while whispering those words over and over.

Vincent apparently heard the man approaching and lowered his pen as he turned in his seat to face the man. "What happened to you?" Vincent asked without any emotion.

"A building fell on me," came the quick reply.

"Well you've looked better, and you've looked worse," Vincent said before turning back to his books.

"Here you go," Chandler whispered while setting the cup of water on the table in front of Vincent. He slowly walked around the table and sat across from Vincent where he felt safer. At least Vincent hadn't grabbed a hold of him, or even spoken rudely for that matter. Chandler felt completely out of place there in his own library, but at least he was becoming somewhat at ease with Vincent.

The man seemed content to just stand, though he paced around a little, limping lightly on his wounded leg. He looked nervous about something, and was obviously upset; not so much angry, just distraught.

Vincent noticed the man's demeanor and paused his writing just long enough to ask, "Am I to assume that things didn't go as planned?"

"HA!" the man said while stopping his pacing in mid step. "It was right there. I actually touched it," the man said while tilting his head back and looking upwards. He curled his elbows and clinched his fist to show his frustration. He somehow managed to carry a smooth tone in adding, "So close...is so worse...than so far."

"What's wrong?" Vincent asked. He was still only paying passive attention, remaining focused on his writing.

"These...These...These kids," the man managed to spit out while casting an eye at Chandler. That caught Vincent's attention. He again turned to look at the man.

"Come now Daniel. Are you saying that some children did this to you?" Vincent asked.

Daniel. His name was Daniel, Chandler noted as he listened intensely to the conversation even though he didn't have a clue what they were talking about.

"Don't mock me," Daniel said while turning his head sharply to look at Vincent and adding, "But you already knew that didn't you?"

Vincent came as close to a smile as he ever did. He used his right hand to turn two pages back in the large book. He glanced at the contents of what he had written on those pages before looking at Daniel and saying, "Yes, I did."

"What else do you know?" Daniel asked with his tone half way between demanding and pleading.

"The usual," Vincent shrugged.

"Where are they now?"

"That, I don't know. They don't even know," Vincent tried to explain.

"Well I need to know. I need to find them," Daniel said.

"I know."

"Of course you know," Daniel said, "You know everything. That's why I'm here."

"Because you want me to tell you?" Vincent asked.

"Yes," Daniel replied with a far more subtle voice than he was using just two minutes ago.

"Then you also know that I can't and won't help you," Vincent explained.

"But this is different," Daniel pleaded.

"How so?"

Daniel pointed at the table where the two books were and said, "Look in your book. It's all right there."

Vincent paused to glance back at the previous page he had just written in. He read a small passage before looking at Daniel and saying only, "I see."

"Do you? Do you really see?" Daniel asked while taking another step towards Vincent and saying, "Do you see what's going to happened, what really happens?"

"Do you think I don't," Vincent asked. His voice carried a more forceful tone than Chandler had yet to hear him use.

"Five children," Daniel began while eying Chandler.

"I know," Vincent interrupted.

Daniel pressed on. He knew he was fighting an uphill battle, but he was determined to make sure that his point was heard. "Five ordinary children; beer drinking, cursing, smoking, disgusting children, have taken what was mine."

"If it was yours, then you would have it," Vincent explained in his soft voice.

"It is mine" Daniel shouted across the table at Vincent.

"Obviously not," Vincent said with a hint of a smile.

"You're happy, aren't you?" Daniel asked.

"I am amused at the irony of the situation," Vincent replied.

Daniel froze in his tracks. He cocked his head to one side and asked, "What irony?"

Vincent placed his pen on the table in front of him. "Here you are jumping up and down, yelling and screaming, flailing about, and whining about how some children took your shiny rock." Vincent froze for effect.

Daniel froze also, and it became obvious to Chandler that Daniel was not used to being lectured to. Daniel held up a hand as if he were about to speak, but was interrupted by Vincent who was clearly not through yet. He used a patronizing tone as he finished, "And you want me to do something about it, or you are going to get mad at me."

Daniel tried to say something, but was again cut off by Vincent, "You talk about how dangerous these kids, but you are no better. You don't understand the responsibility that goes with great power. It's not within your desire to understand. You just want it so you can have it."

There was another pause that allowed Vincent to shift tones again, "Tell me Daniel, who is the real child here?"

Daniel extended his left hand towards Vincent. Daniel's finger tips began to glow bright orange. His left eye lit up with a white glow. Anger was written all over his face. "I should…" he started to say. However, he hesitated his thoughts.

"But you won't," Vincent proclaimed with the highest level of certainty.

The glow faded first from Daniel's hand, then from his eye. He lowered his posture, no longer the defiant man that he had been only a minute ago. Vincent had something over Daniel, and Chandler was racking his brain; trying to figure out what it was.

Daniel's shift in mannerisms continued. His voice got softer, and his words had the appearance of being chosen more carefully, "It's a dangerous situation. You know this."

"Yes, I know," Vincent replied.

"And you are not worried about what these five children are going to do with their new found gifts?"

Vincent raised both eye brows and lowered his chin some to emphasis the seriousness of his words, "I already know what they are going to do. I also know what you would do with this power. You and these kids are simply two sides of the same coin."

"Do you really know?" Daniel asked for a second time that night. "If you really knew, then you'd help me." Daniel's voice had moved from very cocky to pleading, almost as if he were scared. His eyes glowed ever so slightly as he added, "This is going to end very badly."

"Yes, I know," Vincent said. His voice carried a more frustrated tone, obviously over having to repeatedly explain the same thing. "I write the words in this book," Vincent added as he flipped a single page in the large book for effect, "I know what happened yesterday, and I know what's going to happen tomorrow."

Daniel gripped the edge of the table with both hands. He hunched over, and let his head hang low. With a soft voice, he pleaded, "That's why I'm here. I need you to help me stop something bad from happening."

"You know I don't interfere," Vincent replied with an equally soft voice.

To Chandler, it seemed as though everything had peaked with Vincent's firm words. Now, the brief moments of conflict were giving way to a more passive setting. He was about to discover that he couldn't have been more wrong.

"God Damn It!" Daniel proclaimed while slamming his hand down on the book. He leaned in and caste a hard stare into Vincent's eyes, "If you don't interfere then there won't be anything left to write about."

Vincent was quick to react. He grabbed a hold of Daniel's wrist and began twisting while saying, "Don't ever take God's name in vain."

Vincent then gave Daniel a good push that sent him back several feet from the table. As Daniel recovered his footing to keep from falling down, Vincent rose to his feet. "Ne'er in my presence are you to speak with such villainy."

"I'm sorry," Daniel said as he maintained a relaxed composure that was a direct contrast to the sudden stiffness of Vincent who appeared more than ready for a fight. Daniel went on to extend his hand outwards while stepping closer to the table.

"I was beside myself," Daniel added while attempting to shake Vincent's hand. With obvious reluctance, Vincent extended his hand outwards. He didn't say anything, but did reach out and take Daniel's hand. Both men even smiled for a moment, though it was clear that Daniel was wearing the larger of the smiles.

"Whew," Chandler thought to himself. He had never been one for conflict, and had hoped it was all over. This was to be the second time he would be proved wrong on this subject.

Just as Vincent was about to let go of Daniel's hand, he felt Daniel grip hard on his hand. In a fraction of a second, Vincent knew something was wrong, but didn't have time to react. With a firm yank, Daniel pulled Vincent by the arm with so much force that Vincent was lifted into the air and carried across the table. He landed on the floor behind Daniel. Daniel turned immediately to the table and reached for the large book. He slid it towards himself, and flipped back two pages.

For reasons that could only be attributed to instinct, Chandler decided to get involved. With a yell of, "NO!" Chandler leaped towards the table and grabbed a hold of the book.

"Give it up child," Daniel said while trying to pull the book away from Chandler.

Just as Chandler had felt the book being pulled away from his grip, he noticed Vincent standing up behind Daniel. With a single motion, Vincent pulled out one of his daggers and placed it against Daniel's neck.

"Let go of it," Vincent insisted with a calm voice.

Daniel loosened his grip on the book and slowly backed away. As he did so, Vincent turned around to put himself between Daniel and the book.

"I need to know," Daniel said, returning to his pleading voice.

"And you will find out, when the time is right," Vincent insisted. He closed the book, slid it to the other side of the table, and slowly walked around. As Vincent passed Chandler, he gave the teen an approving nod of thanks.

Daniel didn't move. He held his head in a lowered manner, suggesting that he knew he had been beaten. Vincent laid the dagger on the table next to the book as he sat down. "You should know better," Vincent said.

"This is different," Daniel insisted.

"It's always different for someone," Vincent began. He paused and reopened the book. "But I have never once interfered, and I'm not abut to start now."

"What if there is nothing left to interfere with when it is all over?" Daniel asked. The seriousness in his voice could not be underscored. Chandler could sense how concerned Daniel was, not just for his own fate, but for the fate of others. This was, after all, the second time that Daniel had made such an apocalyptic statement. It was as if he felt that five kids somewhere would be able to destroy the world.

Vincent held his ground, "Then so be it." He paused to find his place in the leather notepad before looking up at Daniel one last time.

"Now leave," Vincent said in a manner that suggested it was more than a mere request. If his tone didn't send the point home well enough, he went on to add, "leave now, and I'll forget this ever happened."

"And if I don't leave? What are you prepared to do?"

Vincent reached for his dagger, "Then you'd force me to get involved." Vincent ran a finger down one of the pages of the book and added, "I might even have to rewrite some of the pages."

The point was made, and Daniel stood before Vincent with a look of complete disbelief. "You know what I have to do?"

"Yes," Vincent said softly.

"Are you going to try and stop me?" Daniel asked. He continued to get more and more subdue in both his actions and his words.

"You should know by now that I'll never stop a man from killing himself," Vincent said as he picked up his pen again.

"Someone has to stop them," Daniel said as he started to turn around.

Vincent went back to writing. He paused momentarily to add, "Good-bye Daniel."

Daniel said nothing. He turned to walk away. After taking the third step, he held out his hand and snapped his fingers. In a mere second, he was surrounded by a cloud of black smoke. A second later, the smoke dissipated into the air, and Daniel was gone.

"How did he do that?" Chandler asked in disbelief.

Vincent never looked up, "It's just something he does."

"Can you do that?"

"If I wanted," Vincent shrugged.

"Can you teach me how to do that?" Chandler asked, unsure of exactly what he was asking.

"What is it you want to do?" Vincent asked, "Do you want to act like a child when you don't get your way? Or, do you want to learn how to act in a responsible manner?"

Vincent looked up at Chandler with a solid stare and added, "I can teach you the later. Otherwise, you had better follow him."

Chandler reflected on those words for a moment. As Vincent paused to turn a page, Chandler asked, "He's going to die, isn't he?"

"Yes," Vincent said.

"And he doesn't care?"

"He doesn't believe it. He thinks he can change it."

"Can he?"

"Probably not."

"But, there is a chance?"

"There are always chances," Vincent said. He set the pen down for a moment. He turned to look at Chandler as a serious moment became almost tense. "If I could tell you that some random tree was going to be struck by lightning and fall down tomorrow, would you care?" Vincent asked innocently enough.

Chandler shrugged his shoulders, "Probably not."

Vincent smiled softly, "But what if I told you that you'd be killed by that tree? Then, would you care?"

Chandler hesitated for a moment, but showed himself to be smarter than most people his age, "I guess that would change the dynamics a little, wouldn't it?"

"It's the same with Daniel. He knows that he is probably going to die while chasing these children and this stone of his." Vincent paused for effect, "But if he knows how he'd die, then he could prevent it."

"How does he know that these kids might kill him?" Chandler asked.

Vincent looked directly into Chandler's eyes, "Because I told him he would."

"I thought you said that you don't get involved," Chandler asked. The question was more for clarification than a challenge, though Chandler's tone suggested he was playing 'gotcha' with Vincent a little.

"As he said, this is different," Vincent admitted, "I told him he'd be best to get some help, but he wants the power they have all for himself."

"Why is it so different?" Chandler asked.

"Right now there are five children with virtually unlimited power out there. They have all this power, and no responsibility."

"Gee, what could go wrong with that?" Chandler asked sarcastically.

"Absolutely everything," Vincent replied.

There was another brief pause before Chandler asked, "So how do you know what's going to happen in the future?"

"I don't. I just know what's already happened, and what events are occurring today. Everything flows from that."

"I don't get it," Chandler said with a nod of his head.

Vincent smiled. He glanced around the room before looking at the table. He ran his hand across the table while asking, "If I were to place marble on this table, could you tell which side it would roll off of?"

"No," Chandler said with a shrug.

Vincent smiled again, "But if you saw me push the marble, then could you guess which side it would roll off before it ever got to the edge."

"Well, yeah of course," Chandler said. He paused to think about it for a moment, then added, "But I could never know what side you were going to push it off of before you touched it."

"You could if you knew me well enough," Vincent said. There was a small flicker of light in his left eye as he said that. He shrugged his shoulders in a dismissive manner while explaining, "for example, if you you knew I was right handed then you could be certain that I'd use that hand to push the marble. The most natural motion for me would be to push my right hand across my body towards the left."

A moment of silence fell over the table. Chandler kept thinking it all over. Vincent went back to his copying. He finished one more page before folding up his leather notepad and placing it in his back pack.

"So that leather note pad is where you write down all the things you see?"

"Yes," Vincent said while closing the large book.

"And that book is where you write down what you think is going to happen based on what you wrote in that note pad?"

"That is correct," Vincent said.

"So when you said earlier that you were only copying what was relative, that meant you were only writing down the parts that would apply to the future."

Vincent smiled almost proudly, "I think you're getting it." He paused for a moment and looked down at the book. After a moment, he glanced at his empty styrofoam cup and asked, "Can I get another cup of water please."

"Yeah, sure," Chandler said while standing up. As soon as he rose to his feet, he felt overcome with another of his headaches. Everything in front of him faded to the left as he could also feel himself getting dizzy again. He steadied himself against the table before taking one slow step after another in the direction of the restrooms and water fountains. Vincent only took casual notice of Chandler's condition.

By the time Chandler got to the restroom, he could hardly stand. He spent five minutes holding onto the sink with one hand while splashing water on his face with the other hand. He blinked once, then a second time, and slowly the dizziness faded away. The headache subsided just a little, and he felt comfortable enough to walk again.

As soon as he stepped out of the restroom, he knew something was wrong. It was almost completely black with the exception of the trails of blue moonlight coming in from the overhead skylight. Chandler filled the cup with water and made his way back towards the table.

To little surprise, Vincent was gone. His backpack, his book, even his notepad were missing from the table. In a small bit of irony, the dagger that Vincent had pulled on Daniel was still sitting on the table. Chandler walked over to the table and picked up the dagger. Beneath the blade, there was a single folded piece of paper.

Chandler unfolded the paper and read the words slowly, "Take care Chandler. I've left The Book in your hands and the means with which to protect it. First you have to find it. If you can do this, then all the knowledge in the world is at your finger tips; else it was never there for you to read in the first place. Sincerely, Vincent."

Chandler took one slow look around the library. He refolded the paper and placed it in his pocket. He examined the dagger up and down before placing it in his backpack. With that, Chandler turned towards the front door and walked out of the library with his backpack and skateboard. He'd have the rest of the summer to find the book, or he'd have the rest of the summer to pretend it wasn't even there. If there was one thing that Chandler had learned that night, it was that some things were better left unknown.

The next morning, Chandler went through his usual routine of a shower and clothes, then off to the bus for another day at school. The bus ride was more different than usual. He heard whispers about something that had happened the night before. It wasn't until he got to school that the details were filled in. The previous night, a large building between the suburb of Sugarland and Houston had come crashing down. It was a twelve story bank building, and no one knew why it had fallen down.

As he went through the day, more details emerged. It was hard cutting through the rumors and speculations to get to the facts. Eventually, a few certain facts came about. The police were looking for five of the students at his school. A car belonging to one of those students had been seen racing from the rubble of the bank only minutes after it had collapsed.

The rest of the day passed slowly for Chandler. He couldn't wait to get back to the library. He'd tear the place apart looking for that book. Another part of him was scared. He had to wonder if Daniel would come looking for the book again. He wouldn't have Vincent there to protect him. He again wondered if he wouldn't be better off forgetting about the book. Again, somethings were better left unknown.

to be continued........

THE BEAST

I am the beast that stands alone
I am the king of all others
I go where I please
For whatever reason I please
Any time I please
Intimidation will fill you
When you look deep inside my eyes
But when it is over
I rest to eat
And behind me I leave
The marks of my trait
For the scavengers who circle
Above with hungry eyes
While I return
To my lair for a nap
Where I sit and dream in peace
And ask not to be disturbed
Don't hate me from fear
Rather love me for beauty
Because no place on Earth
Will you find a creature like me

THAT DREAM YOU HAD
LAST NIGHT (FEAR)

do you remember
the dream you had
late last night
do you recall
the fear
the fright

did you awaken
terribly shaken

soaking wet
drenched with sweat

do you remember
the laughing face
of the man
you couldn't escape
it mattered not
how fast you ran

when you awaken
will you be taken

to a place
dreams can't chase

where will you be
when you remember

the dream you had last night

POSSESSION

"welcome to my world,"   he laughed
"do you fear my world?"   he laughed

this is where I always live
this is where you now will live

"you are trapped in here,"   he shouts
"you can't leave from here," he shouts

       the way I show, what you will know
       will set you free, but not from me

          this is my world
          you are my world

          I will own you
          and you will do

          what I say to
          or you are through

"ready to have fun?" he asks
"do you know my fun?" he asks

it is just a game I play
you and me this game we play

the rules are only made by me
and you won't break them, not by me

       the way I show, what you will know
       will set you free but not from me

this is my world
you are my world

I will own you
and you will do

what I say to
or you are through

THE WHITE BAND

Gilborough never liked the rain. It wasn't the dreariness, nor the dangers that came with the bad weather. It was just all that water everywhere; the squeaky and squishy sounds of wet feet in wet socks in wet shoes walking across wet tile. He hated being drenched while trying to talk to someone who was perfectly dry. It didn't make for a professional environment where Gilborough, a Homicide Detective with the Seattle Police Department, felt comfortable questioning a witness.

All that rain also meant that he couldn't enjoy his pipe as often as he'd like. Other than that, he liked Seattle. There might be better places to live, but he knew first hand that there were worse. He had landed in Seattle twenty-two years ago while in the Navy. He grew up in New York, went to college in Miami, and joined the navy to see the world. Seattle was the only place where he felt safe. The only thing he ever missed about New York was family. He had already come to terms with the fact that Seattle is where he'd die. He'd just need to buy a larger umbrella to last him until that day came.

For the moment, he settled for the dry area by the front door to a large Catholic Church. It gave him a chance to relax and enjoy his pipe. Gilborough needed to clear his mind before going inside. He was about bring up some very old business and wasn't looking forward to it at all. While Gilborough puffed on his pipe outside, another man was unloading his conscious on the inside.

It started with the usual, "Forgive me father for I have sinned," routine. Father Donavan listened respectfully, just as he had been doing for close to twenty years now.

The man, Greg, went through the usual list of impure thoughts that he carried with him before unloading the big one. "These thoughts are towards my daughter," Greg confessed. It went beyond just an admission of a guilty act. It was a full confession that poured from his soul.

Few things shocked Father Donavan, but this left him a little speechless. While Donavan listened, Greg went on to add, "She begged me to stop, but I couldn't. I want to, I really do."

"Are you now prepared to stop?" Donavan asked.

"Yes," Greg said through tears.

"Are you sure?"

"Yes," Greg said again.

"Very well, then stop, and say a special prayer to God begging forgiveness," Donavan said before giving Greg penance. Just like that, it was as if nothing had happened.

While Greg was walking out of the confessional, Gilborough was walking into the church. It was an average Wednesday afternoon in the church. There were a few people sitting on benches searching for something. A few others could be seen in front of candles praying for something else.

Gilborough saw Greg exiting the confessional and figured that Donavan had to be nearby. It had been eighteen years since Gilborough had last seen Father Donavan. He had hoped he'd never see Donavan again, but there was news to bring the priest. Gilborough knocked softly on the door to the confessional while asking, "Father Donavan? It's Detective Gilborough with the Seattle PD. Could you step outside please?" Gilborough traded in his usual official tone for something more respectful. After all, he was in a church. As he spoke, Gilborough kept eye-balling Greg who seemed disoriented to say the least.

Donavan emerged from the confessional with a look of obvious concern on his face. The two men stared each other up and down, and took mental notes of how the years had and hadn't been good to each other. Donavan was balding though not too bad. Gilborough had put on some weight, but still looked healthy. Both men were wearing thicker glasses; Gilborough was clean shaved, Donavan wore a goatee. Oddly enough, neither man was showing gray yet. They were still in their forties, that could come later.

"It's been too long," Donavan said while extending his hand.

Gilborough shook Donavan's hand, "I'm afraid it's not been long enough."

"I'm sorry?" Donavan said, not sure what Gilborough meant by that.

"We have a small problem," Gilborough began, wanting to get to the heart of the matter. He glanced around the cathedral before nodding his head to the side, "Can we talk in private?" Gilborough then asked.

"Sure, follow me," Donavan said as he walked towards the front of the cathedral. There was a corner near the entrance that was quiet and away from everywhere. Gilborough knew this corner well. Two of his previous conversations with Donavan had taken place in this very corner. Once they were well away from prying ears, Donavan asked, "So what's on your mind?"

"It's about Harmon Jolston," Gilborough said. He paused and waited to see the expression on Donavan's face.

Donavan began tugging on his goatee. His eyes glanced away as he pondered Gilborough's words, "It's been a long time since I've heard that name mentioned."

"Yeah, eighteen years if memory serves right," Gilborough observed.

"You're right. It's not been long enough," Donavan said. He clasped his hands behind his back and tried to hide the uncomfortable look on his face. He couldn't hide it from Gilborough, not with twenty years on the police force and eighteen of those as a detective. Gilborough knew people, and he knew faces. He'd seen them all by now.

"Can I ask how he died?" Donavan whispered.

"You can asked. I can tell you. But, it wasn't pretty," Gilborough said.

Donavan's eyes gave away his curiosity. He didn't need to speak a word for Gilborough to go ahead and say, "He was murdered."

"How?" Donavan asked.

"We're not yet sure. The coroner is still trying to establish the exact cause of death," Gilborough explained. He displayed an uncomfortable smile as he added, "I don't think we'll ever know what actually killed him, or if any one thing did it."

"What do you mean? What happened?" Donavan asked. The crack in his voice suggested he was more curious than he wanted to be. Deep down, something told Donavan to walk away from the conversation right then and there. However, he was human with human curiosities, and that meant he had to know.

"We found him hanging from a tree. He had been stabbed more times than I could count," Gilborough said.

"Where did you find him?" Donavan asked with a look of shock on his face. If what Donavan had just found out was bothering him, then he was in for an even greater shock. He just didn't know it yet.

"A Cemetery," Gilborough said.

"What Cemetery," Donavan asked.

Gilborough said nothing. He only stared at Donavan with a pair of hard eyes that said, "Don't make me tell you which one."

"Not that cemetery," Donavan asked.

"I'm afraid so," Gilborough said, "About fifty feet from where the five boys had been buried." He paused for a moment before adding, "That's not the weirdest part either."

"How could it get more strange?" Donavan asked with another crack in his voice.

"There was a note reading, 'God's Will Be Done' stuck to his body."

"I'd hardly call that God's will," Donavan said as he developed a mental image of the scene. What he could imagine horrified him. The true horror was that he knew he couldn't even imagine it as bad as it really was.

Everything fell silent between the two men. They both glanced around the cathedral, looking for a way to either extend, or end the conversation. A small amount of added curiosity fell on Donavan, prompting him to ask, "Do you have any suspects?"

"We're tracking down the parents of the five boys he killed."

"Hard to believe they'd wait this long to get some kind of revenge," Donavan noted.

"You'd think, but then you'd be surprised," Gilborough explained, "Sometimes it festers; then one day, they just snap."

Gilborough rubbed on his chin as he thought for a moment, "I doubt it was one of the parents, but then you never know."

"True," Donavan agreed. He allowed another moment of uncomfortable silence to fall over the two men. They had little to say, and nothing in common except a single bad memory. They were both looking around for a way to bring the conversation to a close when Gilborough spotted Greg walking out of the cathedral. Greg still had a look on his face that bordered between disoriented and nervous.

"Just what did you tell that man?" Gilborough asked while nodding his head towards Greg.

"Only what he needed to hear?" Donavan said with a shrug.

"And what did he need to hear?" Gilborough asked.

Donavan gave the, "That is between him and God," reply that Gilborough expected.

Again, silence set in, and both men looked for a way to end the conversation. Gilborough, ever the conversationalist, managed to find the way out, "Well, I'm not sure how much you wanted to know, but I figured you would at least want to be told the basics."

"I appreciate that," Donavan said while once again extending his hand.

The two men shook hands and exchanged brief pleasantries along with requests for the other to keep in touch. Neither man made any promises to that effect; they were in a church after all. Eighteen years had been a long time, but as both men admitted, it hadn't been long enough.

When Gilborough stepped out of the church, he was greeted by the gray clouds that only bring rain. He stood on the steps of the cathedral and lit up his pipe. It was mid afternoon, and he didn't have to be at the station until five. He had drawn the late shift that week. He just wanted to swing by and tell Donavan about the death of Harmon Jolston. He didn't quite get the reaction he thought he would, but then who had ever been able to figure out a priest?

Donavan walked down the main isle of the church as he thought about everything. At the end of the aisle was the the pulpit and alter. Behind the alter, there was a large cross hanging from the ceiling. Behind that, was a painting on the wall; a reproduction of Michelangelo's "Creation."

Donavan stood in the center of the aisle and looked up at the cross hanging behind the alter. Slowly, he knelt to one knee, and said a brief prayer for the soul of Harmon Jolston. He did it more out of habit than anything. Donavan knew exactly Harmon Jolston's soul would end up. Donavan went back to carrying on his duties as a priest. Gilborough ran a few errands before reporting for work that afternoon. Greg finished his shift at work, and went home.

Later That Night...

Greg sat on the couch and watched television for two hours straight after he got home. It wasn't until close to nine that night when he heard a door open in the back of the apartment. He turned his head to look over his shoulder, and noticed a shadow moving down the hall. It was his daughter.

A few months ago, something inside of Greg changed. She changed also. Since then, she'd stayed locked in her room. She'd come home from school, and do her chores before he got home. Then, she'd bury herself in her room with her homework and pray that she didn't see him that night.

It had been a month now, and he'd changed again. He'd made a promise to the effect. He hit the mute button on his remote, and slowly rose from the couch. He walked in the kitchen where he expected to find her, but she wasn't there. If he had been really observant, Greg would have noticed that the knives were all missing from the wooden block on the counter.

Greg turned to walk down the hall to his daughter's bedroom. To his surprise, the door was shut again. He didn't remember hearing her close the door. He softly knocked on the door while turning the knob.

"Hi honey, how are you doing?" He asked with the door only part of the way opened.

She was sitting at her desk and finishing her math homework. She said nothing, and only turned her head an inch to even acknowledge he was there. Greg knew she feared him, but he understood why. He felt an obligation to make everything up to her, and prove that he could be the father he always promised her he would be. To be fair, he did try, but being a single dad just wasn't all it was cracked up to be.

Greg took a few steps into her room. "I know it's not easy honey," he said, though he seemed to stumble on every word, "Since your mom died, I haven't always been there for you."

She said nothing. She tried to finish her last three math problems, but suddenly it became difficult to concentrate on long division. She closed her eyes and wished so desperately that he would go away. Her wish bordered on a prayer. Not all prayers get answered, but some do.

Greg moved a little closer, so close he could almost touch her. Closeness became temptation. "You remind me of you mother so much, and in so many ways," he said while extending his hand out towards her. That's when it happened.

First came the voices, "Don't do it," one voice said. Another voice called out, "You evil bastard!"

The voices came from different directions, almost like echoes. Greg spun around. Out of the corner of each eye he noticed movement, though nothing physical could be seen. Then, as quick as it started, it ended. Silence fell across the room.

Greg turned again to look at his daughter who was down to her last math problem. Two thousand eight hundred and sixty four divided by thirty six was to be the problem that would change her life. As soon as Greg began reaching out to his twelve year old daughter he heard another voice.

"I said don't do it!" The voice called out. There was no second voice.

The next thing Greg heard was the light above him being shattered. That was followed by a series of sensations through his body, like waves of heat passing across his skin from the knives being slammed into his flesh. Greg's body fell to the floor just as she finished her last problem; she hated it when the answer just ran on forever.

Gilborough was eating a burger from one of his favorite places when he got a call. It was dispatch asking him to respond to a homicide. It was more than just a few blocks away, and he certainly wasn't the closest. "Aww com'on," Gilborough pleaded, "I'm trying to eat here."

"Sorry sir, but you were personally requested," the dispatch operator said.

"How is that?" Gilborough asked.

"Why don't you go and find out," came the reply from the operator who was apparently more frustrated than Gilborough.

"Great, the circus is in town," Gilborough replied, displaying his own frustration.

"I'm sorry sir. All I know is that you were asked for by name," the operator replied with a more apologetic tone.

"Okay then, I'm enroute," Gilborough replied as he grabbed his coke and the last half of his burger that he'd have to finish in the car. Gilborough hated eating in his car. It was similar to his dislike of rain. The only thing worse than being wet, is being wet and covered in food.

In what could be called a twist of irony, Donavan had also just finished eating. He was in the process of closing everything down in the cathedral for the night. The front doors had just been locked, and Donavan was watching the candles burn as he prepared to snuff them each out. It had become tradition for Donavan to take notice of every candle before snuffing them. He would ponder what each one was burning for. Was this one for a sick loved one, or that one to help make sure there was food on the table? Which was was simply a request for forgiveness, and which was a request for more than they needed?

Donavan lowered the snuffer over the first candle when he felt a breeze blow past him from behind. He glanced over his shoulder, and a stronger breeze blew in front of him. He also noticed the lighting fade slightly. When Donavan turned again to look at the candles, he noticed that all but the five shortest candles were exhausted.

Donavan cocked his head to the side; observing the oddity of what had just happened. He was about to dismiss it when he heard a voice.

"He's dead," the voice said. It sounded like a whisper, though it carried a faint echo.

Donavan froze in his tracks as he moved his eyes around the Cathedral, looking for someone who might still be in there.

"I'm right here," the voice said before adding, "No, now I'm here. Wait here I am. Over here, no not there." Each time the voice spoke, it seemed to come from a different direction.

Donavan spun a slow circle as he looked around, "Who's there?"

"Just me," the voice said, but again echoed itself, "Not him again. I'm back, remember me? Don't tell me you forgot. It's only me."

Donavan's face turned red with obvious anger. He set the candle snuffer on the shelf in front of the candles as he said, "All right come out. I don't find this funny at all."

"Good," the voice said slowly, "It's not funny. Don't laugh. This is the lesson of a lifetime. It's very real."

"That's enough," Donavan shouted as he continued to spin slow circles while making his way down the isle. He paused and knelt down, and glanced under the pews to see if someone was hiding there.

"Peek-a-boo," the voice said, and echoed, "I see you."

Donavan jumped to his feet as the voice continued to echo, "I'm watching you. I know what you did. Do you know what I did?"

"What did you do?" Donavan asked.

"I killed him," the voice said, "He's dead. God's will be done. My will be done. This will be done."

The last part of the echo trailed off into a breeze that blew through the church. With the passing of the breeze, the five remaining candles flickered, and finally blew out. Donavan spent the next hour searching every square inch of the Cathedral only to find no one.

Meanwhile, Gilborough was pulling into the parking lot of an apartment complex. There were two fire trucks, one ambulance, and six squad cars. Three unmarked cars with lights on top were also present. "This is going to be so much fun. I can feel it already," Gilborough said as he climbed out of his car.

"Who's in charge here?" Gilborough asked the first uniformed officer he saw while showing his badge.

"Well that depends on who you ask," the officer said.

"And if I were to ask you?" Gilborough said with a lot of restraint to his voice.

The cop glanced over his shoulder and pointed at a woman, "Detective Stravinsky is pulling the pieces together."

"Great, thanks," Gilborough said as he walked past the cop.

"Oh and hey detective," the cop said.

"Yes?"

"You got something right here," the cop said while rubbing the left corner of his lips with his index finger.

Gilborough ran his finger across the corner of his lips and wiped away what looked like mayonnaise. "Just friggin' great," Gilborough said to himself as he walked up to Detective Stravinsky.

"Gilborough, over here," Stravinsky called out as she waved Gilborough over.

"Watcha got?" Gilborough asked.

"A homicide. A bad one," Stravinsky said as she and Gilborough shook hands.

Stravinsky and Gilborough had a great professional relationship that went back several years. They always worked well together, and complemented each other nicely. It all came down to the fact that both detectives had so much much in common. Stravinsky was also a non-native to Seattle and had adapted about as well as Gilborough had. She had also put any notion of a personal life to the side, and spent most of her free time either at the station, or in the field working cases. If there wasn't something to work on, she could be found digging up a cold case that had never been solved.

"And what makes this one so bad?" Gilborough asked. To him, dead was dead; it didn't come in degrees.

"Take a look for yourself," Stravinsky said as she led Gilborough over to the coroner's van.

Both detectives climbed in the back of the van, and Stravinsky pulled the tarp away to reveal the body of Greg. He was covered in blood stains. There were five "X"s carved across his forehead.

"Pretty. Someone took their time with this one," Gilborough said as he looked Greg up and down. Considering the amount of blood covering Greg's body, it only made sense that Gilborough didn't recognize him at first. However, as he was looking at the five "X"s on Greg's forehead, Gilborough remembered.

"Wait a minute," Gilborough said. He took a close look at Greg's face before saying, "I've seen this guy."

"When? Where?" Stravinsky asked. The curiosity in her voice was very genuine.

"Today, at a church," Gilborough replied.

"A church? You've gotta be kidding me," Stravinsky said as the two detectives climbed out of the van.

"No I'm not," Gilborough insisted with a shake of his head.

"How does someone go from a church to dead with multiple stab wounds in one day?"

"That's a good question, but then I'd say he has more than just multiple stab wounds."

"Okay, he's a piñata," Stravinsky agreed. She kept walking, leading Gilborough somewhere. Before he could ask where they were going, she went on to ask, "So you're sure it was this guy who you saw at the church?"

"Positive. He stood out, seemed real nervous," Gilborough explained.

"That's interesting."

"Why?"

Stravinsky paused in her tracks. She turned to look Gilborough straight in the eyes while saying, "You were asked to come here for a reason."

"Why, what's up?" Gilborough asked, still curious as to where he was being led, and why he was at the crime scene in the first place.

"Come on. There's someone you need to talk to."

Stravinsky led Gilborough to a pair of squad cars parked next to an unmarked car. Sitting in the passenger seat of the unmarked car was a young girl. The door was opened, and another woman was squatting down in front of the girl, trying to talk to her.

"Dr. Clark," Stravinsky called as she stopped walking and held her arm up, suggesting Gilborough hold his ground.

Dr. Clark stood up and glanced over at Gilborough and Stravinsky. She waved, indicating she'd be right with them before turning around and saying something to the young girl. Then, she made a fast run over to the two detectives.

"How's it going Gilborough?" Clark asked while turning her head to check on the girl again.

"Would be going better if I knew why I was here," Gilborough said. He then nodded his head in the direction of the girl, "Who's that?"

"Daughter of the deceased. That's all I know," Clark said with a shrug of her shoulders.

"She say who did it?" Gilborough asked.

"Nope, hasn't said much," Clark replied.

"Why don't you tell him what she did say," Stravinsky suggested. She braced herself for Gilborough's reaction.

"Okay, what did she say?" Gilborough asked, totally unprepared for what Clark's answer would be.

"She asked to talk to you," Clark said, "She said she has something important to tell you."

"Me?" Gilborough asked.

"She even spelled your name," Stravinsky said, "And that's no small feat."

"From the kettle to the pot," Gilborough replied. He then motioned with his head while adding, "Come on, let's go see what she has to say."

"I'll wait here," Stravinsky said, though Clark followed Gilborough.

Clark just want to be there in case the questioning became too intense for the already traumatized girl to handle. Clark knew Gilborough and trusted him to know where the lines were. She also knew that every once in a while, even Gilborough could honestly forget what someone had just been through while questioning them.

"What's her name?" Gilborough whispered as they approached the girl who as sitting in the front seat of the car.

"She won't tell me," Clark whispered back, "The only thing she said is that she needs to talk to you."

"Lovely," Gilborough said beneath his breath. He walked up to the girl and knelt down on one knee. He was careful to keep a good three feet of space between him and the girl so as to not crowd her. The girl was turned sideways with her legs hanging off the seat. She kept staring upwards, searching through the stars. Gilborough thought she was perhaps looking for hope. He thought wrong.

"Hi there, I'm Detective Gilborough," He said with only a hint of a smile. He wanted to show comfort, but not an over abundance of happiness. She had just lost her father, this was not a happy time for her. At least, that was the assumption Gilborough made.

At first, she said nothing. She kept staring upwards. The sky had cleared up from the rain of earlier. Even through the lights of the city, a few stars could be seen. A quarter moon hung low on the horizon. She didn't appear to be looking at any of those things.

"So what's your name?" Gilborough asked, trying to get her to say something. He was met with only silence. She didn't move an inch, and Gilborough noticed that she wasn't even blinking. There was only the blank stare.

Gilborough glanced over his shoulder at Clark who shrugged her shoulders as if to say, "see, I told you so."

He turned again to look at the girl. He thought for a second before taking a chance and asking, "Do you think you could tell me what happened?" Normally, Gilborough would leave those questions for someone like Clark who had experience with traumatized kids. Gilborough was desperate though. He had to get her to say something.

He braced himself for what ever reaction she might have. It was such a sensitive question who's entire purpose was to get her to recall a bad memory that her fragile mind was most likely trying to bury. He looked close at her eyes, expecting to see a tear. He watched her lips, looking for the quivering action of someone trying to speak. Gilborough got none of that.

She smiled. The corners of her lips curled upwards and a pleasant smile appeared on her face. Her eyes didn't tear at all, instead they began to glow. It was as if she were recalling a fond memory. That's when she turned to look at Gilborough. Her smiling lips spoke.

"I have a secret," She said.

"What's your secret?" Gilborough asked. He was extremely uncomfortable with the idea of playing games at a time like that, but if it got her talking, then he was prepared to do it.

"Oh no, I can't tell you that," She said as if it would be a really bad thing to do.

"What can you tell me?" Gilborough asked.

She leaned in close to Gilborough as she spoke. It was almost like a young child talking to Santa about everything she wanted. There was sincere happiness in her voice. Her smile got a little bigger and her eyes got really wide, "This is only the beginning."

"Can you tell me anything else?" Gilborough asked. A minute ago, he wanted her to talk. Now, he was afraid of what she might say next.

"Yes. I have a message for you," She said.

"What's the message?"

Her smile disappeared, and was replaced with a look of disappointment, "You failed. You had a chance to do the right thing. Now, someone else has to clean up your mess."

"How did I fail?" Gilborough asked, obviously confused.

"I can't tell you that," She replied, "that's the secret."

"Well, can you tell me who's going to clean up this mess?"

The girl, only twelve years old, displayed the wit of an adult when she replied, "Obviously not you."

That was the one that sent Gilborough over the edge. He managed to hide his anger, but it was certainly beginning to boil inside of him. "Do you have any other messages for me?" Gilborough asked, now ready for almost anything that the girl might say.

"Just that he was protecting himself. That's what he was really trying to do," She said.

"Who was?"

"Oh, I can't say."

"Why can't you say? Who is this message from?" Gilborough asked.

She smiled again, and said only, "I made a promise. I'm sorry, but someone has to keep their promises around here." With that, she turned her eyes again to the sky. Her smile faded to a blank stare, and Gilborough knew that she had said all she was going to say.

Gilborough didn't say anything else either. His instincts were to tell her, "to take care, and that everything would be okay." Gilborough just stood up and walked away. Clark followed, but kept turning her head to keep an eye on the girl.

"What was that all about?" Clark asked while trailing behind Gilborough.

"I honestly don't have a clue," Gilborough said out of frustration.

"Surely you must have some idea?" Clark suggested.

Gilborough looked Clark square in the face and said, "No, I don't. It was all psycho-babble to me."

Clark put her hand on Gilborough's shoulder to try and calm him down, "Let me talk to her some more. Maybe I can find something out."

Gilborough pointed towards the girl while never loosing eye contact with Clark, "You've got to be kidding me. That girl's wiring is all screwed up. Hell, she's probably the one who killed her dad." As he spoke, Stravinsky walked up to Clark and Gilborough, though she stayed quiet in an effort to figure out what had happened.

"There's no way," Clark insisted.

Stravinsky cut in, "I agree. She couldn't have done it."

"And what makes you so sure?" Gilborough asked.

"Simple," Stravinsky explained, "you saw how much blood there was."

"Yeah, and?"

"You see any on the girl?"

"Okay, I see your point," Gilborough confessed. He had to admit that she couldn't have made that big of a mess and not have gotten any of it on her.

"Of course none of this tells us who did it," Stravinsky observed.

"I'm sure you'll figure it out," Gilborough said as he pat her on the shoulder. He then turned to walk away.

"You're not leaving me with this mess, are you?" Stravinsky asked.

"You bet I am," Gilborough replied.

"Oh come on," Stravinsky pleaded.

Gilborough only smiled as he pulled his pipe out of his front pocket. Gilborough leaned against his car and stoked up his pipe. As he puffed away, he ran through everything in his mind. He had gotten used to dealing with murders a long time ago. He had even learned to handle the more gruesome cases. However, when it came to dealing with kids, he had always struggled. Kids could make the most irrational of people seem predictable. He never knew how two different kids could handle something so similar with such a different response.

The night would wind down with the girl ending up in a children's hospital before being turned over to her aunt. Gilborough would respond to a car wreck involving an SUV running a red light; killing three people. Stravinsky would spend the rest of the night cleaning up at Greg's apartment and questioning people. Surprisingly, Gilborough slept well that night. Donavan tossed and turned all night.

The Next Morning...

Though he really hated to return, Gilborough's first stop for the day was at the church. Gilborough was religious to a point. He had gone to church often while married. After the divorce, he dug into his job and pushed virtually every other aspect of his life to the side. Outside of work, he hadn't been to a church since his marriage ended. He just didn't have time for it.

Gilborough paused as he walked up the steps to the cathedral. The sun was out with only a few white clouds wisping around. He could see Mount Rainier towering over the city like a guardian. He turned around and took a good look at the cathedral which was a lot more beautiful than he had noticed before. It almost made him a little homesick for New York. The dark gray stone structure reminded him of the architecture that had made the Big Apple famous. In Seattle, everything was modern. He liked it, but every once in a while, it was nice to see something different.

When he entered the body of the cathedral, Gilborough only saw two people sitting on the pews, both looking downward as if in prayer. He slowly walked down the main aisle as he took everything in. He was most awestruck by the large cross hanging behind the alter. It brought everything in the cathedral into focus, and reminded people why they were there to begin with.

Gilborough kept looking around for Donavan, but it was Donavan who found the detective first.

"Hello Gilborough," Donavan said from behind.

Gilborough was only slightly startled. He turned around to see Donavan standing just five feet away. "Where did you come from?" Gilborough asked as he looked behind Donavan for a door he could have been hiding behind.

"Sorry, I was picking up a bible someone left under one of the pews," Donavan said while holding up a small book.

"People forget those here?" Gilborough asked in amazement.

"Forget, intentionally left behind for those less fortunate; we find a lot of them," Donavan explained. Before Gilborough could say anything else, Donavan went on to ask, "So what brings you here two days in a row?"

"Well, it involves a case I'm working on," Gilborough said as he plotted out his choice of words.

"A case you're working on? Does it involve Harmon Jolston? Have you made an arrest in that case?" Donavan asked very curiously.

"Oh no. This is a different story all together," Gilborough said.

"And this different case has brought you here?"

"Yes."

"How can I help?" Donavan asked.

As soon as Donavan said that, Gilborough rolled his eyes as if to say, "So you're actually going to help this time?" However, Gilborough maintained some control and instead only asked, "You remember that guy that was here yesterday?"

"I'm afraid you need to be more specific than that," Donavan said.

"Well, I'm not sure if you remember or not," Gilborough began, "but yesterday when we were talking, there was a guy here."

"Okay, and," Donavan said, suggesting he still needed more information.

"He was real nervous. Remember, I even asked about him?"

"Oh yes, of course," Donavan said as his memory was suddenly jogged, "what about him?"

"How well did you know him?"

"I'd seen him before, but he wasn't a regular member of the congregation," Donavan paused before cutting to the heart of everything, "So what about him?"

"It's actually a little complicated," Gilborough said, not sure how to explain it, or even if he should.

"Is it complicated like the Harmon Jolston case was complicated eighteen years ago?" Donavan asked. His voice cracked as he spoke.

"Actually, in more ways than one," Gilborough said. He paused, putting off the big question, the one he knew he wouldn't get an answer to.

"How many more ways?" Donavan asked with peaked curiosity.

"Dead ways," Gilborough said, "we found him last night."

"How'd he die?" Donavan asked with a soft voice.

"Multiple stab wounds."

"Just like Jolston," Donavan observed.

"And just like those kids," Gilborough added, almost in a dismissive manner. He wanted to see Donavan's reaction at being so casual about such a traumatic event.

Again, Donavan displayed a very reflective expression on his face. He knew where the conversation was going, and he obviously didn't like it. "So what exactly can I help you with?"

"What can you tell me about him?"

"I think his name was Greg. Other than that, nothing."

"Oh come on," Gilborough said with a clear hint of frustration in his voice.

"Really detective, just how much should I know about every member of my congregation?"

"That's more of a question you have to ask yourself," Gilborough said. Before Donavan even had a chance to think, Gilborough went on to add, "Let's face it, this is hardly the first time that a brutal murder is linked to your church, is it?"

"That's not really a fair statement," Donavan said in objection.

"What's not fair is that a girl had to watch as someone confused her dad for a knife block," Gilborough said, not hiding the fact that he was becoming just a little angry. He went on to add, "Now maybe your pathetic conscious can let you sleep at night, but mine won't."

"How is she?" Donavan asked, throwing a curve in the conversation.

"She's screwed up beyond belief, possibly beyond repair," Gilborough said.

"That's a shame," Donavan said with a nod of his head.

"If it was really such a damned shame, you'd be more cooperative," Gilborough said. He quickly followed that up with, "But when have you ever cared about helping kids?"

The anger present in Gilborough's tone of voice was nothing compared to the anger displayed on Donavan's face. He looked Gilborough square in the eyes and said only, "You can leave my church now."

"Yeah, better get out while I'm still alive, right?" Gilborough commented with heavy sarcasm. He started to turn around and walk away, but paused mid step. He looked over his shoulder at Donavan and added, "but I guess as long as I'm not a kid, I'm safe."

"Leave now. Don't come back," Donavan said before he also turned and walked away.

Gilborough didn't say anything else. He walked out of the church as frustrated as he knew he'd be. He didn't really expect Donavan to help.

Gilborough paused on the steps of the cathedral. He was totally furious with Donavan. The worst part was that this wasn't the first time. Eighteen years ago, Donavan had the chance to help Gilborough convict Harmon Jolston of the brutal murder of five boys. Donavan refused. Harmon Walked. It all made Gilborough sick to his stomach.

He was so lost in thought that he wasn't even paying attention as he walked down the steps of the cathedral. He bumped into a woman who was equally lost in thought while climbing the steps.

"Sorry miss," Gilborough said. She barely glanced at him, then quickly lowered her eyes and continued walking.

Twenty minutes later, the woman was sitting in the confessional. She spent ten minutes beating around the bush with all the little things she had done in the past month since her last confession. It took some prodding from Donavan to get the woman to finally talk about what was really bothering her.

"I did something else bad," the woman, named Gina, said.

"Go on," Donavan beckoned.

"In fact, I did a lot of bad things," she said. She fidgeted around in her seat a little. Finally, she got the nerve to come out and say, "I've had an affair on my husband."

"And you've done this once?" Donavan asked.

"No. I don't remember how many times," She admitted. It was the truth, she couldn't count them all. She couldn't even remember all the names.

She and Donavan spent twenty minutes discussing her situation. Everything was only made worse when she said, "I tested positive today."

"You're pregnant?" Donavan asked.

"No," she insisted. Her voice cracked as she said, "HIV."

Donavan said nothing at first. He did everything he could to be comforting. Another five minutes later, Gina was standing at the back of the church, lighting a candle and saying a prayer.

Donavan sat in the confessional and said a prayer for her. However, his prayer was interrupted by a voice.

"What a whore," the voice whispered.

Donavan said nothing. His prayer for Gina shifted quickly to a prayer for the voice to stop. There would be no answer to this prayer.

"She messes around, and her husband has to pay for it? Does it sound familiar?" the voice asked.

"Whoever you are," Donavan began, "You are violating the sanctity of this church."

"Give it up Donavan," the voice replied, "We all know that you violated this church a long time ago. It's not the only thing you violated. Is it? Do you remember? Do you even care?"

There was a moment of silence before the voice spoke again. "I know it's a cliché'," the voice began. There was a pause before the voice seemed to echo, "But. I forgive you father. Fore, I know you have sinned."

Another moment of silence fell over the confession both. The voice let out a deep sigh before saying, "I can forgive you. I just can't forget."

The voice faded away in a series of laughters. It didn't even sound like one person, rather a crowd of people laughing at a comedian. Donavan lowered his head into the palm of his hands, searching desperately to understand his current situation.

That Night...

Gina pulled into the driveway just a little after six that evening. She carried two bags of groceries away from the car and into the house. The steaks were left on the counter to thaw, and the wine went in the fridge. She was immediately off to take a shower and put on something more comfortable. Craig would be home soon, and she wanted to have a nice dinner ready before she talked to him.

Twenty minutes later, she was back in the kitchen wearing her favorite pair of jeans and a comfortable t-shirt. The steaks were cut and marinating while she worked on the potatoes. Just as she was setting the steaks on the stove, she heard the rattling sound of someone opening the door.

She leaned back to peek through the dinning room and into the living room. "Honey, is that you?" She called out.

She heard the door being shut and then heard Craig shout back, "Who else?"

"Who else in deed," She whispered under her breath.

Craig walked into the kitchen, "That smells great sweetie." He walked over to stand behind her. With his hands on her hips, he leaned over her shoulder and kissed her softly.

"Thanks," She said while returning the kiss.

Craig slowly pulled away while saying, "I'm going to shower real quick."

"Take your time," Gina replied, "It will be a while before everything is ready."

Craig blew her a kiss as he walked out of the kitchen. He appeared to move in slow motion with a kind of blur. He disappeared in a series of footsteps that faded into silence that overtook the air.

The silence only lasted a fleeting moment. A single word, "Whore," echoed throughout the kitchen. It was like a harsh whisper fired through the quiet night. A gunshot would have made less noise.

Everything in time froze. She stopped stirring the potatoes, and only stared into empty space. She saw nothing except for the light above the stove in front of her. Both ears tuned out every sound as she tried to listen with the hopes that she didn't just hear what she though she heard.

There was only silence. Even the sizzling sound from the skillet went unnoticed. Unfortunately, the silence was not long lasting. The voice spoke out again, "You are nothing but a whore."

There was a brief pause, followed by what sounded like the voice echoing off into the distance, "So dirty. How do you live with yourself? How do you live? You won't live."

Gina spun her entire body in a slow circle. Her eyes were scanning everything around her. Surely she didn't hear what she thought she did. She had almost convinced herself that there wasn't really anyone in the room. She was just tired and worn out from stress. That's all it was.

Her false hopes were shattered along with her glass of wine that she had been sipping from. She swore it had been sitting soundly on the counter. There was simply no reason for the glass to slide slowly across the counter. Certainly, nothing could explain why the glass flung itself across the kitchen and shattered against the wall. It was only ironic that the wine she had been drinking left a red stain that ran down the wall, and pooled on the floor.

"You think I don't know about you?" The voice shouted out. There was a pause that brought time to a stop. Then, the voice added to its thoughts, "What you did? Who you did? How many you did? And, just how much you enjoyed doing what you did?"

"Stop it!" She screamed out while slamming the spatula down on the stove.

From every corner in the kitchen, she heard laughter. It ranged from mild giggling, to something much deeper and darker. "Ohhhh," the voice taunted, "I bet it's the first time you've said that in a while. Deeper, harder, faster. More, more, more. You want more whore?"

Before Gina had a chance to reply, she felt a blunt object hit her behind her knee. As she was falling downwards, she heard the voice again, "You want more? You want it harder?"

It was then that she felt a burning sensation in her back as a knife slide in three inches below her shoulder blade.

"You want it deeper whore?" The voice called out. She felt the knife repeatedly cutting through her skin as the voice said, "You want it faster?"

She laid there on the floor, trying to see where the pain was coming from. No one could be seen, but the voices didn't stop.

"You want more?" The voice asked with a giggle. It echoed on and was the last thing she heard before being bombarded with what felt like a thousand sharp points of pains.

Later...

Gilborough had just gotten the call to respond to the scene of an apartment fire when he got a second call. This one canceled the first call. The fire was still burning, and the bodies of two people would later be pulled from the ashes of the apartment complex. However, a woman had been found dead by her distraught husband. Though her husband was in total shock, he had managed to ask for Gilborough.

"You have to be kidding me," Gilborough said to the dispatch officer.

"I'm afraid not," the dispatch officer replied.

Gilborough was about to confirm the call, but paused, "Who's on the scene?" Gilborough asked.

"Stravinsky is in charge," dispatch replied.

When Gilborough pulled up to the house, he was met with the expected red and blue light show that signified a crime scene. There was even a police helicopter flying overhead, lighting up the neighborhood with its spotlight. He climbed out of his car and looked up at the helicopter, wondering what, or who, it was searching for.

He walked to the front door of the house which was wide open. There were four cops walking around outside. They were both guarding the place, and searching for anything that might be useful. There was also a cop next to the door who nodded Gilborough in after seeing the detective's badge.

Gilborough moved slowly through the living room while looking at everything. It all seemed normal, but then he also knew that other rooms would probably show themselves to be less than ordinary. He could hear voices in the back left corner, and saw a few shadows moving against the wall near the dining room.

"At least it wasn't in the bedroom," he thought to himself. He hated it when they were in the bedroom. Those were always the worst.

When he walked into the dining room, he saw a forensics officer aiming a camera into the kitchen and taking pictures. Three other cops and Stravinsky could be seen standing behind the cameraman.

"Gilborough, come on over here," Stravinsky said as soon as she saw him.

"Hey Stravinsky, what have you got?" Gilborough asked.

"Take a look for yourself. I think it's another winner."

Gilborough peeked around the corner to see inside the kitchen. The forensics officer with the camera backed up a little to give Gilborough room to look.

"What the hell?" Gilborough asked as his eyes laid sight on one of the most brutal things he had ever seen. He was about to step inside the kitchen when he saw all the blood on the floor. Suddenly the bedroom didn't seem so bad.

"Tie me up and spank me like the evil whore I am," the words, written across the floor in blood, read. Gina was hanging upside down in the center of the kitchen. She had been tied by one foot to the light fixture in the ceiling.

Gilborough stared at the image for a long minute and a half. He didn't say anything, and didn't turn away. He only stared. "This couldn't be happening," He told himself.

"Yeah, it's pretty weird?" Stravinsky observed.

"You don't even know the strangest part about this," Gilborough commented in an unusually soft voice.

"What is it?" Stravinsky asked.

"I saw her at the same church I saw the guy last night at."

"Sounds like you need to stay out of that church," Stravinsky observed. This led to a moment of reflective silence as both detectives took everything in.

"Where's her husband?" Gilborough finally asked while turning around slowly.

Stravinsky nodded her head to the side while saying, "He's outside. Special victim's unit is on the way."

"How is he?" Gilborough asked as he began walking towards the front door.

"I'm not sure how to answer that question," Stravinsky said. She followed Gilborough outside, but turned around at the last minute and said, "Nobody touch anything."

As soon as they were outside of the house, Gilborough asked, "What do you mean by that?"

"I mean he's quiet. He seems distracted, not upset."

"Like the girl last night?"

"A lot like the girl last night," Stravinsky said as they walked towards one of the squad cars. An officer was standing about ten feet away from the car, and another man was leaning against the car. He had a blanket wrapped around himself like a shaw and was staring off into space like a child in the middle of a daydream.

"His name is Craig," Stravinsky said as she paused in her tracks to give Gilborough and Craig some privacy.

Gilborough slowly approached Craig while saying, "Hi, Craig, right?"

"Yes," Craig said without looking at Gilborough.

"You think you could tell me what happened?" Gilborough said, cutting straight to the heart of the matter.

"My wife killed me," Craig said.

Gilborough's brain froze. Maybe Craig misspoke, or maybe he didn't understand the full gravity of what had just happened.

"You care to run that by me again?" Gilborough asked.

"I gave my wife a hug. She gave me death," Craig said. He then opened the blanket that was wrapped around his body to show himself covered in blood.

"Dear God," Gilborough exclaimed when he saw all the blood on Craig. It looked as though Craig had actually given his dead wife a hug as she hung from the ceiling.

Craig said nothing. He pulled the blanket back around himself as he turned to look away. There was only silence. Craig went back to looking out at nothing, apparently searching for answers that weren't there.

"So why did you ask for me?" Gilborough asked.

Craig's facial expression changed from blank to reflective, as if he was trying to remember a piece of information. "Oh yes, that," Craig said.

"Yeah that," Gilborough repeated.

"I have a message for you?"

"What's the message?"

"It's actually a question that I'm supposed to ask you," Craig said.

"Okay, fine, what's the question?" Gilborough asked, growing more and more inpatient over the fact that Craig had to be led like a horse to water.

Craig turned to Gilborough and asked, "How many angels can dance on the head of a pin?"

"Am I suppose to give you an answer to this question?"

"It's just something to ponder?"

"Why should I ponder this question?" Gilborough asked.

"Because it would be easier than counting all of your mistakes," Craig said with a smile.

"What the hell are you talking about?" Gilborough asked with a tone of clear anger in his voice.

"I'm just the messenger. I was only told to pass this on to you," Craig replied.

"Fine, then who told you to pass it on? Why me?"

"I get the feeling that you are being blamed for a lot of it. Not everything of course, but a lot," Craig said.

"What the hell am I being blamed for here?"

Craig turned away as he said, "You'll just have to figure that out for yourself."

Gilborough was totally furious. Two people were dead, and someone was turning it into a sick game. Out of shear frustration, he grabbed a hold of the blanket and pulled it tighter around Craig while saying, "Now you're going to tell me who did this."

"I can't. It's a secret," Craig said.

"You think this is some kind of game?" Gilborough asked, pulling Craig closer to him.

"That's exactly what it is. It's a game detective Gilborough, and you're it."

Gilborough pushed Craig up against the car. "If you want us to have any chance of finding out who killed your wife, then you need to help," Gilborough yelled.

Craig looked Gilborough square in the eyes, and with a smile, said, "The whore deserved to die."

"Then why don't we arrest you. Hell, you are only covered in her blood," Gilborough said as he glanced at Stravinsky. He nodded his head, motioning her to come on over. She was ready to step in anyway. Gilborough was clearly letting his notorious temper get the better of him.

If Stravinsky thought Gilborough was mad already, then she didn't have a word to describe him when Craig said what he said next.

"It wouldn't be the first time you've arrested the wrong person, now would it detective," Craig said in a cold voice.

"You sorry bastard," Gilborough said while pulling out his cuffs, "That's it. Up against the car."

"Gilborough, no!" Stravinsky screamed while jumping in between the two men.

"Oh come on Stravinsky. Let's arrest him for killing his wife," Gilborough said. His face was blush red with anger.

"That's enough," Stravinsky said as she moved closer to Gilborough, trying to get him to back away.

"No. It will be enough when he talks," Gilborough said, backing away slowly.

Stravinsky felt that it was time for Gilborough to leave the scene. "Take a step back," Stravinsky said, "then walk away."

"He knows who's doing this," Gilborough said.

"Yeah. I'm sure he does," Stravinsky agreed, "But we're not going to get him to talk with threats."

Gilborough said nothing. He caste a hard stare at Stravinsky. He paused to turn to Craig, then back at Stravinsky again. He knew she was right, but it didn't change his opinion much.

"You just give me a call if you come up with anything," Gilborough said as if he dared her not to.

"Relax. We'll get to the bottom of this. You're just too close," Stravinsky said.

"Yeah I'm too close. Don't even know why, but I'm too close," Gilborough said out of frustration as he turned and walked away.

As Gilborough was walking away, Donavan was walking into this cathedral. He had taken a long walk that evening to clear his mind. The goal was to get his mind off of everything that was bothering him. It would prove to be a futile effort.

As the door to the cathedral was closing, Donavan thought he heard something. It sounded like laughter, though not a deep laugh. Instead it was something lighter, almost like a giggle.

"Oh no," Donavan thought to himself.

"She's dead," a high-pitched voice echoed through the cathedral.

Donavan took several small steps as he spun a slow circle to look at his surroundings. He didn't say anything. Maybe if he stayed quiet, the voice would go away. He was wrong.

"It's perfectly okay Donavan," the voice said. Then, in typical fashion, the voice echoed off, "It's just you. And just me. And me. And me."

"And, who is the me?" Donavan asked as he looked upwards.

"That's a secret. Five truths. Five lies. In between. The secret lies," the voice trailed off.

"I guess this is some kind of game to you?" Donavan said with a voice filled full of sarcasm.

The air was quickly rocked by a series of laughter before the mysterious voice spoke again, "It's exactly a game. I make the rules. I'll not loose this time. Can the preacher come out and play? You do like to play, don't you?"

The voice trailed off again in a series of laughter. Donavan kept spinning slow circles. Eventually he would be able to see someone. They couldn't be invisible he kept telling himself. Again, Donavan was about to be proved wrong.

He felt a tap on the back of his shoulder. "Tag," the voice said.

Donavan spun around quickly, but there was nothing behind him. Suddenly, he felt a tug as someone grabbed a hold of his right hand. When he turned to look, no one could be seen, but the grip only got tighter. He tried to swing his left hand, but found that wrist also detained. He tried to use all his energy to pull away, but found himself lacking strength.

"You're it," the voice said as another pair of hands grabbed a hold of Donavan by his collar. He could hear the voice up close, and even feel the breathing as if someone were really there. He couldn't see anyone, though something was clearly holding onto, and pulling on, his collar.

Before Donavan could react at all, he felt two separate pairs of hands grab him by his ankles. Again, Donavan tried to resist, but the strength just wasn't there. He tightened up the muscles in his legs, but the hands pulled even harder. Slowly, he felt his feet being lifted off the ground. He was stretched out, and being pulled in every direction while at the same time being lifted into the air. The fist holding his collar only pulled harder, tightening the grip around his throat.

"Do you still want to play this game?" the voice asked. Donavan could feel the breath of someone only inches away from his face. As with before, the voice seemed to echo off, "I mean it was your game to begin with. You wanted to play with me. Do you want to wrestle? Or is it only fun when you get to be on top?"

Donavan was about to scream for help when he felt a hand clasp itself over his mouth. "Shut Up!" The voice called out. "Do you remember that?" The voice echoed on as Donavan was lifted higher into the air, "Do you like being gagged?"

Donavan was unable to speak. That didn't stop him from shaking his head from side to side, suggesting that he didn't like it.

"To bad," the voice was quick to reply, showing how little it cared about Donavan's dissent. "I didn't like it either," the voice shouted with such anger that it echoed from every wall within the church. The painted glass windows rattled as if they were going to break. Even the inner part of Donavan's ears trembled from the shear force that the voice carried.

Donavan could feel the one hand loosen its grip on his collar and the other pull away from his mouth. "This is not the end. Not yet," the voice said. Donavan turned his head to look downward and saw that he was more than ten feet in the air.

"I control you," the voice said. This time there was no echo; only a still calm in the air. The silence gave way to motion as Donavan felt the hands let go of him. He immediately fell to the ground, landing on his back. He didn't even try to move. He could feel the pain shooting through his back and down into his legs.

"I can take you when ever I want, just like I took that whore. Lucky for you, I'm not ready yet. There is one more lesson to learn. It's almost over," the voice trailed off. Donavan could actually hear footsteps as what sounded like a small crowd gathered around him. He still couldn't see anything, but was absorbed with that feeling of being surrounded by people.

"It's bedtime," the voice said quietly, "We'll talk tomorrow."

There was no echo this time. Only a soft spoken voice. An eerie silence settled in, followed quickly by fear. Donavan laid there for almost an hour. It wasn't just the pain he felt shooting in waves down his back, but also the fear that shot up his spine in counter waves.

When he did move, his first motion was to run his hands across his face to wipe away the sweat. An odd thing happened. Instead of removing the sweaty feeling from his face, he felt a cool kind of wetness on his brow. He opened his eyes and looked at his hands. The bright red fluid running down from his wrists and across his palms almost sent Donavan into shock. Donavan immediately looked down at each hand, searching for signs of a wound.

As he wiped away the blood, he could see fingerprints stamped into his skin, but not deep enough to have drawn blood. That's when it hit Donavan, and reality settled in like a pile of bricks on his already fragile soul. The blood was left there from whoever had grabbed him. The same person who grabbed him, had confessed to killing Gina. It must have been Gina's blood.

Donavan didn't know what to do. He wanted to run, but didn't have the strength. It wasn't as if this was something he could run away from anyway.

Early That Morning...

"So you care to tell me what has you so shook up?" Stravinsky asked. She and Gilborough had met at a small coffee shop that they had both been frequenting for the most of their careers. It had become a popular gathering spot for cops; both on duty, and off.

Gilborough didn't answer immediately. He took a slow sip of his coffee as he thought about everything. He had actually given that very question some serious thought over the previous night. After taking a sip of coffee, he finally said, "I don't really know."

"Have any ideas?" Stravinsky asked.

"No. But, then maybe that's it. I feel like something is going on here that we're missing."

"Like what?"

"That's just it, I don't know," Gilborough admitted.

"Stressing the absence of answers?" Stravinsky asked.

"Something like that," Gilborough said with a hint of a laugh. He took another sip of coffee and glanced around at the few people walking by. He turned back to Stravinsky and asked, "Why are you so concerned anyway?"

"Hate to see you loose your badge," She said while staring across the top of her own cup of coffee.

"Oh come on," Gilborough moaned.

"No, I'm serious. You almost lost it last night with that guy."

"He was holding out. He know's who killed his wife."

"And the girl?" Stravinsky asked, referring to Greg's daughter, "Think she was holding out also?"

"Yes," Gilborough said without hesitation.

"So everyone is hiding something?" Stravinsky suggested.

"Basically, yes," Gilborough replied.

"Come on, there has to be something else," Stravinsky said. She seemed concerned for Gilborough. She could tell he was taking everything a bit more personal than normal.

Gilborough took another long sip of coffee before saying, "It just feels like everything is coming full circle on me."

"How so?" Stravinsky asked.

"My first big case as a homicide detective was the Harmon Jolston case."

"And now Jolston is dead," Stravinsky began.

Gilborough interrupted her before she could finish, "And there are more murders occurring around the church."

"I think I understand," Stravinsky said.

"I just have that eerie feeling like this is my last big case or something."

"Oh come on, you have hundreds of bigger cases in front of you," Stravinsky joked.

Gilborough almost smiled, "That can be a good thing. It could also be a bad thing."

"You said it, not me," Stravinsky said. She allowed herself a small pause before asking, "So what is on you agenda for the day?"

"I'm going back to the church. Need to talk to that priest one more time," Gilborough said while finishing off his cup of coffee.

"Think he is holding out as well?" Stravinsky said, almost as a joke.

Gilborough gave no indication that he was joking when he replied, "I think he is holding out more than anyone. I'm just not sure how."

Three Hours Later...

For Donavan, the morning came with not one bang, but many. He found himself trying his best to run towards the front door of the Cathedral. Every step hurt not only his legs, but also his back. Each loud knock on the door rang through his head as if they were tapping directly on his skull. When he opened the door, his pain only grew.

"Good morning," Gilborough said. It only took a second for him to notice that Donavan was in pain. Gilborough was holding a manila envelope, and couldn't wait to show Donavan the contents. However, he was suddenly curious about how a priest gets himself injured.

"Morning. Excuse me if I leave off the 'good' part of it," Donavan said while holding his back with his left hand. He was using his right hand to steady himself by holding on to the side of the door frame.

"Everything okay?" Gilborough asked. He put a special emphasis on the question by motioning towards Donavan's hand on his lower back.

"Yeah, I'm fine," Donavan said, "I just slept wrong I think." Donavan went so far as to let go of his back and try to stand straight. The attempt at displaying himself as physically uninjured failed miserably. The pain on his face was too obvious.

"If you say so," Gilborough said with a shrug of his shoulders. He raised the manila envelope and began to open it while asking, "You have a few moments?"

"As long as it's important," Donavan said. It was clear that that he'd rather do anything except stand around and talk to Gilborough.

Gilborough was quick to show that he didn't care about Donavan's discomfort, "I'm sure this is more important than anything you have planned for the day."

"You just might be surprised at what my days hold in store for me," Donavan said.

"You're probably right," Gilborough replied. He pulled a photo out of the envelope and quickly added, "But this is important none the less."

Gilborough held the photo up for Donavan to see while asking, "You know this girl?" The picture was a close up of Gina's face with her eyes closed.

Donavan hesitated. Of course he knew her, but wasn't about to admit it. He also wasn't ready to lie either. "She doesn't look familiar," Donavan said in an effort to compromise with his conscious.

Gilborough only nodded his head. That answer was close to what he expected. He slid the first photo back into the envelope, then pulled out another picture. "How about now?" Gilborough asked while holding the picture up for Donavan to see.

Donavan's face gave himself away. There was no denying anything at that point. "What happened to her?" he asked. The picture was of Gina, taken while she was still dangling from the ceiling in her kitchen.

"That's a good question," Gilborough said.

"Is it a question that you have an answer to?" Donavan asked while staring at the picture. He could almost feel the pain that she went through.

"I'm actually wondering if you might have any answers," Gilborough said while sliding the picture back into the envelope.

"How could I help?" Donavan asked. The tone in his voice told of how disgusting the idea was.

"Give me a break. I saw her yesterday when I was leaving," Gilborough said, "that's two in a row."

"Two what?" Donavan asked, "Two people from my church who have been brutally killed?"

"You have to admit that it's an odd coincidence," Gilborough explained. He had to fight hard to keep his temper under control. Gilborough wasn't known as being the most diplomatic of detectives. He had a tendency to say what was on his mind and let the chips fall where they may. He was also experienced, and knew this was one of those times were silence could get him further than his usual bitter sarcasm.

That didn't mean that Donavan was going to show the same sort of diplomacy. In fact, Donavan displayed an unusual kind of anger when he observed, "Maybe the real coincidence rests in the fact you were the one who saw both of these people at my church."

"You think this is some kind of game?" Gilborough asked.

Donavan's face turned white with the question. He immediately flashed back to the previous night when Donavan had asked that same question. Only moments after asking that question he had found himself lifted into the air, then promptly dropped to the ground. The entire thought sent a shiver down his spine that reverberated into waves of pain.

"No, I don't," Donavan said, "I take death very seriously."

That's when Donavan heard a sound. A light giggle came from behind him. The nervous priest found himself peeking over his shoulder to see what the sound was. Another nervous shiver ran down his spine when he heard a whisper, "I think the man believes it."

"He disgusts me," the voice then said, speaking just above a whisper. As usual, the voice trailed off in a series of echoes, "I say we kill him now. I say we make him suffer some more. Someone has to die. Say a prayer you evil bastard."

Donavan nearly fell down from spinning around to see where the voices were coming from. He should have already known that he wasn't going to turn around and see someone there. That didn't stop him from looking.

"You okay?" Gilborough asked.

Donavan became extremely dismissive. "I'm fine. Why do you ask?" It really didn't matter how hard he tried to play off his sudden paranoia, he knew he was in trouble. Even an average bystander could tell something was bothering Donavan, so only God knew what Gilborough was thinking.

"Maybe he knows," A whisper said into Donavan's ear. Donavan could even feel a light breath blow across his ear as the voice went on to add, "We both know how stupid he is. Maybe he knows. Maybe he found a clue. Maybe we don't have to explain everything to him."

Donavan's eyes again wandered off to the left, then the right. No matter how well he knew that he wasn't going to see something, he couldn't stop himself from looking.

Gilborough pressed the point by asking, "You sure everything is okay Donavan?"

Donavan gave a moment's thought to the question. He couldn't very well tell a homicide detective that he was hearing voices. At the same time, he felt a strange kind of safety in Gilborough's presence. The voices would only get louder when Gilborough left.

"Yes, I just haven't been sleeping much," Donavan said, only telling half a lie.

"Conscious bothering you?" Gilborough asked.

"No. Nor should it," Donavan stated clearly. His facial expression immediately shifted from distracted to irritated.

"As long as you can look at yourself in the mirror in the morning," Gilborough commented. He had officially given up on ever getting any help from Donavan. That point was driven home when he said, "I'd like to think that if people around me started dying, I would want to help. I'd also like to think that it didn't have anything to do with me."

With that, Gilborough turned and walked away. He never once looked back as he walked down the steps of the church. Donavan waited until Gilborough had made it down the steps to the cathedral before closing the door.

"Oooohhhhh, I think he almost gets it," A voice whispered into Donavan's ear.

Donavan held a tight grip on the door latch, almost using it for support as he heard the whisper. At first, he wasn't going to say anything. Donavan thought that if he just ignored the voices, they would go away. He was only tired and under a lot of stress; that's all it was. Of course, that explained all of the less than normal happenings of late. Donavan couldn't convince himself of that one no matter how hard he tried.

"It's almost over Donavan," the voice cried out in a high pitched scream.

"What's almost over?" Donavan asked in a whisper so quiet that he hardly even had to move his lips.

"The lies. The deceit. The evil. The murders."

"So you are going to stop killing?" Donavan asked.

"There are just two people left to kill. But yes, it will stop."

"Who are these last two?" Donavan asked. There was a clear tremble in his voice. He could only imagine who would be next.

"Oh, that's a secret. It's a secret soon to be told. A secret too hard to hold. A secret that's cold."

The voice trailed off in a way that Donavan was almost used to. A soft wind blew through the cathedral. As the wind blew, the voice reverberated, "It's almost over."

Donavan took a seat on the nearest pew. He didn't know what to think anymore. All he wanted was for it to be over. Deep down, something told him that he shouldn't find too much comfort in that idea.

Gilborough walked up to his car and started to open the door to get in. He was momentarily distracted by a car parked only thirty feet away. Two people could be seen leaning by the passenger side window. Gilborough watched as one of the people wadded up a hand full of money and reached in through the window. When he brought his hand out again, he was holding a plastic bag of something. Gilborough smiled. This was going to be too easy.

He pulled out his pipe. It took two matches to finally light it up. Once lit, he walked in the direction of the car. He was casual in his movements, not wanting to appear as if he were headed towards the car. No, he was just an ordinary person enjoying a stroll down the street. He could smell the rain coming, but was out to enjoy the sunshine while it was there. He actually walked past the car before pausing next to a light post. He took several long puffs on his pipe while glancing around at his surroundings. The street was far from empty, though it was without that hustle and bustle feeling either.

Just as the two men next to the car started to walk away, Gilborough began moving slowly towards the car. There was a lone man sitting in the driver's seat. Gilborough walked up to the passenger side and took a puff of his pipe while asking, "Excuse me, you wouldn't have the time would you?"

"Yeah, it's abut a quarter to eleven," the guy said after looking at the clock on his dashboard.

"Great, thanks," Gilborough replied. He acted as if he was about to walk away, but paused. He took two long puffs of his pipe, then asked, "I'm sorry, one more thing."

"Sure," the guy said. He was experienced enough to know that the best way to get away with being a dealer was to blend in. That meant being polite to the average citizens who would normally loath his type.

Gilborough held out his pipe and asked, "You wouldn't know where I could get something good to smoke in this thing?"

"Like what?" The guy asked.

Only a cop would come out and ask if the guy was selling drugs. Gilborough played it off casually, "Well, I don't want to imply anything, but you look like you know your way around town."

Gilborough paused and looked around, playing as if he were nervous. "Let's just say I'm not looking for anything that can be bought at the store."

The guy only smiled, "I gotcha."

He reached behind his seat and grabbed a backpack. Gilborough held his cool, but kept looking around as if he were nervous. The guy pulled out a small plastic bag of what had to be marijuana.

"You looking for something like this?" The guy asked.

"Actually I'm looking for exactly that," Gilborough said and he smiled and took another puff from his pipe.

"How much you want?" The guy asked.

"How much is in each of those bags?" Gilborough asked in response.

"Two ounces. Should be enough to last a casual smoker like yourself," the guy said with a smile.

"I'll take two bags," Gilborough replied. He reached into the pocket of his overcoat as if he was going to pull out his wallet. Gilborough kept his wallet in his back pocket. The pocket he was reaching into is where he kept his badge, but the guy didn't know that.

The guy dug into his backpack to pull out another bag. When he looked up again, he saw Gilborough smiling while holding his badge in his hand.

"You gotta be kidding me," the guy said.

"I'm afraid not," Gilborough replied. He nodded with his head while saying, "Come on, out of the car."

"This is entrapment, plain and simple," the guy said while climbing out of his car.

Gilborough only laughed, "Yeah, I tricked you into dealing out in broad daylight."

"I'm gonna have your damned badge for this," He said as Gilborough put the cuffs on him.

Gilborough didn't reply. He finished cuffing the man, and called for a tow truck to impound the man's car. They could inventory it back at the station. Thirty minutes later, Gilborough was driving away. The guy was cuffed in the back seat, and a tow truck could be seen pulling away with the guy's car.

The man's I.D. revealed his name to be Jason Tobin. A call to the station showed that this was to be far from Jason's first arrest. He had multiple priors for everything from dealing to breaking and entering. Nothing suggested a tendency towards violence, but then Gilborough already knew that. He never needed to pull his gun, and Jason had practically put the cuffs on himself. He knew the routine, and knew he'd be back on the streets dealing within a couple of days.

Gilborough said little while in the car, and Jason said nothing. Jason knew his fifth amendment rights, and Gilborough knew that nothing said in that car could be admitted as evidence later. Three blocks later, they were sitting at a red light. Jason was looking through the windows and taking in the view. He sure didn't have anything else to do.

As soon as the light turned green, Gilborough hit the gas. Two seconds later, he was slamming on the brakes, trying to stop as fast as possible.

"God Damn It!" Gilborough exclaimed as the car came to a stop and barely missed hitting a small group of kids standing in the middle of the road.

The force of the car stopping so abruptly threw Jason out of his seat. "What the hell is your problem?" He asked as he regained his senses.

"Sorry," Gilborough began while looking over his shoulder at Jason, "Those kids just got in the way."

Jason climbed back into his seat and looked around, "What kids?"

When Gilborough turned to look through the windshield, the boys were gone. "They were there, I swear," Gilborough said as he looked around to see where they had run off to.

"You been smoking any of that stuff that you claim you found on me?" Jason commented sarcastically.

Gilborough didn't reply. He let his heart rate drop a little before hitting the gas again. He thought his near crash experience was over. He was about to be proved wrong. As soon as the car began moving, Gilborough heard a loud, "Bang!" as something hit the top of the roof.

"What was that?" Jason asked while looking upwards.

Gilborough glanced up at the roof of his car for a moment before dismissing it, "Probably a piece of garbage."

Moments later, there were four more loud crashing sounds as something kept hitting the top of the roof. "What is that?" Gilborough was forced to ask while leaning forward to look out of his windshield at the sky. It sounded like a hail storm, but this was Seattle. It might rain all day long everyday, but it rarely hailed.

While Gilborough was leaning forward, something hit the windshield. Gilborough never saw a thing, but the noise was terribly loud. Whatever hit his windshield did so with enough force to leave a series of cracks. "Crap," Gilborough shouted as the sudden noise startled him.

"What the hell is going on man," Jason shouted from the back seat of the car.

"Just hold on," Gilborough said as he swerved into the next lane, looking for a place to pull off the road. No sooner had he swerved then, "BAM!" and something else hit his car. This time it was the hood. Again, Gilborough saw nothing, but something left a dent two feet across in his hood.

"Look man, if this is some bad cop routine, you can give it up," Jason shouted.

Gilborough glanced over his shoulder at Jason and begged, "Just calm down, all right?"

"Yeah sure, what ever," Jason said with a nod of his head. As soon as he said that, his face went from appearing slightly nervous to being scared for his life. "Holly shit!" Jason shouted while pointing at the windshield.

Gilborough turned around again and was stunned beyond belief. Standing on his hood, was a thirteen year old boy. The boy was standing in the center of the dent that was left earlier. He was leaning forward and holding on to the top of the windshield with his hands. His eyes seemed to cut through Gilborough with both anger and determination.

For a split second, Gilborough was frozen with fear and hesitation. He didn't know what to expect next, and didn't know how to react. Any sudden move could throw the kid off his car and into traffic. That split second cost Gilborough everything. It only took that single second for the kid to reach back with one hand and throw his fist through the windshield.

The noise was deafening. The flying glass was blinding and caused Gilborough to lose total control of his car. First he swerved left, then to the right. Each time he turned the wheel, Gilborough over corrected, causing the next swerve to be even worse. The next thing he knew, the car was sliding sideways towards a curb, and beginning to flip.

Gilborough didn't count all the flips, but knew it was more than one. The first flip threw the car across a sidewalk, and the second into a grocery store parking lot. Out of shear luck, the car ended up on its wheels.

Though shaken and rattled, Gilborough was still in one piece. He looked over his shoulder at Jason who was laying on his side in the back seat. He was moaning and trying to move. It was a good sign that he wasn't hurt too bad.

Gilborough tried to open his door, but it was jammed shut. All the windows had been shattered to pieces, with only shards left around the edges. Gilborough struggled a little as he pulled off his overcoat. Once off, he was able to use it to clear away the last of the glass around his window. With that done, Gilborough climbed out through the window.

He ran his eyes quickly around the scene, taking in every detail as only a trained detective could. Traffic on the road had slowed to a crawl as everyone tried to get a good glimpse at the banged up car. Gilborough looked for, but couldn't see the kid that had been on the hood of his car. The fact that traffic was moving at all, meant that the kid wasn't in the middle of the road. Gilborough turned back to his car and tried to open the back seat.

"Do you even know how to drive?" Jason asked as he made his way towards the driver's side door where Gilborough was waiting for him. Jason's movements were only hindered by the fact that he was wearing handcuffs.

Gilborough cleared the glass fragments away from the backseat window. He then carefully pulled Jason out of the car.

"Are you sure you're okay?" Gilborough asked as Jason found his footing.

"I'm fine. But you could take these off," Jason replied while turning around and holding out his hands to display the cuffs.

"I shouldn't do this," Gilborough said while reaching in his pocket to pull out his keys. He quickly added, "Just understand that if you run, I will find you."

Gilborough was just about to slide the key into the lock on the handcuffs when he heard a voice, "Don't do that."

The voice came from above both men, and they each turned around to look. Gilborough was left shocked, Jason only confused. Standing on top of the wrecked car were five boys. They were the same five boys that Gilborough had slammed on his brakes to avoid hitting. In the center, was the boy who had thrown his fist through Gilborough's window.

"I know you like letting guilty men go free," the boy in the center said.

His thoughts were finished by the boy next to him, "But I think it's time we bring that bad habit to an end."

Gilborough stared in total disbelief. "I know you, don't I," Gilborough said slowly.

One of the kids standing on the roof of the car squatted down so he could look Gilborough in the eyes. "You might remember me, but you sure as hell don't know me."

Before Gilborough could respond to that, or even completely ponder the words, it was too late. The boy sprung off the roof of the car and lunged at Gilborough. The boy grabbed a hold of Gilborough by the throat while driving his knees into the detective's chest. For only being eleven years old and weighing barely over a hundred pounds, the boy jumped with enough strength to send Gilborough falling backwards.

The force of the boy's knees driving into Gilborough's chest left him breathless. As soon as they were on the ground, the boy reached for Gilborough's waist and pulled out the detective's gun.

"Well what do we have here?" The boy asked while pulling the hammer back on the revolver.

"Is it loaded?" one of the boys standing on top of the roof asked.

The boy with the gun smiled. He turned to Jason and raised the gun while saying, "There's only one way to find out."

Jason panicked. He started looking around frantically, trying to find a way out of his situation. "Hey man, I didn't do nothin' to you guys," Jason pleaded.

"That really doesn't matter," the boy with the gun said. He waved the revolver in a circle for effect.

Jason's immediate instinct was to run away, but it was to late. Before he could move, he felt two pairs of hands grab him by each shoulder. A third pair of hands grabbed him by the neck and began lifting him off the ground. Jason kicked his feet, but with his hands cuffed behind him, he was unable to get any leverage. The boys held him against Gilborough's car with one of the boys standing on top of the car and holding Jason by the neck. The other two boys held on to his arms and stretched him out along side the car.

"Come on, let's find out how many bullets are in that gun," the boy holding Jason by the neck said.

"But I didn't do nothing," Jason pleaded again.

"Of course not," One of the boys behind Jason said.

Another boy added, "You didn't sell drugs."

"And you didn't sell drugs to kids," A third boy observed.

A forth boy added, "And of course you didn't sell any bad drugs."

The boy with the gun wrapped up the sarcasm, "And two people didn't die from your bad drugs. There also isn't a little girl out there wondering when her mom will wake up from the coma she is in from your damn drugs."

The hammer fell on the gun, and a molten hot piece of metal was launched into Jason's knee. Jason kicked with pain and screamed out in agony. He tried to use his other leg to kick away from the car, but the boys had too good of a grip on him. They might have seemed like only eleven and twelve year olds, but they had the strength of giants. The boy with the gun only smiled as he said, "You didn't do nothing."

"You did something," another boy said.

"You did something very bad," the boy holding Jason by his neck added.

"Now we're going to do something," the boy holding Jason by his left shoulder said.

The boy holding Jason by his right shoulder added, "We're going to do something very bad."

With that, another shot was fired directly into Jason's stomach. He flinched with pain and screamed out again, but it was to no avail.

"Stop it!" Gilborough shouted as he climbed to one knee.

The boy with the gun spun around quickly and pointed the gun square between Gilborough's eyes.

"You're lucky that there is still a lesson for you to learn," the boy said. He pulled the hammer back a third time. His eyes never left Gilborough's eyes. Slowly, the boy turned his arm to point the gun at Jason.

The boy smiled while staring down at Gilborough. His smile seemed to curl up even more as a third bullet flew from the barrel and pierced Jason in the center of the skull.

"He was very bad," the boy said.

The three boys holding Jason let go, allowing his limp body to fall to the ground. The boy that had been holding Jason by the neck added, "But we are so much worse."

Another boy on top of the car asked, "How many bullets left?"

The boy with the gun looked at the chamber of the revolver before replying, "Two."

"And two lessons left to be taught," another boy said.

Gilborough had a second gun in his glove compartment, but there was no way he could get to that. He also knew that he couldn't run fast enough. He decided to take a long shot and reason with them, "I really don't think that there is a lesson you can teach me."

One of the boys jumped off the roof of the car. As soon as he landed, he said, "The fact that you would even say that suggest the contrary."

The other three boys on the roof of the car also jumped down. The boy with the gun backed up so he was closer to the other four boys. He slowly lowered his gun. There was a moment of silence as the five boys gathered together in a tight circle.

"Find us," one of the boys said.

"Don't make us find you," another added.

"It's almost over," said a third boy.

"You know where," a forth boy said.

The boy with the gun smiled again as he said, "Hurry, you don't want to miss this."

And like that, they were gone. They just vanished before Gilborough's eyes. There was no smoke, no bright light. They didn't slowly fade away. One second they were there, and without even blinking an eye, they were gone.

Gilborough's instincts where to call for back up and deal with the death in front of him. He looked down at Jason who was laying face down on the concrete next to the banged up car. Something else told Gilborough that he needed to hurry if he was going to prevent anything else from happening.

He reached through the the passenger window and pulled his back up gun out of the glove compartment. From there, it was a six block run back to the church. Gilborough was in his mid forties and hadn't exercised in years. He stayed in shape just enough to pass the physical at work, but that was it. Somehow, this lack of physical conditioning didn't keep him from running the whole way. He never got tired, and never even came close to running out of breath. He just didn't think about it.

His thoughts had strayed back eighteen years. He had only been promoted to detective a month earlier. The call came in that someone had found something at one of the beaches. He didn't sleep for a week after that. He and nine other cops along with two coroners and three medics spent the night pulling body parts out of a shallow grave.

They were slowly able to piece together the bodies of five young boys. Fingerprints on a knife found near the scene led them to Harmon Jolston. After being followed, he was picked up while leaving Father Donavan's church. This was of special interest because the boys all attended Sunday school at the church.

Unfortunately, that was the only evidence that linked Jolston to the boys. As a result, he was acquitted. The truly frustrating part was that Harmon Jolston had apparently confessed to Father Donavan that he had committed the crime, but Donavan wouldn't testify. Gilborough never did forget the faces of those young boys. Watching those same five boys kill Jason, sent a cold chill down Gilborough's spine.

"There is no way it could have been them," he kept telling himself as he ran one block after another. They had been dead. They had been mutilated. As much as that bothered Gilborough, he couldn't help but think, "Why now?" Even if it was possible, why wait eighteen years. It wasn't even the anniversary of the killings. There really was no rhyme or reason for it all.

By the time Gilborough got to the steps of the cathedral, his adrenaline had given way to fear. Was he too late? What would he find? What did they want with him? Those questions kept echoing through his mind as he climbed the steps of the cathedral.

The door to the cathedral opened slowly. Gilborough peeked inside, not wanting to rush into a dangerous situation. He didn't hear anything, so assumed it was safe. The sound that the door made when it closed startled Gilborough. It was mostly his nerves. He walked into the main body of the cathedral and saw no one.

"Hello?" Gilborough called out, "Donavan? You here?"

In the back, Gilborough could hear the squeaking sound of a door opening up. This was followed immediately by Donavan's voice calling out, "Yes. Who's there?"

Somehow, Gilborough found the energy to run a second time as he bolted down the main isle of the cathedral. He ran past the alter and towards a door in the corner where Donavan was standing.

"I was hoping that I had seen the last of you," Donavan said as soon as he saw Gilborough.

"Well the feeling is mutual, but we have bigger problems," Gilborough said as his run came to a stop.

"Such as?" Donavan asked. His tone suggested that he was less than trusting of anything Gilborough had to say.

"We need to leave. I don't have time to explain it," Gilborough replied. Gilborough's tone, his facial expression, even the way he was looking around nervously, suggested that Donavan would be wise to listen.

With a very straight face, Donavan asked, "Is this about what I think it is?"

Gilborough slowly nodded his head yes. This answer worked best for both men since neither one of them cared to discuss what they thought was going on. Gilborough had the advantage of having actually seen the boys who were supposed to have been killed eighteen years ago. Donavan had only been hearing voices. Neither man assumed that their version had more credibility than the other.

As much as Donavan disliked Gilborough, he decided the best thing he could do was to follow the detective out of there. Neither one of them said anything. Gilborough turned to walk away. He wanted to get out of there as soon as possible, and he knew Donavan was going to follow. Donavan never thought twice. He hopped a couple of times on his bad leg to catch up with Gilborough. Both men walked past the alter and towards the main isle of the cathedral.

They were half way down the aisle when they both heard a voice. "And where do you think you're going?" Someone said from behind them in a voice that echoed.

Another voice quickly added, "I say we send the bastard to hell."

"In a hand basket?" another voice said with a laugh.

"He can have my casket," a fourth voice suggested.

"He can rot on the beach for all I care," the fifth and final voice said.

Both men turned around slowly. Gilborough knew who was talking, but Donavan was still under the assumption that he was just hearing the voices that seemed to have no source. He was about to be proved wrong one last time.

All five boys were standing on the cross that was hanging from the ceiling behind the alter. The same boy that had shot Jason was holding the gun. Gilborough knew that the gun still had two shots in it. He had to only assume that the boys were holding one shot for him and another for Donavan.

"Who are you?" Donavan asked. Maybe it was the lack of light, or maybe he had repressed everything from his memory. He really couldn't remember the boy's faces.

"Who am I?" One of the boys asked. He jumped from the cross, flew through the air, and landed on the alter. "You really don't remember who I am?" The boy asked.

Another boy shouted, "Come on Zach, show him."

That's his name, Donavan remembered; Zach. The boy holding the gun was named Rob. Two of the other boys were Tony and Mike. The fifth boy's name was Danny.

Zach spun around quickly and lowered his pants to moon both Donavan and Gilborough. "You remember this?" Zach asked.

He turned around again while pulling his pants up. "You remember giving me your love?"

Donavan's face turned white. This couldn't be happening. It couldn't be real. As Donavan came to grips with the situation he was being faced with, the four boys standing on the cross leaped off. Danny and Mike landed on the left side of the cathedral. Tony landed on the alter next to Zach. Rob, the boy holding the gun, landed on the ground in front of the alter; only ten feet away from Gilborough and Donavan.

"You really don't remember us?" Rob asked. He held the gun by his side as if he had forgotten it was even there. Gilborough's eyes never left that gun. He knew they had every intention of using it.

"No, I remember," Donavan said, though his voice cracked on every syllable.

"Do you remember everything?" Danny asked as he and Mike approached from the left side of the cathedral.

Donavan paused. He remembered, but was too ashamed to talk about it. It took him a few moments of reflection to finally admit, "Yes. I remember everything."

Tony jumped from the alter to the edge of the balcony that looked out over all the rows of pews. He seemed to balance perfectly on the edge as he looked down at Donavan. The tone in his voice was almost festive-like as he asked, "So you know why we're here?"

"I have a good idea," Donavan said.

"Well come on, let's hear it," Mike said as he and Danny took a few steps in Donavan and Gilborough's direction.

"What do you want to hear?" Donavan asked. He took a mere half a step back, wanting to put as much distance between himself and the boys as possible.

"I wanna know why you killed me, you evil bastard!" Zach shouted as he held out his hands for effect.

"Come on, confession is good for the soul," Rob said as he looked downward. He smiled when he glanced at the gun. That smile sent a bolt of fear racing down Gilborough's spine.

"You should know this better than anyone," Danny said.

"I didn't want to," Donavan said in a whisper.

Gilborough's jaw nearly dropped. He looked at Donavan while asking, "You killed them?"

"No," Donavan said at first.

Zach reached behind his back. In one motion, he pulled out a six inch long knife and threw it at Donavan. "You lying bastard!" Zach shouted as the knife flew through the air.

Donavan never had a chance to react. The blade flew into his right shoulder, causing Donavan to spin around and fall backwards. He landed on his knees, and used his left hand to keep from falling down all the way. It didn't hurt as much as he would have thought, but the pain was still there. He winced and grimaced, but never felt the need to scream out.

While Donavan tried to find the strength to stand up again, Gilborough decided to take matters into his own hand. He reached for his holster and pulled out his second gun, hoping it would have some effect.

"That will be enough," Gilborough said.

Rob's face lit up with a bright smile. He tugged his right shoulder and lifted his own gun up while saying, "And what are you going to do detective?"

"How do you kill what's already dead," Zach asked while jumping down from the alter and landing next to Rob.

Tony added, "You can't stop us."

"It's almost over anyway," Mike said. The frequency with which the boys kept saying that sent a shiver down Gilborough's spine.

"You still don't get it, do you?" Danny asked.

"You died. It's over. The people responsible have been dealt with. What else is to get?" Gilborough asked.

"You stupid bastard," Zach shouted.

"I'm dead. That evil pervert had me killed," Zach pointed at Donavan for effect. He took several steps forward as he went on to add, "He got his twisted little pleasures."

"What did I get?" Tony asked.

"I never got to date a pretty girl," Mike added.

Danny drove the point home when he said, "I never got to know pleasure."

"Not until now," Rob said while pointing his gun at Gilborough.

"So you only get pleasure from revenge?"

"When you're dead, it's all you have," Tony said dismissively.

"Come on Rob, put the bastard down," Mike said as he took a couple of steps towards Rob.

"Rob took careful aim at Donavan who was barely standing. He was holding his right shoulder with his left hand and hunching over a little from the pain. Gilborough aimed his own gun at Rob. "You don't want to do this," Gilborough said.

"Someone has to do something," Danny said.

"You sure as hell didn't do anything," Mike commented.

Tony went on to add, "You're still not doing anything. He's right there. He abused five kids. As soon as he thought they might say something, he had Jolston kill them."

"What are you going to do?" Zach asked.

"I'll arrest him, and lock him away forever," Gilborough began. He paused to look down at Donavan before saying, "I'm sure he will confess fully. We won't even need a trial."

"Not good enough," Rob said while taking a step forward and pulling the hammer back on the gun.

"The days of getting to just confess, and move on are over," Mike said with a voice so smooth, it sent a chill down Gilborough's spine.

"Come on Rob, do it" Tony said.

"Show them what real penance is," Zach added.

"No! Don't do it!" Gilborough shouted. He knew it was too late. Instincts took over and Gilborough dove to push Donavan out of the way.

Rob let loose a single shot, and half a second later, so did Gilborough. The bullet would have gotten Donavan in the center of the chest if Gilborough hadn't reacted as fast as he had. Instead, the bullet ended up in Gilborough's knee. The shot that Gilborough fired went nowhere.

It flew out of the barrel of his gun, and quickly slowed down as it approached Rob. The young boy was actually able to reach out and grab the bullet in mid air. Gilborough had to fight an intense series of pains to stand up.

As he rose to his feet, he found that he was surrounded by all five boys. They were perched on the backs of the pews like birds waiting to soar down on their prey. He looked over his right shoulder, and saw Donavan trying to climb to his feet. Frantically, Gilborough looked around for his gun, but couldn't find it.

"Searching for this?" Zach asked as he held out Gilborough's second gun.

"I wonder if it's loaded," Danny observed.

Zach drew a large smile on his face as he used a single motion to point the gun at Donavan and fire a single shot. The bullet flew into Donavan's leg, sending the priest back to his knees again.

"Yep, it's loaded," Zach said as he glanced at Danny.

"Then let's do this," Tony shouted. He jumped off the back of the pew and flew through the air, landing gracefully behind Donavan. He grabbed Donavan by the back of the neck and lifted him into the air.

Danny and Mike followed suite and grabbed Donavan by the arms. Together, they lifted Donavan fifteen feet into the air. Donavan screamed for mercy, "This is God's house!"

"We're just cleaning it up for him," Mike whispered into Donavan's ear.

"Do it!" Danny shouted.

Zach lifted the gun upwards and fired the remaining bullets into the body of Donavan. All Gilborough could do was watch, and pray they didn't save any bullets for him. When Zach fired the gun a last time and it only clicked, Gilborough felt a moment of relief. He knew then that it was over. He looked up and watched as Danny, Mike, and Tony let go of Donavan's limp body. He crashed to the ground and shattered a single row of pews in half.

"Oh detective," Rob said.

"What?" Gilborough asked. He kept holding his knee which was throbbing with intense pain. He looked over at Rob who was pointing Gilborough's first gun directly at him.

"I still have one bullet left," Rob said.

"It's over," Gilborough said as he stared at Rob.

"Not yet," Rob replied.

"Almost," Mike said while landing on the ground behind Gilborough.

"But, not yet," Danny said.

"One lesson left," tony added.

Zach threw his gun to the side as he walked over towards Gilborough. He looked up at the detective and asked, "Do you get it now? Do you understand why we did what we did?"

"I think so," Gilborough said through the pain.

"Ohhhh, 'think' isn't good enough," Zach said. He looked over his shoulder at Rob who pulled the hammer back on the gun.

"Okay. I get it. You're angry that I didn't arrest Donavan to begin with," Gilborough said.

"Good answer," Rob said as he lowered the hammer on the gun again.

"Now tell me detective," tony began.

"How many other guilty people have you ignored?" Mike added.

"How many innocent people have you wasted time with?" Danny finished.

Gilborough thought for a second. Slowly, and with measured words, he said, "I don't know."

"Good answer," Rob said. He lowered the gun by his side.

The five boys grew together as a group in front of Gilborough. Zach stared at Gilborough while saying, "You could have prevented this."

"You would still be dead," Gilborough observed.

Rob's face grew very reflective, "The only thing worse than death..."

His thoughts were finished by Mike, "Is knowing that the person who killed you is still out there."

"Worse than that," Tony observed.

"Is knowing that he's making other people feel good about doing bad things," Danny added.

Rob brought the thoughts to an end, "It breeds an evil cycle."

"And the cycle just ended?" Gilborough asked.

Rob glanced over at Donavan's dead body. He then turned back to Gilborough and said only, "yes."

With that, the five boys turned and walked away. They stopped at the door to the cathedral. Rob turned again to Gilborough and raised the gun. He smiled as he said, "And remember, I still have one bullet left."

COLLECTED

and now it's here
and you are asked
just what have you collected

with a bundle of time
and bottle of wine
just what have you collected

tell me what have you collected
what is it that you take with you
when you cross into the next life

what have you learned
and what have you earned
and what all have you collected

and now time's due
and your life is through
just what have you collected

so you got your toys
conquered girls or boys
but from this what have you collected

you have memories
hot dark wet dreams
and from this what have you collected

pictures taken
promises broken
which of these have you collected

tell me what have you collected
what is it that you take with you
when you cross into the next life

what have you learned
and what have you earned
and what all have you collected

WAVES OF LIFE

Golden. That was the only word to describe it. Not red, not orange, and not yellow, though these colors were present. They blended together into something else. The sun rays were scattered low across the horizon and gave the drink Tequila Sunrise its name.

He stood on the pier and spent a full hour watching the sun rise. It had a cleansing affect on him. The pure sun, the fresh air, and the wide open sea came together and freed his mind from the bonds of day to day life. Just a half a day earlier, he had felt completely trapped in his office on the fifteenth floor of a downtown Houston skyscraper. From his window, he could look out over the entire city, but still felt trapped in a room measuring twenty foot by twenty foot.

Now, he could not only look out over the wide ocean, but he could see the entire world ahead of him. It was all there for him; no bindings, no restraints. He was only limited by human desire.

"This is what God intended," Gary thought to himself, "He gave us this beautiful world, and left it for us to enjoy."

The entire meaning of life stared at him through the sunrise. He would quit his job on Monday and live life in the sun if only he felt that such dreams could be real. The irony was that his job had allowed him the luxury of being there that morning. Being the chief financial officer of a mid sized oil company had given him the salary that let him buy a small boat. This job had also grounded him in a reality without dreams, and confined him to that office.

This was his newest hobby. After forty-three years, he had done everything from collecting coins, to deer hunting. Gary had skied across a lake, and down three mountains. Once he had hiked the Grand Canyon, and twice he had taken up golf. His last hobby had been fly fishing which led to deep sea fishing. That had led to his purchase of a boat six months ago.

This had been his most expensive hobby so far. After doing all the research, as he was prone to do, he finally settled on a twenty footer with an on board motor. Secretly, he called it his yacht. Though it fell far short of being a real yacht, it was a monster of a boat for just one person. He had been out in his boat four times now. Each time, he had ventured further and further from land, and had stayed out longer.

His last trip took him a full five miles out. He had gotten so lost in time that he didn't make it back to shore until after dusk. He couldn't get over how peaceful the sea was at night. It was almost as if the moon sang a quiet song to the water below, calming the ocean and sending it to sleep. His current venture out was going to be an over night stay. He had packed a cooler full of water and soft drinks along with all kinds of sandwiches to last him for a sleep over with the sea.

Once the sunrise fully gave way to the daylight, Gary decided it was time to set off. He loaded his cooler, a pillow, and a blanket in the boat. He also took a fishing pole and two books, just in case he actually got bored. Maybe he'd spend the day reading, maybe he'd try to catch something from the water below. Maybe, he'd do nothing. For the first time in his life, he really didn't have a plan. He didn't even want one. All he wanted to do, was escape.

Two hours later, he was almost completely out of sight from land. He could see a brown strip of Galveston beach stretched across part of the horizon behind him. To his left, he could see two oil rigs in the far distance. There were a few other specs on the water that he assumed were boats, but they were so far away, he couldn't tell. He liked it that way.

Straight ahead of him, he could see two blues blending together to make a horizon between the water and the sky. They came together in a grayish color. He looked at the horizon like it was a great curtain that was hiding something, and he could only wonder what it was.

The engine on his boat had long been turned off, and he was left drifting where ever the waves took him. He was laying down on the front of his boat with a book. He had started it three times, but kept putting it down. He couldn't stop staring at the horizon in the distance and wondering what lay out there. He actually went so far as to ponder filling his boat with tanks of gas and venturing all the way out to the gray horizon.

The idea made him laugh. He knew it would be like chasing the gold under a rainbow. No matter how much gas he had in his boat, or how fast he went, the horizon would always be ahead of him. It was like a carrot hanging in front of a donkey that kept him going. The only difference was that Gary knew the carrot would keep moving. That kept him where he was, happily afloat without a worry in sight.

The surprising part for him was that he had even made it that far out. Gary had never been a huge romantic or dreamer. He had climbed the corporate ladder by always focusing on the goal in front of himself. If it wasn't real, or wasn't achievable, he didn't bother. Yet there he was, pondering what secret dreams the unknown sea held.

A mere twenty minutes later, Gary was faced with what could only be called irony. It seemed as though the dream was chasing him. The horizon that he thought was gray because of the blues of the sky and water blending together was slowly growing into a line of clouds that were getting both closer and darker. That's when it hit him. In his exuberance to get to the sea, he had forgotten to check the weather. The man that had planned every detail of his entire life had overlooked this critical bit of information.

He again looked around and noticed how alone he was out on the sea. Apparently, this was because he was the only person who didn't know about the tropical storm that was supposed to roll on shore that day. It was quickly dismissed as nothing more than a ruined weekend. Gary gathered up his towel and soft drink from the front of the boat. By the time he started up the motor, the gray clouds had taken over more than half of the sky, and the first few drops of rain fell on his face.

Like most tropical storms, they come out of nowhere, and strike with lightening speed. This was to be no exception. Twenty minutes into his trek towards shore, Gary was in the middle of a full storm. The rain was the least of his worries. The wind was a distant second. The waves had gone from one foot, to more than eight feet. A larger boat would have had no problem with this, but his twenty footer had gone air-born twice as the sea sank from below him. The third time would prove to be the worst.

He cleared the top of a wave and was dropping to the ocean when a gust of wind blew him sideways. When the boat hit the water, the nose went in the side of a wave which yanked the boat to the side. This ultimately flipped his small craft forward, sending the tail over the nose, and ejecting Gary from his beloved boat.

He hit the water fast and hard. The shock of everything left him instantly confused. His face was burning from the impact with the water. As soon as he managed to get his head above water, a nine foot wave came crashing down on him.

Again, he came to the surface and tried to get his bearings. He could see his boat floating upside down about thirty feet away. Between him and his boat was the life jacket that he had delayed putting on.

He managed to ride the next wave as he bobbed high into the air before sinking down again as if he were on a roller coaster. He could feel the weight of his khaki shorts and polo shirt becoming totally absorbed with water. It only added to the sinking feeling from the next wave collapsing on top of him.

He didn't know how far underwater he was, and he wasn't even sure which way he had to swim to get to the surface. The moving water sent him bouncing around beneath the waves. As the seconds ticked away, so too did his air supply. The burning sensation in his lungs was a sharp contrast to the cold water surrounding him. The only thing he knew was that he needed air, and that meant finding his way to the surface.

Gary kicked hard with his legs while simultaneously grasping at the water with his arms. He extended his left hand upwards while kicking; trying to grab at the surface of the ocean. That's when he felt something. He clinched a fist with his fingers and grabbed what felt like another hand.

Five fingers wrapped a tight grip around his wrist and gave his entire body a good yank, pulling him towards the surface. As the hand pulled him, he used his feet to give one last kick. He broke the surface of the water with a violent lunge. His entire body cleared the water line and his mouth opened wide, trying to take in as much air as possible.

When he fell to the water, he landed on his back. Gary tried to stay afloat as he took three more deep and refreshing breaths of air. Everything was suddenly at peace in his life as he realized just how close he had come to death. To his dismay, everything was also at peace with his surroundings. He slowly opened his eyes and saw the sun glaring down brightly on his face. He could feel the warmth. More importantly, he could not feel the wind or the rain that had nearly taken his life. There was only the sun and a clear blue sky.

He turned his head slowly, trying to take in everything around him. That's when he saw the man who had apparently saved his life. The man looked to be in his forties, though Gary could tell nothing more than that. He had long black hair that was graying with age. It was tied back in a pony tail that hung over his shoulder. His face was hidden behind a ragged beard. The only thing Gary could see behind the beard were a pair of heavy eyes.

The man was leaning over the edge of a small wooden boat with a paddle fastened to each side. The boat measured about twelve feet long and had at one time been painted white, though only remnants of that paint still remained. He reached out again and grabbed Gary by the shoulder. With one strong yank, the man pulled Gary out of the water, and half way into the boat. Gary kicked with his legs and grabbed with his hands to pull himself the rest of the way into the boat. Gary got some help from the man who grabbed Gary from behind and gave him another good yank. The man's strength flipped Gary over. He landed dazed and confused on his shoulder.

Gary rolled over in the small boat and grabbed his shoulder which he knew he had bruised by landing on it. He slowly sat up as he looked around at his surroundings. He was awestruck over the sudden absence of the storm. The light from the sun was actually rather blinding, and caused Gary to squint his eyes as he looked around in a full circle. Behind him, he could see another, larger, wooden boat. This boat was at least four hundred yards away, but Gary could tell that it was a sail boat.

He turned around again to look at the man who had just saved his life. "Thanks," Gary said while extending his right hand.

The handshake that Gary was hoping for never materialized. Instead, the man took a more hostile approach towards Gary's show of gratitude. The man swatted Gary's hand away with a force equal to what he had used to yank Gary into the boat. The man then reached to his side and produced a gun which he pointed at Gary's chest. The gun appeared to be an antique. It had a flint lock firing mechanism like that of a musket from more than a hundred years ago.

"Hey, sorry," Gary said, "Just being appreciative."

The man waved his gun at Gary while saying something that Gary didn't understand. Gary leaned his head towards the man and tried to listen to the words, though their meaning escaped him. From the way the man waved his gun, Gary could only assume that the man wanted him to scoot back. Gary did just that. He pushed back with his feet until he was sitting on the other side of the small boat.

Only when Gary was as far away as he could get did the man lower his gun and tuck it in his belt on his side. That's when Gary took full notice of the man's attire. His pants were loose fitting and black, though very dirty and with more than one minor rip. His shirt was bright red and also loose fitting, though with just as many nicks and tears as his pants. Around his waist, he wore a wide brown leather belt. It was inside of this belt that the man tucked his gun. On the other side of his belt, the man had a long knife tucked away.

The man looked around for a moment, as if he were attempting to find his bearing. He looked over Gary's shoulder before nodding his head in Gary's direction. Again, he said something that Gary couldn't understand. It sounded like Spanish, though not exactly.

"I don't understand you," Gary said with a shrug of his shoulders.

The man grabbed the handle to one of the paddles, and pushed it in Gary's direction. He spoke again, this time with a clear tone of anger in his inflection. The man pulled out his gun, pointed it at Gary, then waved it above Gary's head. At the same time, the man grabbed the handle to the other paddle and pushed it in Gary's direction. Gary glanced over his shoulder and noticed the large sail boat in the distance. He looked back at the man who continued to wave the gun over Gary's head, apparently pointing towards the larger ship.

With slow motions, Gary placed each hand on one of the paddles. The man lowered his gun, and Gary assumed that it was his job to row the small boat towards the larger ship. It didn't seem that hard at first. The waves were calm, and the boat was not that heavy. However, as the minutes quickly passed by, Gary could feel his arms burning from the strain. The ship didn't look that far away, but that was only one of the illusions of the ocean. The flat surface always made objects appear within an arms reach, even when they were miles in the distance.

Gary paused for a bare moment to rest his arms. No sooner had he removed his hands from the ores, than the man raised his gun again and yelled something that Gary didn't understand.

"All right, all right," Gary said, "Give it a break."

Gary went back to paddling the small boat, and in twenty minutes that passed like twenty hours, they were coming upon the ship. Gary was awestruck. The ship look as if it had been ripped from the pages of a history book. It was solid wood and measured over a hundred feet long. There were two large masts towards the center of the ship with several smaller ones on each end. At six points along the side of the ship there were cannons. They were real cannons. Gary couldn't believe it.

His attention was distracted by the man who yelled something at him. Gary turned his head and saw the man pointing with his gun again. When Gary looked at where the gun was pointing, he saw a rope ladder being dropped from the side of the ship. Gary looked up and noticed three men standing at the top of the ship. He couldn't tell much about their details because the sun was directly behind them.

With a little work, and a lot of yelling from the man in the boat, Gary managed to position the small row boat directly below the rope ladder. The man fastened the rowboat to the larger ship with a rope. Once the rope was fastened, the man waved his gun towards the rope ladder. He again yelled something that Gary couldn't understand. The message was clear enough, and with wobbly legs, Gary stood up in the boat.

Somehow, he managed to grab a hold of the bottom rung of the ladder on his first attempt. This was no small feat considering how the waves kept raising and lowering the boat he was standing on. Once he had a grip on the ladder, he faced the daunting task of trying to climb this ladder. The hard part was really just getting past the first several rungs and finding a place to use his legs. It was a test for his arms which were already tired and worn from the rowing. However, with the motivation of a man standing below and yelling while simultaneously waving a gun at him, Gary made short work of it.

By the time he made it to the top, Gary was perhaps as exhausted as he had been in years. He spent sixty hours a week working in an office. He wasn't used to such physical exertion, and it showed in his face. As soon as his hand grabbed the top rung, one of the men on the deck of the ship grabbed Gary by the back of his shoulder.

With a single heave, the man pulled Gary from the ladder and onto the deck of the ship. This man looked similar to the man in the rowboat—only thinner and a bit younger. There were two other men beside him, one was blond with shoulder length hair.

The third man had long black hair that was more neatly combed than the rest of the men. His beard was trimmed and groomed, and his clothes were in far better condition than the rest of the men. He was obviously the leader of the group; a point driven home by his dress, as well as his mannerisms. He stood back and calmly directed the other two men on the deck. Where everyone else felt compelled to yell and scream, this man spoke with a softer tone.

The leader looked down at Gary and said something while pointing off to his left. As soon as the leader spoke, the two other men picked Gary up by his arms and began dragging him across the deck of the ship. At that moment, Gary didn't know what bothered him more—being yanked and dragged around, or just not being able to understand what everyone around him was saying. Maybe if they could just communicate, then he could talk them into treating him better.

The two men dragged Gary fifteen feet across the deck towards one of the main mast. "Come on guys, please let me go," Gary pleaded.

However, his pleads were met only with a stronger pull as the two men launched him towards the mast. Gary landed on his stomach only inches away from the mast. He could see the hands of another man tied to the other side of the mast. Before Gary could even react, one of the men grabbed him by both hands and yanked him up. The other man picked up a piece of rope and threw it around the large mast.

Together, the two men tied Gary's hands behind the pole. They ran a second piece of rope around the pole and across Gary's chest, just to make sure he couldn't move. They walked away and left him sitting there, tied to the pole of a ship old enough to have have participated in the Revolutionary War.

The two men walked towards the leader and the man who had plucked Gary out of the water. The four men glanced at Gary. They all produced smiles that seemed anything but friendly. Gary lowered his head and wondered when he would wake up from this dream. It had to be a dream. It would explain everything except for one small detail. Nobody ever assumes a dream is, indeed, a dream.

Gary watched the four men walk towards the other end of the ship. There was an eerie kind of silence that slowly crept into Gary's mind. He could hear the steps of the boots from the men, though that sound faded as they distanced themselves. He could also hear the sounds of the sea, though that was only in the distance. He was after all, a good thirty feet above the water, and near the center of the boat. The water broke softly against the side of the ship, though Gary could only hear the occasional large wave. There were seagulls in the distance, and an odd one here and there would drift close enough to offer Gary a single squawk.

Gary didn't know how long he had been sitting there when the silence was broken. It seemed like an hour, though it could have been as little as ten minutes. When the silence was broken, it wasn't by some strange sound that would have fit perfectly with the surroundings. Instead, it was a simple voice.

"Not too nice are they?" The voice asked. There was a touch of laughter to the heavily accented voice. It came from whoever was tied to the other side of the pole.

"Excuse me?" Gary asked.

"Those gents could use a lesson in manners, wouldn't you say?" The voice, clearly English, said.

"I'm sure you'll be successful in teaching them," Gary replied, making a sarcastic remark about their current situation. It was obvious that being tied down didn't put someone in a position of teaching anyone a lesson.

"You never know, I just might," The other man said with a hint of laughter in his voice. There was a pause, and any hints of humor faded from his voice as he added, "Someone here needs to be taught a lesson."

"Whatever," Gary dismissed, still trying to figure out when he would wake up and realize that this was all a bad dream.

"Whatever indeed," The man said in a voice that trailed off into little more than a whisper.

Several long minutes passed without a word being said. Occasionally, one of the men from the ship would pass by. A few would look down at Gary, most wouldn't. No one said a word to him. Something in Gary wanted one of them to talk to him; to say he was free to go, or tell him everything would be all right. Another side of Gary was afraid they'd say something; who knew what fate they had in store for him?

Not long after arriving on the mysterious ship, Gary watched as the men began to move rapidly around the ship. The sails were raised on the mast, and the men all worked together to pull in the long and heavy ropes attached to the two anchors.

"What's going on?" Gary asked, mostly to himself, though he was hoping the man on the other side of the pole might have an answer.

"They got what they want, mate," The man said, "they are sailing for home."

"Where is home?" Gary asked.

"Barcelona."

"Barcelona?" Gary asked with a clear tone of confusion in his voice. A nearby man on the deck turned to look at Gary upon hearing the city's name. Gary quickly looked away, and the man went back to pulling on a rope that raised a sail on the mast.

"Yes sir, you and I are guest of the Spanish crown."

"You've got to be kidding."

"Nothing to joke about in these waters, mate," The man said.

Gary let a moment pass before asking, "So why are you here?"

"Surely the same reason as you," came the reply with the usual bit of laughter.

"I doubt that," Gary replied with a long sigh. He really had no idea why he was there, or even how he had gotten there.

"Come, come now," The man said, "you're a thief the same as I, and you'll hang for it the same as I."

"A thief?"

"Aye, a bloody no good pirate. A scourge of these here parts," The man said with an even deeper laugh.

"You have no idea who I am, or what I've done," Gary insisted. He went on to add, "But I am certainly no pirate."

"Nay mate. You might not ride head long into the wind with cannons a blazzin', and you might not even know what it's like to swing from one ship to another with a knife in your teeth," The man paused and allowed himself a slight chuckle, "But that don't mean you've never run off with gold that ain't your own. Nor does it mean that you never caused another man's fate to be lowered like a ship falling beneath the view of them there waves."

Gary listened to the man, wondering who he thought Gary was. The entire story was too surreal. Here he was in a situation that Gary was so far from understanding. The more he thought about what the man had said, the more nervous Gary got. He couldn't help but wonder what the man was ready to accuse him of. Even more than that, he had to wonder who the men on the ship thought Gary was, not to mention what they were ready to accuse him of. A kind of nervous paranoia fell over Gary.

He didn't say anything else to the man, and the man said nothing else to Gary. He watched as the hints of land disappeared into the distance until it was only water that he could see in every direction. Gary kept his mind busy by watching all the men on the deck of the ship. He couldn't help but get nervous every time one of them would come near him.

The sun made a slow descent across the sky until there was the orange glow of the dusk sun bouncing off the clouds in the distance. It wasn't until then that Gary began to feel hungry. His twist of fate had left him so nervous that he had forgotten about such needs. Gary's hunger suddenly faded when he saw the man assumed to be the captain along with two other men approach him. They stopped by the large mast and talked among themselves.

They carried on a five minute conversation while occasionally looking at Gary, pointing in various directions, and looking around the ship. Gary knew he was a topic in the conversation, though he had no idea to what degree. Eventually, the three men moved to the other side of the pole and continued the conversation while looking at the other man.

Their conversation extended another ten minutes before the three men wandered off. Again, there was silence that was anything but peaceful for Gary. As much as he wanted to be out of his current situation, Gary would have settled for knowing what the men had been talking about. It was hard enough to not be in control of his fate, it was even harder to not know what that fate was.

"Do you know what they were talking about?" Gary finally asked of the man tied to the other side of the pole.

"Yes," The man said with less of a festive tone in his voice than earlier. He didn't elaborate any, and let the silence speak for him. Obviously it wasn't good.

Gary let a few minutes pass before gathering the strength to ask, "What were they saying?"

The man spoke slowly as he said, "Don't ask questions, the answers to which you don't want."

"I need to know something," Gary said, almost pleading.

"Very well then," the man said, "We are to be hung under the full moon."

The severity of the statement didn't strike Gary as much as the confusion of it all. "I thought we were going to Barcelona?" Gary asked.

"They changed their minds. Seems as though we are dead weight. Plus they are running low on food; dead men need not eat."

"I still don't get it. Don't they know I haven't done anything?"

"Come now Gary, you know what you've done," the man said.

Gary was immediately confused as he whispered his own name "Gary?"

He turned his head to try and look around the pole, "How do you my name?"

"The whole world knows your name. At least they will," The man said with a laugh. Before Gary could say a thing, the man went on to add, "The whole world hates you, and they can't wait to see you hang."

The man paused and chuckled briefly before adding, "Some say hanging is too good for you."

A cold chill ran down Gary's spine. He had to admit he might not have been the best person in the world, but no one hated him. In fact he was rather proud of the fact that most people who knew him seemed to like and even admire him. It really wasn't arrogance on his part. He couldn't remember the last time someone had made a negative comment about him; at least not that he knew of.

Sitting there and listening to this, Gary couldn't help but wonder who these people thought he was. He decided to press the matter a little by asking, "So can you tell me exactly what I have done?"

"Nothing that I haven't done," The man said casually.

"That's vague," Gary insisted, "Give me specifics."

"You want specifics boy?" the voice asked, "You want me to name all the lives you have ruined? All the people who's homes you've all but burned down and taken away? I can't name all the elders who lost their very nest egg to your ego."

"The names go on and on," the voice said.

"You don't even know who I am," Gary said with a clear voice of frustration.

"Don't I?" the voice asked, "Think hard boy. Remember all that treasure you hid, all that gold you moved around?"

"I've never taken treasure. I've never even seen treasure," Gary insisted.

"Then why are you here?" the man asked with a chuckle.

"I don't know, but I never took any treasure or any gold," Gary insisted again.

"Oh you didn't take it all of course. You left a little. You stacked it just the right way so it would look like it was all still there," The man laughed, "But it wasn't all there, was it?"

"I told you once, and I'll tell you again that I never took anything," Gary said, though his voice cracked on his words.

"We'll these guys are sure you did. So I guess it's them that you'll have to convince."

"You seem even more ready to convict me than they are," Gary said.

"I just hate to see a guilty man profess his innocence. If you've done something, then be proud of it at least. If you have to lie about your actions, then were they ever worth acting?"

"What about you? Why are you here?"

"I already told you. I'm a thief, a bloody pirate. They know it, and I know it."

"And it doesn't bother you to know that they want to hang you?" Gary asked.

"Of course it bothers me, but at least I know why I'm being hanged," The man said, not hiding any pride about what he might have done.

The conversation fell silent from there. The sun finished its descent which gave way to the darkness of night. Slowly a full moon began to rise over the horizon. It wasn't like most full moons that Gary had seen. It was larger and brighter than any he had remembered, although he had to admit that he'd spent little time in his life ever studying the moon. There appeared to be a halo around the moon with a light so bright that the stars seemed faint.

He kept closing his eyes, telling himself that it wasn't real. Every time he would open his eyes again, the moon would stare down at him even brighter than just moments ago. It was very real. He thought about saying a prayer to ask for a way out, but he opted against it. He had never been much of a church goer, and felt embarrassed to suddenly call out for help from a God he never knew.

Just as he felt his hunger return again, he saw the captain of the ship along with five men walking towards him. His hunger immediately went away. They gathered around the pole and talked amongst themselves for several minutes. The captain leaned in and looked Gary square in the face while saying something to one of the men behind him.

"What did he say?" Gary asked of the man on the other side of the pole.

"He wants to make sure they have the right person."

"They don't, tell them they don't," Gary pleaded.

"Save it boy," The man laughed, "I done made peace with my evils. I suggest you do the same."

The captain motioned towards Gary and the other man. Two of the captain's men moved towards the pole. They first untied the man behind Gary. They stood him up and kept him facing towards the back of the ship. The men then untied Gary and stood him behind Gary's would be companion.

"This can't be happening," Gary said with a pleading voice.

"But it is," The man said.

"It just can't," Gary insisted as he was pushed from the back, indicating he should move forward. The man in front of him started walking, and Gary followed suite. The man was dressed similarly to the other men on the ship. His hair was short like Gary's, though nothing of his face could be seen.

They walked slowly towards the back of the ship. Gary could see a larger group of about twenty men standing near the back of the ship. There was also a rope hanging from one of the smaller mast on the very back of the ship. Beneath the rope were several small crates. When they got to within twelve feet of the rope, one of the men put his hand on Gary's chest, indicating he should stop walking.

"Oh my god," Gary exclaimed, "They really want to hang us."

"Tis a lynching indeed; right and proper to tell the truth," the man said.

"I still don't see how you can be so calm about this," Gary said with a nervous voice.

"I know what I did. I know I deserve worse," the man said.

"But I didn't do anything, I swear," Gary insisted for the third or thirtieth time that night. He would proclaim it a thousand times if he thought it would help.

"You just keep telling yourself that. But, I'd recommend you come to terms with your evil," the man replied.

One of the deck hands pushed on the back of the man in front of Gary. The man took a few steps forward, but then paused all the sudden.

"It's been a pleasure knowing you Gary," The man began. He slowly turned around to let the moonlight reveal his face to Gary as he said, "What ever you walk away with from this place tonight, understand one thing. Confession is good for the soul."

When the light fully illuminated the man's face, Gary was left in total shock. It was like staring into a mirror. The man looked identical to Gary, right down to the small mole high up on the left cheek.

"It can't be," Gary said as he looked into the man's eyes.

"It be mate. And all things being equal, I'd rather be me than you," the man said. He winked once at Gary and added, "At least I know the evil that I've done."

Gary's knees became weak, and he nearly fell to the ground. One of the men next to him had to grab a hold of him by the shoulder to keep him on his feet. "This can't be real," Gary murmured to himself.

"You'd better hope it's real," Gary's would-be twin said as he was guided towards the stack of crates beneath the rope. The man took a step up on one of the crates before pausing to look at Gary. He smiled, and there was a small flash in his eyes as he said, "The alternative you are about to face could be much worse. It would be better to be hung quietly on the back of a ship, than in full view of the entire world."

With that, he turned around and climbed atop two more crates. The captain climbed behind him and put the rope around the man's neck. The captain then climbed back down the crates and gave a long speech that Gary didn't understand. The Captain repeatedly pointed towards Gary and his would be twin while talking. More than once, Gary could hear the man's voice rise to the point of near shouting. After giving his speech for several minutes, the captain looked up at the man and seemed to ask a question. The man turned to look at Gary, and smiled. He then turned back to the captain and nodded his head.

With that, the captain gave the crates a firm kick and they flew out from under the man's feet. He dropped like a rock, and the rope pulled tight on the man's neck. His body fell limp, and his eyes closed instantly. The deck hands around Gary moved closer to get a good look at the man's dead body.

Gary panicked. He just wanted to enjoy a day out on the ocean away from everyone. He wasn't trying to run away for good, just for a day. He certainly wasn't out to get hung for something he was sure he didn't do. That's when Gary looked down and realized that he wasn't bound in any way. The closest person to him was five feet away. He slowly turned his head around, and saw no one behind him. A way out was forming for him. It was far from perfect, but it beat hanging from the end of a rope.

Gary took one more look at the man hanging from the end of the rope. He swore it could have been his twin brother, or even Gary himself for that matter. The only thing Gary knew was that he didn't want to end up like that. In a second, he took off racing towards the other end of the ship. Within the first few steps, Gary could hear the captain yell something. A second later, every man on the ship was chasing after Gary. He could hear their heavy footsteps pounding the wooden deck of the ship. He had no illusions of out running them. These were hardy sailors, and it was, after all, a boat.

Half way down the ship, Gary veered off to the left side of the ship. He ran towards the ledge and jumped up to the railing. Gary never looked back as he dove over the side of the ship. His plan was to hit the water and keep swimming until he found shore somewhere. What Gary hadn't factored into his escape plan was the fact that the ship's deck sat thirty feet above the waterline. He hit the water like a brick. He felt a tingle in his neck, and for a second he lost consciousness.

As soon as he opened his eyes, Gary felt his air supply escaping him. He made a frantic push towards the surface. Within a few feet of reaching the surface, Gary felt a hand grab a hold of his wrist. There was panic as Gary remembered only hours earlier what had happened when someone tried to pull him out of the water. Gary pulled hard and broke the grasp. He then gave the water a good kick as he pushed for the surface.

Fear and instinct took over for Gary who breached the surface. He allowed himself to take a single deep breath before submerging below the water again. He was determined to keep fighting his way through the water, and away from his captors. As soon as he fell below the surface, the hand grabbed a hold of him by the collar and yanked him above the water.

"Calm down and get over here," A voice shouted to him.

Gary wasn't about to calm down. He only had escape on his mind. He was so focused on getting away that he didn't even realize that the voice was an English one. He pulled hard, but who ever had a grasp on him pulled even harder.

"Stop kicking already," the voice insisted.

It was only then that Gary realized that it wasn't one of the men on the ship after him. He stopped kicking and allowed the man to pull him through the water. When Gary turned around, he was greeted by a man in a bright orange jump suite. He was in a small rubber raft with a larger Coast Guard cutter behind him. Something told Gary that he was safe. Perhaps what comforted Gary the most was the rain. It was pouring down, and that meant he was back in a world that made at least a little sense.

Gary completely relaxed, and allowed himself to be pulled into the rubber raft. Once inside, the coast guard officer started the small outboard motor on the raft, and headed back towards the cutter. Five minutes later, Gary was sitting in the cabin of the cutter with a towel wrapped around himself.

"Your lucky to be alive," A medic said as he walked into the room.

"You have no idea," Gary said with a deep reflective sigh.

"Didn't you know there was a storm coming in today?" The medic asked. He pulled out a thermometer and placed it under Gary's tongue.

"Nope. It wasn't in the news," Gary mumbled with the thermometer in his mouth.

"You've gotta be kidding me," the medic began. He nodded to a folded up newspaper on the other side of the room while adding, "It was a front page story in the paper."

"I guess I missed it," Gary shrugged. At that moment, he could have cared less. He was safe and that was all that mattered to him.

The medic seemed to want to press the matter. He stepped over to the table to pick up the paper. "Here, check it out for yourself," He said while handing the paper to Gary.

Gary opened it up to the front page. Sure enough, there was a story taking up the bottom left eighth of the page. A tropical storm was expected to make landfall that afternoon. Gary shrugged his shoulders again and set the paper down by his side. That's when he noticed the lead story in the paper.

"Leading Oil Company Under Investigation for Shifting Losses," the headline read. The name of Gary's company was the first word under the title. It wasn't until the second paragraph that Gary's name appeared along with the CEO and the president of the company.

"I don't believe it," Gary said while continuing to read.

The medic took a slight interest in Gary's comments, and peeked over at the newspaper as people are prone to do. "Oh yeah, that," The medic said. He pulled out a small light and grabbed Gary by the chin. While using the light to examine Gary's eyes, the medic went on to add, "This city's gonna wanna hang those boys if they end up making out like pirates while thousands of people loose their jobs."

The medic click the light off as he said, "Some say hanging is to good for them."

Not to be

sit in the dark and stare at nothing
burn a match and I light a candle

I have my doubts and I'm not sure this time
don't think it's something I can handle

but it's here and it's there
and it's nothing new to me

and I'm here
and you're there
again, nothing new to me

and we worked
and we failed
I'm so sorry that I didn't try harder

but I know it's just not there

guess I knew it from the start though
but I didn't care, didn't want to know

so tired of being all alone
I was fed up and then so were you

I was here
you were there
only a matter of convenience

then we met
then we fell
I'm so sorry that I did not catch you

but there was no one there to catch me

THREE WORDS

three little words
that's all they are
three little words
fall from a star
three little words
can travel so far
three little words
capture a heart
three little words
never apart
three little words
from my lips flow
I love you
it's not that hard

NEW START

well I still don't know what happened
what could have gone wrong
it seemed fine all along

there was a certain kind of rhythm
it was like a song
we just sang along

I felt a special kind of magic
felt it in my heart
then it fell apart

you never took the time to say goodbye
just drifted apart
to look for a new start

9 1 1

society changed by circumstance
with lives lost in an instant

a flash of light a sonic boom
and our world shatters in glass

we try to watch we close our eyes
we take it in and we deny

there is sadness
and we fall down

and then we cry some more
want to do something

there is anger
call to action

and then we pause ourselves
won't do the wrong thing

resolve to act
but not react

we control
our existence

don't stand alone but stand the same
can't move on our knees

as darkness falls we see the light
tomorrow is a new day

there is sadness
and we fall down

and then we cry some more
want to do something

there is anger
call to action

and then we pause ourselves
won't do the wrong thing

(WTC) What's This Crisis

what life   what loss   what waste

what has come
and from where
where's the voice
does someone care

a mother here
a father there
another body
do they care

what life   what loss   what waste

the sound I heard
the sight not seen
the blood I taste
oh what a scene

the count goes up
still not there
the end's in sight
but who knows where

what life   what loss   what waste

what's the goal
mission please

why the fight
why not peace

to make a change
to state a case
to move a cause
it's still a waste

what life   what loss   what waste

FOUR WINDS

the four winds blow
north east south west

and you prepare
to take that quest

you're not alone
in a corner

look in the air
what do you see

the future there
for you and me

it's a dream
a fantasy

it's the place
you want to see

sneak up on you
from somewhere

but you don't see
and you don't care

the four winds blow
north east south west

and with you
I'll take that quest

SPIDER

8 legs move
dance a groove

through the night
filled with fright

you can't see
and you can't hear

you can't be
this full of fear

but while the moon
comes so soon

so too arrives
the spider lies

it spins a web
upon your soul

will you awake
this you don't know

spin a web
tell a tale

shadow moves
across the floor for you

while you sleep
it will creep

to your bed
then you are dead

WE DANCED

I held her closely
tightly
gently

moved across the floor so gracefully

spun her once
spun her twice

pulled her in
smells so nice

and we danced
like we never danced before

and we danced
moved all across the floor

the tempo pulsated
to it we gyrated

it beat out loud
moved a crowd

we didn't care
we didn't share

it was our dance
we slide through the air

and we danced
like we never danced before

and we danced
moved all across the floor

PASSED

things come so slow
and go so fast
perhaps that's why
we dwell in the past
why look forward
it's all back there
but can't go back
can only stare
at what has been
at what was said
at what we did
and what we had
but pause again
as you will see
the future there
for you and me

WHAT IF

what if I never
said hi again

what if nothing
more could have been

what if you never
said g'nite again

what if we'd both
been sorry then

what if we never
spoke again

CHOOSE

two doors staring right at you
you pause
which will you choose

one door right
one door left
how much money
how much love
will you trade
for the other one

will the one on the left
be your final death
will the one on the right
finally give you the might

toss a penny through a tornado
where it lands
decides where you go

you'd be better off
simply walking off
but when you walk away
you never seize the day

WICKED

I dance
I jump
I scream
I'm wicked
are you afraid
and when I smile
that devious smile
the one that says
I know what you don't know
that's when
I'm being wicked

IN HER LIFE

She's still looking for the reasons
trying to find an answer
to all the questions
in her life

But through all the changing seasons
she can't find the way
just make it day to day
in her life

Not sure what she's supposed to do
maybe no one does
there is no map
in her life

And there's no one there to help her
she's there all alone
she can't find a home
in her life

Sometimes she looks back again
the way it was back then
and she can't lie
about her life

She sometimes gets the feeling
that there might be hope
there is a dream
in her life

THE GARDEN

Take me to the garden
Where the ripe fruit grows

Take me down the path
That's said to be paved with gold

Let's go for a long walk
Find a nice peach tree

Sit and have a long talk
Am I here, is it real

Or is it a dream that I feel
All is good all is right

Everything is a beautiful sight
But this is how he had made it

This is how it's meant to be
Like it was in the beginning

We just weren't around to see
So take me to the garden

Where the fruit is always ripe
Let's go for a walk in the garden

And see all his wondrous sights

NAVIGATOR

in times before the times of now
the sailors sailed upon their bow

moving forward not looking back
using stars to keep their track

with the light
that shined
so far away

and the fear
was left
in the last day

be my navigator
and set a course upon the stars

you can be the sailor
I'll take your hand, we'll travel far

you're eyes they shine and cut through night
they lead the course through wrong or right

guide my future, guide from my past
to distance shores where love does last

with beauty
that shines
upon my soul

and last
forever
this much I know

be my navigator
and set a course upon the stars

you can be the sailor
I'll take your hand, we'll travel far

Halloween

creeping crawling
hear them calling
hear your name
are they insane
scratching biting
there's no hiding
you can't escape
it's your fate

they come for you
they come tonight
they come right through
the dark of night
you think you're safe
it's just a mask
that's when you hear
that deep dark laugh

they laugh at you
cause you are through
they laugh again
just one more sin
it's no big deal
this pain they bring
yes, it will hurt
yes, they're insane

that shadow moved
look that one too
where will you run

what will you do
you think you're safe
just Halloween
only a shadow
no cause to scream

you can't be safe
on Halloween
you can't be safe
when they are seen

Memory of a Dream

you never told me

if you found what you were looking for
if you found out just who you are

you never came back

from that place that you went off to
said you were just passing through

and you faded
like a memory from a dream

I still remember

the first time that we danced
the way our eyes fell into a trance

the dream remembers

of the chance that you had beside me
of the chance you took and left me

and you faded
like a memory from a dream

and you never told me
if you found what you were looking for

you just faded
like a memory from a dream

NIGHT MARE

Night Mare
please leave me alone

please stop stalking me
please graze somewhere else

Night Mare
lack of want of you

lack of consciousness
lack of will to fight

Night Mare
dark beast causing fear

dark dreams filling me
dark night will not leave

Night Mare
makes me want to cry

makes my heart beat fast
make me want to die

Night Mare
I ask you to go away

I beg you to go away
I'm lost so please go away

Night Mare
stalking another prey

stalking another night
stalking eternally

SHADOW DANCE

she moves
with waves of passion
silk skin
her only fashion

and she moves so slow
with no place to go

heart beat
sets the rhythm
her eyes
do the stealin'

and she'll reach inside
a dream you think you've died

one word
she will whisper
close your eyes
and you're the listener

to her every breath
for you there's nothing left

she stares
and cuts right through you
you freeze
unsure what to do

and you're hypnotized
simply mystified

eyes open
and she is gone
look around
there is no one

was she ever there
or just a dream you dare

SEPARATE

He's just a man
Taken for all and all
Try to walk strong
But sometimes he falls

Like when he looks
Deep into her eyes
That's when he starts
When he realizes

He is he
She is she
Separate
Just simply two

Never to be
A he and she
Separate
It will always be

Sometimes he dreams
When he sees her smile
That it was he
Who made her happy for a while

But then he looks
Deep in her soul
A slow tear falls
Because he knows

Never to be
A he and she
Separate
Just simply two

Never to be
A he and she
Separate
It will always be

Missed...

And I try not to remember

Make a point not to think back

And the time just passes by

I really should know better

But then we all do sometimes

Another second races by

Tomorrow will be different

I said the day before

Can't stop time if I tried

She looked so pure and graceful

Just like she always did

And a tear fell from my eye

And he couldn't wait to hold her

Just like I always did

another tear just races by

And then she said I do

And then he said I do

Can't stop the tears if I tried

RAIN DANCE

The stars aren't shining down tonight
And the full moon is no where in sight
But that's ok
A sprinkle here, a sprinkle there
Brings out something special in the air
And that's ok

A lightening streak
The thunder speaks

And that's ok with me
Cause you are here
Next to me
Side to side
Cheek to cheek
Toe to toe
Don't you know
We're dancing

Barefoot in the rain

A giant Splash, we're up to our knees
I speak of love, you know what I mean
Ok now, please do not fear
Listen so close, and you will hear

A lightening streak
The thunder speaks

And that's ok with me
Cause you are here

Next to me
Side to side
Cheek to cheek
Toe to toe
Don't you know
We're dancing

Barefoot in the rain

Help

let me help
what little I can
let me help
let me take your hand

no guarantees
I can't hang the stars
no guarantees
but I can take you far

it's not an offer
but a promise I make
these aren't just words
but a promise I make

LIE

I lied
no wait
that isn't true
it just a secret
that I kept from you
it was no big deal
no need to cry
it's just a secret
that I had to hide
it wasn't an attempt
to play some game
you'll understand
if I don't say her name

Best Friend

My best friend
Is all I need
Is all I want

Feeling of closeness
always understand

look in those eyes
and I comprehend

nothing left hidden
nothing unsaid

a shared union
one hand in hand

we dance in tandem
on the same wave

and know each other
sharing the same page

I love

just my

best friend

always

BIRD

as I sat in the clouds one day
I watched a bird try to fly away

spread its wing, tried to soar
but that old bird could fly no more

took a glance, looked up, looked down
tried to smile, but could only frown

it took a second, longer yet
and that old bird made one last bet

took a leap, nothing but faith
but right on down, that bird did race

there was fear cast from his eyes
the tears raced down, that bird did cry

the tears so many, fell like rain
with ground approaching, he braced for pain

but tears collected, to a pool
beneath the bird, that leaped like a fool

it wasn't over, not for him,
for that old bird, learned then to swim

his life was over, but a new one dawned
fore that's the day, I named him swan

ROSE

here's a rose for all the children
here's a rose for all the wives
here's a rose for all the parents
who ever really tried
I picked a rose of beauty
I smelled a rose so fresh
I closed my eyes and dreamed
of an aroma so sweet
so give a rose to a girl
give a rose to make her smile
give a rose and hold her hand
if even for just a while
there are roses red like wine
you'll see roses blue like sky
but the rose that stands out brightly
is one pure and white like mine

WALK

coat wrapped up
safe from the chills
take a long walk
over those hills
I remember the bright days
I remember the shine
there was warmth back then

move down the road
walk past the trees
wander the woods
just looking for me
I remember not being alone
I can recall a time together
we shared our warmth back then

two miles from no where
five years from then
I might turn around
but who knows just when

DANCING ALONE

I danced all alone
I stood—just me
I never really knew
just what alone could be

then I met you
now I can relate
to just what it means
to be the only
oh so lonely

I take another step
in love with you
leave behind the shadows
that I knew
just staring at a future
built with you

THE FOOL

I watched a fool
watched as he sat
sat and did nothing
but sat like a fool

he had it all
all in his hand
holding everything
I never had

but I watched the fool
open his hand
and throw it away
now a lone fool he stands

SECOND

in a second
that's
all it takes
one time tick
one time with fate

can you wink your eye
envision why
can you accept
this time you tempt

that fleeting moment
last chance to have
to take the future
no time for past

there is no difference
between now and then
it's all the same
except just when

YOUTH

our wild youth is calling
asking, wondering why

they raise their heads, stare deeply
new world through their eyes

their youth is just for today
their smallness will not last

their vision of the future
is molded in our past

TAKE ME

you wrap yourself around me
never let go of me
breath deep, inhale my soul
take from me all that I know

and you consume
just all of me
you slowly take
all that was me

into your life I'll fall
tread fast after your call
never look back behind me
nothing left there for me

and you consume
just all of me
you slowly take
all that was me

your words fall so softly
yet still they somehow rock me
make me shake and make me quiver
want to be alone never

and you consume
just all of me
you slowly take
all that was me

the stars shine through your eyes
talk to me, hypnotize
you look and I am yours
into my life your love pours

and you consume
just all of me
you slowly take
all that was me

WARNING

I better warn you here
before you go too far
I know you want her now
but don't go rushing in

the pain that you might feel
from wanting her too bad
could be even worse
than never having had

this is something I can say
from experience
once I held her hand
then I pulled her in

but the smile that she gave to me
was the last one she did

before she said good-bye
and left me standing there

and now that I sit here
explaining this to you
I can say I know the pain
that you will go through

so before you make her yours
you better understand

that sometimes it just might be better
to loose without the love

cause I will always have
her passion in my heart
and I will never be able
to let go

so slowly go to her
but be prepared to wait
guard you heart, your feelings too
before it's too late

L O S T

I had a dream
I saw you float away
watched you walk and
wander astray

didn't know what you were searching for
but you were searching all the same
maybe you were just afraid
of playing that same old twisted game

I am everywhere
I am there to take your hand
but you walked away
walked on to another day
all alone
won't let me in

I had a dream
I saw you walk away
and I was there
to take you far away

but you still weren't sure just what you wanted
you couldn't talk to me, try to explain
maybe you were just afraid
that I would bring that same old pain

now where are you
with empty hands
and no one there

    to take you in
      all alone
still won't let me in

CREATE

create
make
something new
from inside
your head
bring together
not torn apart
create
what you know
throw out
ideas
create

LAUGH

don't cry
just laugh
don't sigh
find a laugh
inside
deep laugh
can't hide
can't cry
just laugh
inside

NOT OVER

not over

not yet

in me

fight left

not closed

no doors

can go

so far

clinched fist

will fight

not over

not yet

SEASONS

and it felt like summer
sunshine
brightly
open up my eyes
such a lovely sight
hot days
it's just like passion
we share together

and it felt just like autumn
signs of
changes
as we grow together
enough harsh weather
colour
what for
but to show us the way
together

and it felt like winter
ice cold
now old
what once was bright
has faded fast
maybe never meant to last

and it felt like spring
survived
the day
ready to write the next chapter

to take the chance
so new
me and you
moving out of the cold
go together growing old

STORMY NIGHT

I felt the storm
I heard the thunder bolt
I saw the lightening streak
never felt so weak
so all alone
future so unknown
I saw the lightening in your eyes
heard your thunder cries
and I felt the wind
from you again
another fight
stormy night
that was the night the storm brought no rain
but carried plenty pain
all the same
damage done
nothing won
another fight
stormy night

CONFLICTED

don't read too little
don't read too much
into what I say
or how I touch
what drives these words
I don't know myself
what drives me away
is a cry for help
smooth skin on skin
and I don't know why
I pull you so close
then run and hide
lack of balance
security
never understood
what my life needs

LEARNING IT'S NOT LOVE

there use to be a kind of passion
something like a fire
when we kissed, when we touched, we she smiled

we were just like kids
living day to day
sharing everything

but
what once tasted
like the sweetest of wine
seems
to have gone sour
through the many ticks of time

late at night
looking in her eyes
learning it's not love

and now I have to learn

learning it's not love
maybe something else
there maybe someone else
but this was not love

late at night
looking in her eyes
learning it's not love
a habit formed

that habit breaks
and shatters a heart on the way

new life begins
the old one ends
left to make it day to day
and learn
it was not love
learning it's not love

SMILE

I lost my smile
where did it go
who had it last
I do not know

I gave a smile
to a pretty girl
she took my smile
she broke my world

who had it last
what was her name
I trusted her
life's not the same

I had a smile
now wear a frown
such is my life
turned upside down

my face I'll hide
from everyone
I lost my smile
this face I'll shun

look in the mirror
what do you see
I see a man
but it's not me

he has a stare
that's lost in time
his eyes don't move
they wont stop crying

he has no smile
no smile like me
I have no smile
I can not be

RESCUE

take me with you now
away from this nightmare
this dream is too real
I'm trapped inside my mind

awaken me into your world
rescue me with love

it's your beauty that I need
look into your eyes
but all I see is white
that slowly fades away

I so miss your touch
warm skin against mine
this cold wind blows so fast
tornado of confusion

open up my eyes with your soft kiss
awaken me into your world
rescue me with love

spineless full of fear
hunched over, half a man
hide behind a dream
that's fast becoming real

a thousand years I could fall
and never land upon the earth

or I could crash into your soul
catch me falling with your love

kiss me and open my eyes
awaken me into your world
rescue me with love

Obvious

look and see
it's there before you

behind you
all around you

engulfing you
what you searched for

even longed for
said a prayer for

begged and plead for
too busy searching

always looking
sometimes hunting

open your hand
open your eyes

open you heart
touch, see, and hear

it's not difficult
or impossible

less exertion
more passiveness

more awareness

MR. DEATH

you mock him
he mocks you too

don't know what
you're going to do

you stare so hard
he stares right back

ready to unleash
a heart attack

you laugh out loud
he chuckles deep

ready to bury you
beneath six feet

you come to know
and understand

what it means to be
gripped by death's hand

tossed around
like a a rag doll

to take your life
he makes this call

what life means
he doesn't care

your feelings
he'll never spare

WHISPER

A soft voice tells you to stop
right in your tracks

better look back
no one there

no shadow moves
just you and your intentions

better think twice
better use caution

It's the whisper to your soul
foretelling things untold

whispering to your soul
telling you what you already know

random words floating around
mixing of sounds

mixing of truths
what will you do

it's the whisper to your soul
foretelling things untold

whispering to your soul
telling you what you already know

HIDE AND SEEK

when the lights go out
do you scream and shout
do you feel the fear
of them standing there
will you play the game
will you hide in shame
when the lights go out
will you go about
searching for
who's behind the door
when you've been picked
when you are it
how fast will you chase
better set your pace
they have the lead
hiding in the tree
just might be worn out
when the lights go out

SEVEN DANCING ANGELS

seven angels
dancing on pins
dancing for love
dance against sin
dance for you
dance for me
watch them close
can you not see
they dance around
like prancing clowns
with happy faces
dance happy paces
their steps you trace
as evil they chase
with robes that flow
and wings that blow
a flutter of air
as they dance sans care
these seven angels
will dance again
they dance each time
there is a sin

Good-Bye

this is where I get off
this is where I say good-bye
this is where my train stops
the road ahead is not mine
the past has been pleasing
though not always easy
so say good-bye to me
because I am leaving
you can go forward
I'll just turn left now
we might meet again somehow
but our time is through now
I'll find my own way
start a brand new day
you can leave or stay
but please don't go my way
each step that I take
will separate our fates
cause there's nothing we can make
so say good-bye, it's getting late

HAPPY THOUGHTS

think happy thoughts
they say to me
think happy thoughts
and thus you'll be
these happy thoughts
can cure all ills
these happy thoughts
can make you well
I saw a happy thought
once upon a time
but this happy thought
was not mine
this happy thought
belonged to a child
with happy thoughts
of running wild
but happy thoughts
elude forever me
a happy person
I can never be

BAPTISM

I've never been one
to run from the rain
because I can see
what no one else can

the prickles of water
striking my skin
each drop of water
removes one of my sins

the water falls down
It's a baptism from above
the thunder will roar
just god showing his love

the lighting will strike
I now see the light
baptism by fire
a new life I make

this rain once washed
the sins from the world
from this rain I can feel
my sins lifted from my shoulder

I can stand taller
not weighted down
and not fear the sins
of those all around

LITTLE OLD WOMAN

"You're gonna die," she said
"Won't be long boy, and you'll dead"

Her eyes burned and spit of fire
But wrinkles told of age and tired

She screamed again and waved her hands
Shouted loud, "You're gonna die man!"

She seemed so certain, she had to know
Maybe those fiery eyes had touched his soul

He stared confused, unsure what to say
This wasn't how, he'd planned his day

This little lady seemed out to kill
But death that day was not his will

He turned and tried to walk away
She quickly followed, no, this was his day

"You can run from me, but not from fate,"
"I know that you have a date."

"With a rocky stone, and a wooden box,"
"It's over soon, your fate is locked."

She talked with a screech, and screamed so loud
She had the attention of a gathering crowd

She grabbed her heart, and started to yell
Then to the ground, the little woman fell

And at that moment, someone did die
And at his feet, the dead one lie

TALKING TO BONES

I can talk to the dead
you know

I can hear where they want
to go

I can hear what they have
to say

They tell me how they love
to play

I sit on the ground and talk
to bones

I hear them knocking on wood
their homes

They tell me secrets I don't want
to hear

I can feel their presence
is near

Would you like to talk to them
as well

Or maybe go to their world
and dwell

I sit on the ground and talk
to bones

I hear them knocking on wood
their homes

CONFESSION

With my last breath
I must confess
I will bear witness
To an act in time distance

I once crossed the line
I committed a crime
I knew not why
But he had to die

With my bare hands
I killed a man
He stood not a chance
It was his last stand

I looked in his eyes
I watched him cry
I took my time
Blood ran red like wine

Now I lay here
With my own death
And I don't fear
It's all so clear

Fore you will see
The death of me
Just as when
I saw the death of he

It Rained on Christmas

that's the Christmas
that it rained

when his car
was swept away

he missed a curve
and went astray

flew through the air
now she's all alone today

and now
Christmas cries for her

the rain
will fall like tears

and the lightening
shows her fears

of being alone
talking to the thunder

she's all alone
because now

it always
rains

on Christmas day

LEARN TO LIVE AGAIN

she has that hungry look
glaring in her eyes
another day not tasting
what is offered of her life

for too long
she's been looking
for divine intervention

but now it's time
for her to learn
to live again

she spent too much
time pretending
but the feelings of loss
were too unrelenting

had the dreams
and was afraid
to ever live them

but now it's time
for her to learn
to live again

Power of Love

two people
separated by fear

two people
never felt so near

one man
knows what she wants to do

one woman
unsure what he's going through

two people
there is no distance

two people
drawn by circumstance

one man
finally discovers love

one woman
throwing away distrust

two people
discover the power of love

two people
learning to share their love

MOONLIGHT

an ocean
can keep them
from touching

and yet
their hearts
beat as one

they both stand
in the light
of the moon

the gray light
shines down
on them both

together
they can finally
find love

and its pull
can join them
once again

they'll never
be too far
apart

as long as
they hold tight
to the light
of the moon

THE WEB

one dream dies

one left alive

nightmare caught

tied in a knot

good dream leaps

your life it keeps

into your soul

the good dream goes

and thankfully

nightmare not free

to take you in

and make you sin

just one more night

sound sleep in sight

above your head

you keep the web

THE MOUNTAIN CRIES

mountain proud
and so strong
rises high into the air

the sunrise
breaks the night
caste down its warm stare

the mountain
slowly cries
into long cold streams

tears fall
into creeks
over boulder like cheeks

collect
just like tears
in the palms of your hands

the sunlight
hits these tears
like a mirror in the sand

and displays
the mountain
standing above it all

with these tears
that it cries
the mountain never falls

Turn Around

turn around
take a single moment
to reflect on the things
that you have done with your life

turn around
if only for a second
to glance back and see
what you have witnessed with your eyes

behind you
lies all of the answers
to all of the questions
you'll ever want or need to ask

behind you
there is a trail
that leads to the future
count the footsteps you've left in the sand

in your past
lies the ghost
of your very soul
it's who you are now and who you will be

in your past
the very seeds
of your whole life
were planted and from there it grows

0-595-33349-4